The Tarczal Alliance

J. Paulette Forshey

DISCLAIMER

All the characters in this book have no existence outside the imagination of the author and have no relation whatsoever to anyone bearing the same name or names. They are not even distantly inspired by any individual known or unknown to the author, and all incidents are pure invention.

Website: www.jpauletteforshey.com

Cover design: Rachel Connor

Editor: PS Ritchey DBA: Old Mill Publishing
oldmillpublishing@gmail.com

Also By J. Paulette Forshey

A Tango Trinity
Cat and the Wizard
Miracles from the Heart
Passionate Cooks
The Estate
33 Days Til Christmas

Acknowledgements

To my husband for believing in me and helping me make my dreams come true.

My heartfelt thanks to Pam Ritchey's Old Mill Publishing and the many hats she wears as editor, formatter, this book wouldn't be here today without all that you did to support its creation.

To Rachel Connor for the fantastic cover she blessed on this book.

The Tarczal Alliance

New Orleans 1925

THREE HUNDRED FIFTY-FIVE years of life had not made Logan Kincaid immune to the smell of death.

"You didn't have to kill her, you son of a bitch!" Logan's teeth clenched as he faced the fiend standing at the end of the pier, the chill of the night air fitting with the grisly scene.

Franchot glanced at the woman in his arms, her throat gaping from his vicious attack. He dropped her like so much rubbish, wiping the blood from his lips. "That's what happens to bait you send out. Come closer, Jean-Pierre. I tire so of this cat and mouse game. Come and let us finish this dance." Franchot taunted Logan using his birth name, stretching out his arms in welcome.

With a roar, Logan charged. He slammed into Franchot's mid-section and they crashed into a stack of barrels. The barrels barely moved. Franchot brought his clasped hands down on his back. Logan grunted as the wind was knocked out of him, fanning his anger even more.

"Young Flora was much sweeter than the *putain* you hired tonight to distract me," mocked Franchot, his attempt at distraction making Logan even more determined to focus on his foe.

Sucking air painfully into his lungs, he jerked Franchot sideways off his feet. Logan landed on the bottom, grimacing as his shoulder crashed into the wooden decking. He would be damned if he would let this animal get the upper hand. He had waited too long to collect his debt.

Crack! The impact of Franchot smashing his head into Logan's dazed him and the men broke contact to scramble away from the other. Franchot made it to his feet first and pulled out a knife.

Logan jumped up and back to dodge the swipe of Franchot's blade before the steel could leave its mark on his face.

"You bastard!" Logan growled, circling to attack. "Flora was an innocent!"

"Innocent? The slut was cheating on her husband with *you*!" Franchot lunged at Logan who quickly side stepped but not before the knife grazed him, sending a searing pain through his side.

"I was going to take her away and marry her," Logan ground out, as blood dripped from the wound.

"Marry a monster? Really Jean-Pierre, did you think she would?" Franchot gave a merciless chuckle.

"I'm not a monster." Grabbing Franchot's arm, Logan struggled to take the knife from him. Franchot twisted and his fist found Logan's jaw. Despite the blow, Logan held on, and both men now clutched the hilt.

"Flora didn't believe that."

Franchot struggled to push the knife into Logan.

"No, not after what you did to her." With ebbing strength, Logan forced the knife's blade to turn toward Franchot.

"I did what you were afraid to do. I showed her what we truly are." Franchot thrust his leg between Logan's trying to knock him off balance.

Logan could not stop himself from responding to Franchot's taunts despite the fact he knew he was only trying to divert him. "What *you* are!" Logan spat, twisting to pull the knife closer to Franchot's chest.

"What *we* are!" Franchot snarled as he shoved Logan toward the end of the pier.

"I'm nothing like you." Flora's face flashed before Logan's eyes and a great strength surged in him. With a roar, he thrust the blade down to sink deep into Franchot's chest. He stepped back as a dark stain spread over the bastard's shirt.

Franchot looked down at the knife protruding from him, a chilling laugh slipped from his fanged mouth. His feeder teeth were reacting to the blood. "But you will not have the pleasure of seeing me in the cold hard ground." Then he turned, stumbled, to plunge off the dock into the dank, dark, muddy waters below.

"Damn it," Logan cursed. He owed it to Flora to make sure the bastard was truly dead. Despite diving in after him, he could not find Franchot's body. As he pulled himself out of the water, Logan noticed a large gator swimming by and allowed a satisfied grin to lift his lips. He hoped the poor animal did not suffer indigestion from his next meal.

With limb-numbing exhaustion, he dragged himself to his feet and away from the bloody scene of the battle. It had taken him five years of chasing Franchot, but he could rest now, knowing the only woman he'd ever loved, Flora Rainey, had been finally avenged.

Chapter One

In each of us is a need—or a fear, if you will—
to be loved.

Present Day

THE PROFILE ON her stated she was in her early thirties, and hmm, those years fit her like a thong on one of Hef's bunnies. Logan Kincaid relaxed against the old oak, letting a wide grin slide into place. He watched the woman cross the street. Pretty didn't describe her; knock-out did. He'd recognized her from the scholarship file picture when she arrived at the outdoor market. Long blonde hair, longer legs, and intelligent green eyes, all his weaknesses rolled into one.

✧   ✧   ✧

CHIN HIGH, SHOULDERS squared, Allyson Weston exited her car and walked to the courthouse patio. A cloud passed over the warm, noonday sun giving her a sudden chill. The previous night's dreams and the past tugged at her memory. But, the harder she tried to draw those thoughts to the surface, the more they eluded her. A shiver rocked across her stiff shoulders from the emptiness of the elusive dreams. Her hand fisted at her side. *No, I won't give in to self-doubt. This is my time. My chance to live my life, not the life someone else wants me to live.*

She shook her feelings off and crossed the street, stepping up her pace. At her wrists, wide bracelets, almost medieval in their simplicity, of silver and hammered copper glinted in the sun. Her hands bore rings on every finger, slender whispers of silver, some resembling twisted vines, roses, and a couple with polished earthy stones. Her earrings of metal and stone flashed color, brilliance, tinkling with each movement. The light brush of metal against her neck shored her resolve. Her uptight, control-freak, estranged husband would've hated the flashy earrings which only made her love them more. The divorce couldn't be finalized soon enough for her.

The weekly farmer's market and college's annual art department display were this weekend. Only the best of the best presented. Allyson wandered through the market, while discreetly evaluating the competition's artwork. She required the ensuing year's Thomas Rothwell Art Scholarship to fund the next step to her freedom. She had talent, but being better than the best wouldn't be enough. She'd upped her game to make the scholarship list. Halfway through the displays, one piece captured Allyson's attention, and sunk her heart. The artist's work shone.

"Brazenly grandiose."

The man's voice came from behind her. Rich, warm, baritone, like melting chocolate surrounded by a hardened shell. "Conceited, too," he added. A strange buzzing began in her head following his words.

"Conceited?" Allyson shot an incredulous glare at the voice and connected with a face capable of making angels weep from its chiseled masculine beauty. Ebony hair with a touch of wave brushed his collar, onyx eyes danced with intelligence, a slender, trim, rakish beard—a pirate's beard—the color of jet lined his jaw then darted upward to frame a firm mouth made for pleasure. Or sin.

"Stop him!" The shrill cry stabbed the air from across the square. Tennis shoes pounded the ground. Rubber slapped against concrete, the sound reminiscent of feral drummers in the distance. A shaggy-haired young man raced through the displays, a bright green and pink woman's purse clutched to his chest. An officer lumbered behind.

"Excuse me," the man said to Allyson in that melted chocolate voice. He thrust a bag into her hands and stepped in front of the running teen.

The young man, busy glancing behind him at his pursuers, didn't notice the barrier in his path until too late. He ran head-on into the man's chest. The colossus didn't budge, and he now towered over the inept robber with his fist tangling in the young man's shirt.

Slowly, he lifted the boy off his feet, bringing them nose-to-nose. The teen gulped loudly, still clutching the purse to his body.

"I don't think pink and green are your colors, son." The man gave a rumbling chuckle as he plucked the handbag from the boy. The officer and the bag's owner joined them.

"Officer, I think this belongs to you." A smile creased his bronze, aristocratic face, and he lowered the boy to the ground, giving him a small push. The boy landed in the officer's hands. The red-faced deputy wheezed while he cuffed the boy, whose shoulders slumped in defeat.

The hero-of-the-moment gave a short bow to the bag's owner, a middle-aged matron who twittered like a schoolgirl at the gesture. She held the bag high in the air. "He got my bag back! He got my bag back!" she exclaimed and twittered more.

The deputy led the boy away, tossing instructions and gratitude over his shoulder in equal measure. "Thanks Mr. Kincaid. Can you stop by the station later on to file a report?"

"Yes, Deputy," the man agreed to the request.

The woman followed, browbeating the would-be thief with each step.

"Now, where were we?"

The champion grinned at Allyson like a wolf that had just spotted his dinner. She stood before the stranger and his masculine presence lapped around her like waves on a beach. He towered over her five foot six height by a good foot. She guessed him to be slightly older than her, at least in his late thirties or early forties. He had the aura only maturity gave; a complete confidence which made men wary and women draw closer. His clothes were casual, but expensive, and accented the expanse of his shoulders and slim waist.

"Hello, again. Thank you for holding my purchases." The corners of his onyx eyes twinkled as he relieved her of his bag.

"Mrs. Kostanoski will be singing your praises from now to next year." Allyson stared at his face and sighed inwardly at the beauty of it as the annoying humming returned to her ears.

"Who?" His gaze never wavered from hers.

"The woman whose purse you recovered?"

"Only trying to help out." He smiled, and her mouth went dry. Allyson found herself staring at his mouth and the base of his throat. Primal instinct told her his mouth would no doubt be demanding and passionate on the lips of the woman he chose. She blinked trying to figure out why his neck and the beating pulse drew her attention. The artist in her made her fingers itch with the urge to sketch his face, to try to capture the essence that made him, him. Allyson shivered as fear and excitement skittered along her skin. She glanced up to his eyes only to find she'd been caught ogling him and blushed clear to the roots of her hair.

✧   ✧   ✧

THE WOMAN'S FLEETING inspection caused Logan to pause and suppress the grin threatening to creep across his face. He knew he should stop; she had no defenses against his decades of experience but a primal need drove him on as he observed her tremble. The last time a woman caused him to lose restraint was ninety years ago. An intriguing, yet disturbing revelation, since that was when he'd sworn off relationships.

"You disagree the painting is showy?" He turned the subject back to the painting, and with practiced ease, he returned what he surmised was a compliment from the flush blooming on her cheeks. He indulged himself by allowing his gaze to rake over her. A whine like a mosquito's settled in his ears.

"The artist captured Kandinsky's style completely," she sputtered.

Logan didn't give a damn about the painting or the artist. He wondered if the large, dark purple sweater that hung mid-thigh on her was an attempt to hide her body. If that was her goal, the tight black stretch pants and thigh-high, ebony, suede boots were a poor choice. Any movement pulled the sweater tight like a second skin over her compact, lithe body.

"Absolutely. He copied a style. You wouldn't have, Ms?" She fidgeted, and the movement caused the sweater to pull snug over her breasts making them stand out like ripened fruit and accented her flat stomach. *Nice. Bet that stomach quivers when a tongue is run over it. Wonder what she'd do with a tongue in her belly button? She's probably a giggler.* He licked his lips. *And a squirmer.* It was apparent she had no idea what she did to him. He didn't mind. Several parts of his anatomy were already stirring in response. Her front equaled the heart-shaped derriere he'd seen earlier while she browsed the competition.

"Weston. Allyson Weston. How did you know I paint?"

The tiny frown across her brow made him want to laugh. So this was Michael Weston's estranged wife in the flesh. During the job interview Michael had constantly moaned and bitched about his soon-to-be-ex-wife. So far, from what he'd seen, he wouldn't kick her out of bed for eating crackers. Guess Michael didn't grasp he'd let go of an extraordinary woman. Logan let his gaze travel down to her legs, dancer's legs, long and well-defined. Legs any man would enjoy wrapped around him.

Smoothly, Logan reached down, slipping his hand under hers bringing both up to eye level. "You have paint under your nails." His thumb brushed the skin of her knuckles.

"Oh."

Quickly, she withdrew her hand from his. She folded her arms across her mid-section, lifting the orbs and tucking her hands safely under her arms.

Logan's smile widened. "Do you have family in town?" His attention wandered back to the boots she wore. The way they encased her legs from toe to over the knee were a wonderful enticement. His imagination flared to a deliciously wicked conclusion when she interrupted his assessment of her intriguing appendages.

"An STB."

How fresh, honest, and naive she was. Logan bit back a chuckle. Heroes and bartenders: everyone trusted them, confiding intimate details of their lives they'd never reveal to anyone else, an interesting quirk of human nature. He arched an eyebrow in query, and she clarified. "Soon-to-be-ex-husband."

He stopped himself before he could lick his lips. At the same time, the essence of her blood rose from beneath her skin to mingle with the pungent leather of her boots. He inhaled more deeply, drawing it inside him, and swirled his tongue in his mouth to better experience the bouquet. Sweet, delicate, and exotic. Fit for the gods. He stopped his feeder teeth from slipping into place. A taste of her blood would never be enough, and an ocean too little for a man to quench his thirst. Stunned, he wondered where that thought came from, while trying to wish away the growing arousal in his groin. The whirr in his ears grew a little louder.

This woman didn't have the wide-eyed inno-

cence… *Stop it!* He wouldn't allow the memories of
the other one to fill him. He banished those reminis-
cences from his mind and focused on the woman
before him. Her femininity and something else tugged
at his masculinity like nothing else ever had. It puzzled
him while the small, annoying noise continued in his
head, distracting him. He stepped closer to her.

She shifted back a step. He'd invaded her space,
and she didn't like it. Interesting. What or…who
made her this way? Had Michael injured this free
spirit? Instantly, Logan hated the man for that reason
alone. Her almost belligerent question pulled his
attention back to her. "If you don't like the painting, is
there any you do like?"

"Do you have any here?" he asked leaning into
her, waiting for her to move back.

Surprisingly, this time she didn't.

HE LEANED BACK, arms folded across his chest as she
stared at his hands.

He wore an antique signet ring on carefully manicured hands, hands sinewy and muscular like those of
a laborer. In a tuxedo or tatters, this man would always be tall, dark, polished, and imperious.

"No, I don't, but you already knew that, didn't
you?" She sighed. One could blissfully, and willingly,
drown in those bottomless eyes. She knew his

kind…handsome, sharp dresser, sexy as hell and he knew it and used it to get what he wanted. Michael had been like that and she'd gotten suckered in and over her head before she knew up from down. *Not happening again* shouted a tiny voice in her head.

"Losing my touch, am I?" He gave a deep, warm laugh. His onyx eyes twinkled again. He moved closer, and she wondered how his dark hair felt. It appeared incredibly silky. "Here I'm trying to impress you." His spicy, masculine fragrance enveloped her. Her body responded to his scent with a languorous warmth curling low in her belly. *Knock it off libido; we agreed no more* shouted that voice in her head, louder.

"How else could I engage you in a conversation or get this close to you?" It was strange. This man aroused her senses and made her contemplate ideas she hadn't considered in a long time. She stepped back. The whine diminished slightly.

"It's been a while since one's come my way, but I'm still aware of a pass being made at me. Thanks, but no thanks. I don't mean to be rude, but I've recently ended one relationship, and I'm not ready for another." She straightened and lifted her chin. *You tell'm girl!*

"I'm concentrating on my career and a life on my own." She was sure he'd understand her self-imposed unavailability. Small talk would follow. He would later forget the whole episode. She felt flattered a handsome stranger had noticed her. But, while she'd probably succeeded in chasing him off, she now felt let down and the reason eluded her.

"Oh, I get it. You're doing the whole artist suffering for their work thing." He nodded his head. "Depriving yourself of carnal pleasures and the delightful entanglements which go with them?"

"No, I'm not depriving myself of anything. I just don't want to make the same mistakes twice."

"Then it's possible you could be interested."

"No it isn't. Look you seem like a nice guy…"

"I am."

"I'm not interested. A man-a relationship-isn't in the picture right now."

The corners of his mouth twitched with a smile, and inwardly, she cringed at the unintended pun.

"Logan. Logan, there you are." A brunette half Allyson's age came toddling up on ridiculous high heels, in a too-short skirt, and a too-low blouse. "Didn't you say to meet you over at the courthouse steps? We really need to get back." The woman wrapped her arms around one of his, completely ignoring Allyson and declaring Logan hers.

"Stacy, don't be rude." He reprimanded the dark-haired woman-child who pouted at the scolding.

Years of good manners reared their ugly head, and Allyson heard herself say. "It's been nice meeting you." Then, to her chagrin, she found herself giving him an apologetic smile from sheer reflex before turning and leaving. *Why do I always have to be nice?*

Be the appeaser? She gave a little sigh. *Why were men all like Michael? Can't one man in the universe be faithful?* Ever since it became known to the public she was going to be a divorcee, scum bag after scum bag had hit on her. Were they any good men around? She reached the curb waiting for a car to pass before crossing and felt his gaze on her back. Allyson turned to see the stranger staring at her. He gave her a dazzling smile, which took her breath away and made her heart skip a beat.

Once back in her car, her fingers beat a rapid cadence on the steering wheel. The noise had gone, replaced with the slippery excitement of the stranger's attention. Funny, it still gave her goose bumps. It felt nice to have someone not find fault with her for a change. She sat at the stoplight wanting the feeling to last a little bit longer.

✦   ✦   ✦

LOGAN USHERED STACY back to the car unceremoniously. Once inside, he started the vehicle. "Stacy." His gaze never left the road.

"Mr. Kincaid?"

He noticed caution replaced the seductive purr in her voice, it pleased him, but she needed to learn a lesson.

"I believe you'd do better as a feeder with another Tarczal house." He clenched and unclenched his jaw

"Don't you agree?"

"Yes, sir," the girl whispered.

"How would you like to visit Europe?"

"Yes, sir, I'd like that."

He didn't give a damn what she liked, the twit's little display of jealousy was annoying. No woman owned him. The blame lay in his lap for choosing someone so young to accompany him on this outing. What had he been thinking when he invited her? Unfortunately, he'd have to handle this diplomatically, no need for her to file a grievance with the feeder's union.

"Good. When we arrive at the estate, I'll have my driver take you to the airport."

She smiled, seemingly delighted.

Chapter Two

"THREE HUNDRED YEARS ago we were considered fierce warriors." Logan grunted as he ran across the racquetball court of his Baneridge, Ohio home. "Now we're forced to confine our aggressions to a small blue ball." Logan growled in disgust, barely dodging the blue ball, which whizzed a little too close past his head. "And, I guess each other." Logan saluted his best friend with his racquet. "Nice try St. Clair, but as usual you're aim is off," he happily informed Nairn. He relished playing against another Tarczal. It made the game much more interesting. With a normal human, he had to show restraint or risk injuring his opponent.

"Sure, Kincaid?" Nairn St. Clair snorted, and sent the orb flying again. "By the way, you've got a spy in your company."

"Like hell I do." Logan cursed running to catch the sphere, and quickly returning it to Nairn.

Nairn had accomplished his distraction. "Exactly what I said." He leaned into the serve. "Didn't think you'd be so stupid." The blue sphere shot out again.

Logan charged the ball, smacking it harder than he expected. It connected with the sweet spot of his racquet, sending the orb to the front wall.

"Who?" he demanded. His sneakers squeaked against the glossy wood floor of the racquetball court. Smack. The sound of high velocity rubber colliding against bare skin echoed off the court's high white walls. His racket caught nothing but air.

"Damn." Nairn picked up the ball, and went to the serving line. They both wore the tight fitting shorts and the wrist and headbands of the sport, opting not to don shirts. Bare skin made the game more interesting.

"Sting?" Logan taunted. They'd been at it for a good hour, and he'd purposely pushed his friend hard. Nairn's ponytail sagged with sweat.

It amused Logan when people mistook Nairn's surfer dude image of sun bleached blonde hair, scruffy jeans, and baggy sweaters, and equated it with a laidback attitude and dim intellect. It only took a closer study of his friend's ice blue eyes to see they were those of an intelligent predator who waited and hoped for his prey to make a mistake. And, if they didn't do it fast enough, he'd nudge them into making one.

"Hell, no!" Nairn bounced the ball once and struck it forcefully on the way back up from the rebound, sending it flying off the wall in front of him. "First impressions made me think Franchot and the crap he pulled, but he's been gator bait for decades. Right?"

"You know it is." Logan's jaw clenched.

Nairn went on. "The trail had all his dirty ear-marks. Imagine my surprise to find it's your new man, Weston."

"Michael?" Logan's shoulder grazed the wall surface leaving a bit of bare skin on it. "Can't be."

"Yep and yep." Nairn sprang forward hitting the sphere before it bounced off the floor, sending it with lightening speed back to Logan who had taken the time to glance at his shoulder.

"Damn." Logan recovered, and sent the ball flying to ricochet off the wall. "And I approved his hiring."

"I noticed." Nairn grunted and ran to confront the speeding object. "Slipping in our old age are we?"

Logan slammed the ball back to him making Nairn scramble to hit it. "Who you calling old? I'll always be younger than you."

"Why do you think he's here?" Nairn laughed scoring another point.

Logan shrugged. "Industrial espionage? Religious fanatics? Who knows? We've got a possible break-through in the AIDS lab which looks promising." *Am I slipping, letting a spy get close?*

"I still can't get past the idea some of those fanatic idiots would rather kill the infected instead of cure them. Stupid." Nairn shook his head.

"They're scared."

"They're stupid."

Logan had to agree, but he tried to be the bigger, levelheaded, man.

"On the subject of scared and irrational, the paper pushers have been busy lately." Nairn hit the ball on the fly.

"Okay I'll bite, why?" Logan smacked the ball propelling it against the front wall sending Nairn scrambling.

Nairn made the shot but it flew to collide with the ceiling. "Damn, fault!" He twirled the racquet in his hand. "We've had an influx of Machavaya immigrants to the area."

Logan stepped into the service box, bounced the ball once before sending it flying. "Machavaya, hmmm, any idea why? They usually don't amass unless there's a celestial event or catastrophe."

"I asked their leader for an explanation in case we needed to prepare for something big. I like having all our bases covered." Nairn met the sphere and returned it viciously.

"And…."

"Supposedly a legend is about to be fulfilled."

Logan distracted by the blue object's destination asked, "Which one, they have a slew of them."

"Kharizan and Alaza." The ball landed in a fault area and Nairn went over to pick it up.

Logan halted in his tracks. "The warrior and the blood witch, really? They believe the nonsense of a new dawn of that pedigree is about to be implemented?"

"Hey, I've checked with my dad, you know how he

and your Aunt Maryse keep up on these things, and a lot of unusual thing are going on." He bounced the ball repeatedly off the floor, catching it in his hand each time.

"Thought you weren't a believer."

"I'm not but if you show me enough evidence to the contrary…." Nairn shrugged.

Logan shook his head in disbelief, a grin spread wide on his face. "You're all nuts." He ran after the ball his friend let fly. The burn of muscles felt good after sitting behind a desk.

"Enough on that subject, let's get back to the cure, how promising is the advance?" Nairn breathed heavily. He ran to catch the ball, slamming into the wall to catch up with the sphere, sending the hard rubber ricocheting off the wall.

"Good enough to eradicate several strains and prolong life expectancy in common humans." Logan grinned starting to breathe hard too.

Nairn paused mid-stride. "It would definitely increase our food supply. Not to mention how it would help the coms. This reminds me. How's the surrogate blood program going?"

"The PFC." Logan stopped too and observed Nairn raise an eyebrow. "Sorry, downfall of working with scientists. PFC is the Perfluorocarbon blood. They've found while it's filling, tests show our bodies don't receive any nutritional benefits."

Nairn blew out a breath. "Crap, it doesn't do us

any good."

"At least it doesn't have the hemophilic-like side effects that popped up with regular blood serum." Logan sighed.

"What a disaster. I lost five good men with the experiment before they discovered the problem." Nairn gave a disgusted growl.

Logan shook his head. "You'd think with the great minds and centuries available to the Tarczal race, we'd be able to come up with an alternative to feeders."

"It's not like the feeders don't benefit from their association with us." Nairn shrugged. "Humph! Time." Nairn grunted, letting out a breath. He went over to grab a towel, wipe his face, and retrieve a bottle of water.

Logan scrubbed a hand over his face. "True. I contacted the local group earlier to send a couple of them over today."

"Figured you'd need a pick-me-up after our game?" Nairn chuckled.

Logan laughed. "Figured *you'd* need one."

"Anyone I know?"

"I asked the local group to send two over. I didn't care who." He no sooner finished the sentence than giggling and excited whispers echoed off the tile walls as the girls came towards them.

Two young women appeared around the corner. They were identical in every way, from their lime-green polished toenails peeking out of open-toed shoes to their blue-black hair and lavender eyes.

"Hey, it's the twins! Marcia. Paige. What're you doing here?" Nairn held out his arms, and the young women ran to him full of youthful energy. "Last time I set eyes on you two you were knee-high to a grasshopper. What are you doing here?"

"You asked for feeders." They squealed in unison giving him a peck on the cheek. "And, here we are!"

Logan's mouth thinned into a scowl. "A mistake's been made. I don't take nourishment from underage donors." He stood and reached for the phone on the wall. "You're what fifteen at the most? You know the rules. Feeders must be at least twenty-one."

The twins shook their heads in mock disgust. "We turned legal last year. We're seniors in college Mr. K., we graduate in the spring." Logan noted Paige still answered for the two of them—a childhood trait.

"My college?" Logan asked.

Paige gave a short laugh. "Of course! Tilendale is the best liberal arts college around."

"Good, I built the town and college with the expectations our people would use both to their and our, advantage."

"Yea, pretty brilliant, even for you." Nairn snickered at Logan's eye roll. "Using a college town to camouflage the coming and goings of our nourishment providers." He turned his attention to the young women. "They grow up too fast." Nairn grinned, wiping an imaginary tear from his eye with one hand, while clutching the other to his chest. "Who wants who? And please tell me this isn't your first time."

Marcia tsked. "No, we've done this before." Nairn patted his lap. "Let's get this done." The lean young woman wrinkled her nose.

"We're doing this before you shower?"

"Yep, sorry girls." He chuckled as Paige sat on his lap.

Logan raised a skeptical brow. "You're really old enough?"

"Yes, Mr. K. I've done this lots of times."

A little lie, despite her bravado. Seasoned feeders didn't squirm. Marcia wiggled her tight little bottom all over his lap. Nothing sexual, just pure nervousness.

He tilted her head, stretching her neck taut. The artery pulsed with the liquid of life. Logan smelled the flush of heat warm her flesh, while her skin prickled and the hair stood up on her neck. Baby soft, supple, not accustomed to repeat piercing…yet.

He let his breath dance across her skin and felt her involuntary shiver in response. He elected to stop her torment and get on with it. His extra set of teeth slid into place behind the front two. He began to feed.

Young feeders mistakenly equated the act with sex or romance he mused. For him it was nothing more than a meal, appreciated, well paid for, but still a meal. The excitement had long since faded.

Her blood filled his mouth, warm salty, coppery, the bouquet exploded over his tongue. Then like an excellent wine, layers of other smells and tastes surfaced. Flavors floated up. Smoky, woody, and tangy. It amazed him how a person's life, and health, rose to unfold itself to him from a simple sip. Depending on the person's heart rate, the meal could be savored or quick. This girl's would be a fast food snack without the toy surprise.

Within minutes, Logan and Nairn had taken their fill. Before the girls left, each man thanked them. Logan reminded them to make sure they reported the donation for the month.

Logan wiped his face and the back of his neck. "How about a sauna?" He picked up his sports equipment and stuffed it into its bag.

"Sounds great." Nairn flashed him a wide grin gathering his things, then paused. "When'd you put in a sauna?"

Logan headed for the door.

"The workers finished last week. After living in Europe, I missed having access to saunas and opted to put one in here."

They trudged down the hallway to where the cedar-lined sweathouse was tucked neatly into a recess in the fitness room. Striping down, each dumped their clothes in a hamper and grabbed a clean towel before entering the bench-lined room. Logan turned the heat up on the already smoldering stones then slowly added water. Steam wafted up while he and Nairn leaned back to enjoy the moist heat.

Relaxing, Nairn moaned and stretched out his long legs. "By the gods, this feels good."

Logan closed his eyes and nodded. They sat in silence for several minutes.

Logan grinned. "Glad you took my offer to set up the Janissary's Academy here." He then chose to pull his friend's chain. "It's a relief you didn't let personal feelings get in the way."

"Change the subject, pretty boy."

Logan chuckled, "Why don't you two kiss and make up?"

"I said let it go." Nairn threw his water bottle, aiming for Logan's head.

Lucky for Logan he saw it coming and caught it in time. "You're here earlier than expected." He swiped his forearm across his brow, mopping the beads of sweat dripping from his hair, clearing his throat. "I'm glad the Alliance finally gave the go-ahead for a central training facility for the security teams. It's the second best decision they've made in a long time."

"And the first? Making you their attorney?"

"The vote on that decision is still out. No, jackass, I'm referring to my predecessor turned Alliance member, Thomas, recommending you taking over the academy. In only seventy-five years, you've turned the Janissary into the most elite group of law enforcement on the planet. They make the rest of the world's Special Ops nothing more than crossing guards."

Nairn accepted the compliment. "Thanks. Now

can we get back to the topic you're avoiding? Spy. Weston. You know Michael's in the middle of a divorce?"

Logan gave his friend an annoyed stare. "Yes, he mentioned it in passing." Much to Logan's annoyance, he remembered Michael lamenting on it several times in fact. Like he cared about the man's personal life. Weston. *Boy, I never envisioned that one coming. Could I be slipping? Nah.*

An impish grin lit Nairn's face. "I'm guessing he's been enticed with easy money for the information. The usual bait."

"Michael doesn't work in any sensitive departments, doesn't have any reason to be there. He's a paper pusher," Logan said more to reassure himself then answer Nairn. He took a deep drink from his water bottle. "If he visited those areas, I would have been alerted."

"Could it be personal?"

Logan stared at him disgusted and grumbled, "God, I dunno. Maybe I dated his grandmother or made a bad business deal with his dad years ago. But, shit, you'd think I'd remember something like that. Can't be."

Nairn grabbed a towel to wipe the perspiration off his chest. "I think he's working for a bigger fish. A person who knows how you do things. The credentials Michael gave you came back clean." He dried his face and tossed the cloth aside. Nairn arched an eyebrow.

"Your interview with him didn't send up any red flags, did it?"

Logan gave a Gaelic shrug. "Not really. Though, he was a little twitchy during the interview. I chalked it up to nerves." He blew out a pent-up breath.

"I think there's a way to keep him off guard until we can figure out if he's working on his own or in conjunction with another party."

"You've been checking him out."

"Why I get the big bucks. You should check out Michael's ex."

Logan gave him a sly glance. "I already have, it would seem."

Nairn grinned. "You have? Why? When?"

Logan laughed. "Yesterday's art show."

"Oh? How'd it go?" Nairn cocked an eyebrow.

"She's hot, and she needs the scholarship I put in Thomas's name."

Nairn motioned for Logan to toss back the water bottle. "Thomas has never forgiven you for it." He took a swig from the bottle. "I hear the wife is pretty."

"Extremely. With long blonde hair all the way down to her tight little ass."

"Sweet." Nairn wiggled his eyebrows.

Logan laughed. "You better not let you-know-who hear you. She'll hand you your junk on a silver platter." Nairn's on again-off again romance with his girlfriend, Salina DeBois, was well known. Being off at present, unfortunately, they were both too pig-headed to admit they were right for each other.

"Can we not talk about her?" Nairn grumbled.

Logan held up both hands in truce then laughed. "I guess the hunt for the scholarship winner is over. I've always enjoyed being a patron of the arts."

Chapter Three

THE NEXT MORNING, Allyson couldn't shake the lingering grip of last night's sleep. Even scrubbing her face hadn't helped. Sseven nights in a row, Allyson had dreamed. After each trek into the realm of sleep, a will-o'-the-wisp memory attached itself to her. Each night she caught a glimpse of a bit more, yet never enough for a complete recollection.

She sighed, focusing on shortening her grocery list to the basics. Too many needs and not enough cash, she hated living this way. On the other hand, it was better than living with Michael and his putdowns.

The man's image from yesterday popped into her head. "Like every other guy, slime." She grimaced. "Out of sight, out of mind, and they feel free to wander." Annoyed, she snapped the pencil between her fingers in two. "I swear I think men need a collar, leash, and chastity-belt to keep them faithful."

In an instant, the painting from yesterday's exhibit swam before her and she blinked it away. How could she compete with such talent? Sunlight bounced off her own work decorating the walls of the living room drawing her attention. Her precise watercolors, calm and gentle, hung quietly on one wall. They garnered praise from many, but bored her. While her true love of creating screamed, 'LOOK AT ME' on the other walls. Bold, vibrant, brilliant swaths of colored, in-your-face designs grabbed the viewer by the throat demanding attention. Michael had hated her work so she'd kept them hidden in a spare room closet. The minute he walked out the door, her art came out to be displayed. Maybe she needed to begin her new life in the same way.

A knock at the door startled her. She swallowed a sob rising in her throat. A deliveryman stood there with a large package and a clipboard in his hands.

"Mrs. Weston?"

"Ms. Weston."

"Sorry, I have a package for you. Please sign here."

Allyson scrawled her name then handed back the clipboard, which he tucked under one arm, then picked up the package. "Where do you want this, it's a little heavy."

"Please put it on the table."

He laid the package on the table and left.

Allyson stared at the plain brown box. The logo of the college art department glared across the return label jolting her back to yesterday. Reading the label, a memory of musky cologne sprang uninvited to her senses and his autocratic maleness filled her mind. A card stuck to the outside of the box. Carefully, she opened it with trembling hands and read the short note scrawled in a bold, masculine hand.

May this remind you of your goals.

A single "L" signed the card.

Allyson tore open the box, and annoyance coiled in her stomach as she slid the item out of the container. Damn, it was the painting she'd admired from yesterday.

She had to return it. Accepting the canvas from Logan would cause too many problems. Allyson sank into the nearest chair rubbing the ache that throbbed across her brow.

✧   ✧   ✧

THE ART DEPARTMENT professor, annoyed at the possibility of losing a large commission, and having to repeat himself, glared at her.

"Mrs. Weston, I've explained. The gentleman paid cash."

Allyson let the Mrs. slide.

He continued, "We cannot credit a refund to his account. We don't accept returns or have the room for them. Which is why we sell the art-work and it helps fund our department. All sales are final."

Allyson lugged the painting back into the trunk of her car, slamming the lid closed. Great! Stuck with a painting costing who-knew-what. If Michael noticed it, he'd think she had the money to waste on trivial things or worse, his attorney would. Those two weasels would put their pointed little heads together and have her paying alimony to Michael.

Oh, Mr. Logan Kincaid better take this painting back or she'd shove it down his arrogant throat.

✧   ✧   ✧

ALLYSON FUMED...AT Michael...at the world...most importantly, at Logan Kincaid. She'd spent too many years being told what to do, and not doing what she wanted. No man, no person would to tell her what she could or couldn't do. Not anymore.

She half-expected the young male attendant at the gate to give her a hard time, but he'd smiled and waved her through. Odd, but then maybe that was all his job entailed. On the other hand, perhaps he smartly recognized an angry woman and intelligence told him to not mess with her.

Whatever the reason, Allyson drove down the winding driveway to the mansion. The locals had dubbed it simply, 'The House'.

From the road, one could see only the lines of its rooftops and chimneys. The many peaks and stacks made it appear a tiny village, not one dwelling. It was the oldest residence in the county. Pulling in front, she sat in the car for a moment trying to calm her rage. Composed, rational, but firm, she would let him know he'd toyed with the wrong woman.

Making her way to the front door and up the few steps, she paused to a take a deep breath to relax and absorb the grandeur of the massive oak entranceway with its recessed stone. She jabbed at the doorbell.

This house—immense residence—that should have been bustling with noise and activity, sat strangely, eerily quiet. Several minutes passed before she heard the faint sound of approaching high heels on a wooden floor echoing through the door.

A woman answered. Definitely not a servant and not the brunette Mr. Kincaid had with him at the courthouse square.

The woman wore her red hair short, her hazel eyes sparkled against a peachy complexion. Her clothing consisted of an expensive midnight blue leather skirt and a silk blouse in cool teal. Long, tan legs stretched from the skirt to nestle in to-die-for classic black and white Zebra-striped Manolo Blahnik's.

Good grief, does he have his own harem? Wife, maybe? Mistress, perhaps? Lover, most surely. Allyson wondered how to handle this.

"May I help you?" The woman's speech dripped with culture.

"Yes, I am here to see Mr. Kincaid," Allyson's voice broke with an embarrassing squeak, while she reminded herself not to fidget.

The redhead eyed her for a minute and then noticed the box leaning against Allyson's leg.

"You're lucky. He's chosen to work at home today. Please, come in. Do you need help?" At the shake of Allyson's head, she gave an elegant shrug. "I'll see if

he's available to visitors. Please wait here in the foyer."
She stopped and turned back to Allyson again. "Your
name, please. And your business with Logan?"

"My name is Ms. Weston, and my business with
Mr. Kincaid is personal." The entire world did not
need to know about this.

The smile the redhead gave her made Allyson realize there had probably been many women who
received gifts from the man this beauty warmly re-
ferred to as Logan. A wife, or lover, how did she
handle these situations with such aplomb?

A clock loudly ticked the seconds away or could it
be the sound of her heart? Allyson used the time to
study her surroundings. Polished oak and scented
cedar were everywhere—floors, paneling, and the
staircase. Doors with glass insets, frosted, etched, or
both, glinted brilliantly. A chandelier, of Austrian
crystal woven together with delicate silver tendrils,
hung in a large room to her right. The day's sunlight
glistened sharply from its many facets.

A door down the hallway opened and the woman
stepped out.

"He'll see you now."

Allyson hefted the re-boxed painting in her arms
and walked to the door the redhead held open. An
instant after she passed through, the door closed
behind her. Once again, the sharp clack of high heels
on wood faded into the distance. The hair on the back
of Allyson's neck prickled at the sound. She imagined

the clatter lent urgency to the woman's retreat, but dismissed the notion as childish.

Funny, why had she chosen the word retreat?

Sunlight streamed in from the side windows of his home office and spilled across the mahogany desk. Logan Kincaid sat behind it wearing a smug, self-satisfied expression. Relaxed, he still exuded a powerful, feral elegance. He rose and came around the desk, only to lean back on the front of it, legs crossed leisurely at the ankles. He wore an expensive tailored suit, a sharp contrast to her unglamorous jeans and sweatshirt. The droning which began in her head upon entering became louder.

"Ms. Weston, welcome." Logan smiled.

"You're quite resourceful. You found out where I live." She scowled at him.

"I asked around."

Seeing a small sofa nearby, she plopped the painting onto it. "I'll bet you did." Allyson mumbled. "I can't accept this."

"Why?"

"I don't know you."

"That can be remedied." A wicked smile danced across his face.

"I believe I made myself clear."

"The gift makes my intentions clear." He unfolded his arms to press his palms against the desk behind him.

"Really? What does your little friend, what's her

name, Stacy, have to say?" She all, but stomped her foot. "Or the woman who answered your door?"

Logan enjoyed the way she stood, arms crossed, chin up. "Stacy is an employee who over-stepped her bounds. Salina is a good friend."

"Stacy didn't act like an employee. Does she know it's all she is?"

"The girl's position here has been made quite clear to her. Now there isn't any reason we can't proceed."

"There is no 'we', and there's not going to be any 'proceeding.' Here's your painting back, please leave me alone."

"You don't want to be alone, Allyson." His voice purred, and the serious glint in his eyes put her on alert. She stepped back.

"Leave me alone, or I'll take steps to insure you will."

"A threat?" He straightened, uncrossing his legs to close the distance between them and then stopped. At that moment he realized she truly believed he couldn't be attracted to her and that spurred his desire more.

"Take it anyway you want. Goodbye, Mr. Kincaid."

Turning, she quickly stepped out of the room. She found herself almost at a run heading for the front door. Her hand touched the doorknob and she heard him laugh, a full, reckless sound sending tingling sparks of excitement down her spine. She bolted out the entrance.

✧   ✧   ✧

HIDDEN IN THE foliage shadows along the driveway, he observed the woman leave the sanctuary dubbed, 'The House'. He'd waited many years for Kincaid to show more than a passing interest in a woman. Decades rolled along, but finally Kincaid had. About time.

The Alliance said he was one of them. The Alliance said they accepted him, but they hadn't. They all lied. He deliberated how to deal with them. Being a dead man gave him more freedom to do what he pleased. To all of them.

✧   ✧   ✧

SALINA POPPED BACK into the office, finding Logan alone and laughing. "She left fast. Did you find out what you wanted to know?"

"No. Which is why I need you to do a favor for me." Logan stood in front of the loveseat. The now empty box lie on the floor, the artwork rested on the sofa. He ran a finger across the frame thinking about the woman, glad the buzzing in his ears was gone. Then he straightened and walked back over to his desk. Rounding it, he stepped over to a file cabinet and withdrew a folder. Grinning, he handed it to Salina. "We've found the recipient of the Thomas Cedric Rothwell scholarship for the arts." He surveyed her while she glanced at the name on the folder.

"You're well aware it's illegal."

"I'm an attorney. I can find a loophole in any- thing." He'd gone to sit in his chair, leaning back, with hands clasped behind his head.

"Logan…" Salina's lush lips now pursed into a thin line. He'd pissed her off. "You really think it's a good idea after what happened?"

He waved a hand dismissively. "A small, tempo- rary setback in my plans."

"Temporary setback? How can you be sure? She returned your gift."

"Ms. Weston left angry, confused, and a little frightened. She really believed I was hitting on her." He cringed inwardly at the fact he'd been doing that. "I made the painting a test."

"A test? Oh, and how did Ms. Weston fair?" Logan didn't miss the sarcasm in Salina's voice.

"She passed with flying colors." He wondered where the hum had come from, now that it had disap- peared. "Ms. Weston could've kept the painting or had it sent back by messenger since selling it was out of the question. Instead, she chose to personally bring it to me. She doesn't have a clue what her husband is up to. I can use it to my advantage."

"You surmised all this how? Oh, I get it. You've been checking her out."

"Of course. The Weston's are going through a messy divorce."

"I've heard." Again, Logan ignored the disdain in her voice.

"Ms. Weston is in dire need of money, but she still has her pride. It will gall her but she'll have to accept the scholarship." Logan put his feet up on his desk.

"You really think she will? What about the student who really qualified for the scholarship?"

"She will. Don't worry I've arranged for the other student to receive a generous, anonymous gift. Everyone is happy."

"Ms. Weston won't be," Salina warned.

"Not yet, but she will be in time." A smile played on his lips. "Set up a dinner so we can bestow the check on Ms. Weston."

"Who else do we invite?" He heard her resignation. She'd accepted her part in the charade.

"The committee who handles the leg work for the scholarship, of course."

"Michael Weston is on the committee."

"As one of my loyal staff, Michael's required to show. I want to see how this is going to play out." Logan straightened then leaned forward on the desk. "Besides, there's the possibility he still loves her. I need to know all my advantages."

"Advantages?"

"Separated or not, if the woman I still loved received such a gift, and I found out, the gift giver would be choking on the canvas shortly thereafter." Logan tapped the desktop with his fingers. "My guess is Michael will be happy to pawn her off and jump at the chance."

"How is a dinner party going to help?"

"I need to know which way the wind blows with Michael. You're going to flirt with Michael, and I'm going to, how do they say, chat up Ms. Weston."

"I hope you're not asking me to…"

"It won't go that far." Logan laughed quietly. "I won't ask you to take one for the team. I'm not that much of a monster, no matter what the staff is saying about me sending Stacy off, and besides, I don't need Nairn pissed off at me, too." He ignored the daggers she shot at him. "You're going to do a tiny bit of harmless flirting. I want to see how Michael reacts."

"I still don't get it." Salina sighed.

"Michael has his own agenda for worming his way into Kincaid Enterprises. I want to shake him up. Let him think I could be interested in his estranged wife. Michael may think he's got an in. Maybe he'll spill information or at least let his guard down."

"You think he's low enough to use his wife in such a manner?"

"Yes. Michael isn't intelligent or clever enough to pull this off himself. He's working with someone else. I have to figure out which one of my enemies it is, and if they want me discredited or dead."

Logan leaned back and began reading the papers on his desk.

"Have you taken in to account you might be using an innocent woman in all this?" Salina asked.

His attention on the paper before him, he scornfully replied, "No woman, especially a beautiful one, is ever truly innocent."

She blew out a breath.

"Oh, and Salina?" he added smoothly.

"Yes?"

"Ring up a feeder for me will you, I'd appreciate it," he commanded, still focused on the papers on his desk.

Chapter Four

AFTER LUNCH, LOGAN decided to take a walk through the training facilities hoping it would take his mind off of a few things. Like how he had a spy in his company, how he'd pissed off his friend Salina, and the Weston woman.

Allyson. His groin tightened at the thought of her curves and those huge green eyes. Bet they darken to a rich emerald when she climaxed. *Don't go there; she's a complication you need to steer clear of right now.* The picture of long legs wrapped around his waist popped in his mind's eye, a groan slipped from his lips. A quick glance around assured him he was alone and his involuntary utterance had gone unheard by others.

His pace quickened and he mentally shook off those images forcing himself to a leisurely stroll while resisting the urge to scratch the crawling sensation under his skin into submission. How had his life turned upside down? He worked hard to keep his life smooth, uncomplicated after *her* death. For a brief time he considered the Janissary way of life, but his mentor, Thomas Rothwell, suggested his talents lie elsewhere and persuaded him towards more academic challenges. When his mentor became an Alliance member, Logan took his place as the Alliance's coun-selor. While others used brute strength to settle differences, he used cunning, words, and polite civili-zation as his weapons. Why did this woman disturb him so, why did he crave her and by the gods, why did that buzzing accompany her presence?

Logan paused outside the patio doors to view his own personal kingdom. Manicured lawns and gardens softened the many buildings dotting his property. It pleased him that the structure sizes and growth of purpose numbered in the double digits. He'd arrived in the area in 1836, and found the gentle hills and lush valleys to his liking. With a plan in mind, he'd staked out the land he'd wanted. He wanted a house. Not just any house, a large home; a place for family and friends to gather. Being an only child, he longed for a well populated brood of his own with the perfect mate at his side. The search for a spouse had ended in tragedy and the thought of siring offspring died too, but he still proceeded to build the town of Baneridge. His town, discreetly and generously seeded with Tarczals and coms. A year later, Baneridge was officially founded and a year after that Tilendale College launched its first classes.

When his best friend needed a place to start his academy, offering his home seemed logical. He didn't regret the path he'd taken; it suited him well. He was damn good at his job and he served the Alliance and its people with satisfaction. But on occasion, like yesterday, the urge to beat something or someone to a pulp gnawed at him.

It was Allyson's fault; she stirred these emotions awake in him. He closed his eyes dismissing her and clearing her from his mind as he reached for the door to the facility. A crash and a thud followed by a groan and the odor of pungent sweat soaked bodies hitting the floor, or a wall, or another body echoed down the hallway in near defining waves, assaulted his senses. He itched to ditch his suit and join the men in hand to hand training. He schooled his features, no emotion leaked from his face. His heart swelled with pride for his friend as he strolled past each area studying the men locked in one form or another of combat.

Nairn didn't permit wooden katanas here. There were no pulled punches. Lethal steel and full contact ruled these classes. If you weren't good enough to defend yourself from injury, you shouldn't be in here. Only a small percentage of Janissaries made it this far, and by the end of the two year class, a handful at best would graduate.

Logan felt pride for his friend, remembering Nairn's idea and dream of making the Janissary more than they'd ever been. Before; they existed as separate groups trained by individuals. A plan that really hadn't worked for decades, in truth it was full of pit falls and un-cooperation. Under Nairn's plan, no longer did each group work alone; beneath his tutelage they became one, selecting the best from each, blending them into a single working entity. The men from that first group were charged with instructing the next generation of security for the Tarczal race. Satellite schools were set up all over the world but the 'graduate' school was here. In this place, the selected students honed their skills and those from that batch were incorporated into the elite of the elite.

Nairn surprised him when he sought out not only the warrior types but the artist of complex paper trails. The disadvantage to a long life and slowed aging process resulted in having many relocations and new identities. In the past, each family was responsible for their own rearrangements. Unfortunately, due to the urgency of these moves, too many costly mistakes had been made. Dates, birth and death not matching up, or worse, crossing over from one family to another, causing the outside world to question and pry. Logan let a full blown smile spill cross his mouth. Many lives had been saved thanks to Nairn's dream turned reality, by his men hidden in the background filing the right paper work at the right time. While the Janissary artisans of paper outnumbered the muscle of the Alliance it was the muscle that drew the awe of the populace.

Logan halted, the scent of blood, fresh and alive tickled his nose, he inhaled deeply and the aroma caressed his palette to settle happily on his tongue. Ah, someone hadn't moved fast enough. He followed the scent to one doorway. A student lay on the floor inside the room bleeding profusely from the nose while Gideon Alloway, Nairn's right-hand-man-in-training, stood over him lecturing the downed man.

"I don't understand how you got this far with all your 'tells'? You lead with your left every time and your opponent learns this quickly. How? Because you drop your arm and roll your shoulder right before you do. Every-Single-Time." Gideon offered the man the advice and his hand, helping him up. Then Gideon noticed him. "Sir, what may we do for you?"

"Nothing, just observing."

"Right, sir." Gideon nodded before turning back to the student, who, thanks to some tissue stuffed in each nostril, had the bleeding under control.

Logan grinned and headed back down the hallway. The boy was learning, Nairn did well choosing him. He stopped and observed several other classes in session before heading to his friend's office. Much was being accomplished here and it all happened when Nairn took his first step in the long process of convincing the Alliance his ideas were valid. The Tarczal's security needed to move forward and the first thing had been to enlist the oldest warrior to join him and the Janissary.

Tracking down the man took nearly a decade since he rarely spent much time in one spot. Giovanni Maria Alessandro Conte Di Cavour aka Sandro was a loner, to the point of being a boarder-line rogue; when Nairn found him in a back alley dive in Belize spoiling for a fight. As Logan remembered the story Nairn told, Sandro had been sitting at the bar drinking, most of the patrons were giving him a wide berth. Except one young Turk looking to prove he was cock of the walk. The insolent pup kept the insults up until he kicked off a rollicking brawl which was fine by Sandro. It ended with him and Nairn, back to back, fighting their way out. Well, to be truthful, Sandro did most of the fighting while Nairn watched Sandro's back, keeping the slime from a sneak attack. But Nairn's style of fighting and Nairn himself impressed Sandro to the point he agreed to listen to his proposal. Sandro consented to joining Nairn's Janissary and in return Nairn gave him full reign to choose the five men he wanted in his group.

And choose he did. Big men, impressive men, all around six foot seven and taller, muscle and strength rippled over their bodies. Single minded, driven men who lived in the shadows of society on a regular basis. Men who had no one to miss them should they fall, but they never fell. Time and again they completed each mission without fuss or fan fair.

Logan halted at the door to Nairn's office, it was open but spying him on the phone he paused. His friend, deep in conversation, didn't notice him standing there. When he clicked off the cell-phone, Logan knocked.

"Hey, come on in, what brings you to this part of complex?"

"Needed some air."

"So you left the sweet smell of the white collar business side to come visit the sweaty smelly, testosterone side, huh?"

"Something like that, but no…a reminder on my calendar popped up and I decided a walk would do me good."

"Reminder of what?"

"Sepelio Six mission, how long have they been out this time?"

"The Destroyer Six." Nairn leaned back in his chair, arms behind his head.

Logan recalled the day Sandro's group chose their moniker. Sepelio meaning to Destroy, something the group of six men did with glee on a regular base.

"They've been out a little over seven months. Sandro wanted to try and infiltrate one of the Hawthorn facilities." Nairn chuckled. "Hawthorn, gawd what a name, guess they thought they were being clever when they chose that."

"Yeah, naming themselves after the tree they make their stakes and bullets from wasn't a very smart move. You'd think, too, that after all these years they'd realize we're not like the monsters of legend and movies. We die like anyone else, no magic spells or wood involved." He shook his head. "By the way, did Sandro or you choose this mission?"

"I did, or maybe I let him talk me into it, I'm not really sure. I do know I'm starting to think I should've sent another unit."

"Sandro never has hidden his hatred for old Zachariah Vincenzo and the cult he spawned, not that I blame him." Logan mused.

"You two have that in common, going after the man that killed the woman you loved."

"Unlike me, Sandro never got to finish what Zachariah initiated."

"You got your revenge. Sandro's was taken from him when the bastard died of old age but not before leaving his legacy of hate."

"The Vincenzo family has grown and so has their 'Hawthorn' followers. So when are Sandro and the unit due back?"

Nairn leaned back in his chair. "Sandro runs a tight group, normally not breaking silence until they are half way home. Which should be any day now."

"Good, I might need them with this problem."

"Which one?" Nairn laughed.

"The spy, you dolt."

"Don't think I can handle that?"

"I think when Salina finally hunts you down, you're going to have your own problems."

"Only if she finds me before I see her coming first."

"You two need to work things out."

"And you need to get laid and off my back."

Chapter Five

A WEEK LATER, Logan recalled Nairn's words as he anxiously watched the entranceway of the banquet room for Allyson's arrival. It shouldn't matter, her being nothing more than a means to an end, but he couldn't help but watch for her all the same.

"Mr. Kincaid," a gentleman said.

Logan answered with a quick, "Good evening," but his attention wandered. Allyson had entered the room.

She wore a snug sleeveless little black dress and her hair was pulled up on her head, tendrils of silken tresses wafting down here and there. She reminded him of the ladies-at-court during his youth. He remembered well the lessons learned at the hand of one generous raven-haired lady in particular.

"Good evening, Allyson," he said, stepping up behind her.

Startled, she turned and glared at him. "What are you doing here?"

He lifted a brow. "Hi to you, too."

"I'm sorry. I didn't mean to be rude." He watched as she smoothed a hand down the front of her dress in an attempt to hide her nervousness but it only exaggerated the way her breasts swelled above the neckline.

Nice.

"Do you donate to the scholarship or something?" she asked, dragging his attention away from her breasts.

"Or something," he answered, and the buzzing began again. Why did he take notice of that damn hum every time he came within five feet of her? It annoyed the hell out of him.

She rubbed her temple for a second and he wondered if she felt it, too.

"Headache?" he asked all the while wishing his would disappear.

"No, I'm a little nervous."

"Ah," he said, leaning closer to her, enjoying the light floral scent clinging to her skin. "If there's anything I can do to help you relax, let me know."

She blushed at his implied suggestion then immediately lifted her chin to feign composure. "I'm fine, thank you."

"Too bad," he said, lifting a curl from her shoulder, appreciating its silky texture. His gaze locked with hers. "I think we both could use a respite." If possible her blush deepened but a waiter called him away before she had a chance to retort.

"Have fun." He tipped his head slightly then grabbed a glass of champagne from a passing waiter and handed it to her.

✧   ✧   ✧

ALLYSON HELD THE glass with a trembling hand, watching the broad back of Logan Kincaid walk away from her. She wanted to knock the drink back in one gulp but the way her head buzzed, she might pass out if she did. The man totally unnerved her. She'd be dishonest with herself if she didn't admit to having a thought, or two, or three of him and her naked on a bed. But that's all she was going to do. Getting involved with a man like Logan Kincaid could spell disaster. Lost in her own world she didn't see her ex approach.

"Good evening, dear."

Allyson almost choked on the champagne but Michael probably planned his surprise greeting for such a purpose. She turned to face him.

"What do you want?"

His mock surprise almost choked her again. "What? No pleasantries? Not nice of you considering I sat on the committee that picked the scholarship winners." He grabbed a glass of champagne from a passing waitress. Based on the glaze in his eyes, he'd all ready had a few.

"Of course," he continued after he gulped the drink, "you weren't one of those winners."

A knot formed in her stomach. "What are you saying?"

With the shrug that never failed to infuriate her, he stared at her cleavage.

"Let's just say you must have used other than talents to win the scholarship." He lifted his glass toward Logan, who stood with his back to them across the room. "Spread your legs for him, did you, sweetheart?"

"You bastard," she whispered, but Michael only chuckled and walked away. He made her feel like nothing. He always did.

She found her seat, and did her best to enjoy the evening, but Michael's implication tainted her joy over receiving the scholarship. She hadn't slept with Logan, but she acknowledged to herself that is was what he wanted. His sexual interest in her wasn't exactly subtle.

Did he think her a high-priced call girl?

Didn't she truly earn her scholarship? The more she deliberated, the angrier she became. When the dinner ended she sought a chance to speak with Mr. Kincaid alone.

"You rigged the scholarship," she ground out.

"No, I didn't."

"I shouldn't have won."

"Really? Who should have?"

"I don't know."

"Then how do you know you didn't win?" Logan arched one eyebrow.

"Because Michael said."

"Michael doesn't know bull."

"Demons!" A disheveled woman burst into the room and headed directly toward Allyson and Logan waving a Bible over her head screaming. "We have among us one who's been demon spawned!"

"I have the protection and strength of the Lord Almighty. We will drive you out, monster!" she screamed.

Two security guards quickly moved to intercept the woman. Logan placed a hand on Allyson's elbow, steering her toward the other side of the room.

"Come with me, Allyson," Logan commanded, and she let him maneuver her further away. The sensuous freedom of his stride, his vital nearness, all had a disconcerting effect. Her senses set off alarms but she had no idea how to resist the enticing waves swirling around and pulling her closer to him. They reached the hallway on the other side of the room. Allyson peeked over her shoulder to see the security guards had the woman and were leading her away, while she continued her tirade.

"We will find you again, foul creature, and we will destroy you and those who would consort with you!" The woman screeched, and the guards all but carried her out the door.

"I'm sorry, Allyson." He scanned the room they'd exited, his concentration seemingly excluding her for the moment. Fascinated, she stared and watched him for only a second before it dawned on her that the woman's words had actually upset him. Before she could ask why, he swung his gaze to her.

"The scholarship is yours, Allyson. Keep it or

don't, it's up to you," Logan snapped curtly. "You'd be a fool not to accept and I seriously don't think you're a foolish woman."

Taken aback by his sharp tone, she said nothing.

A security guard came back into the room giving Logan the all clear sign. Logan steered her back into the room. "Showtime, Allyson. Smile for the crowd and the photographer." The smile on his lips belied the roughness of his voice.

People mingled around them, nervously laughing and making small talk about the crazy woman. Allyson half-listened to the uneasy chatter and soon others drew Logan away into the crowd.

For the rest of the night, she was conscious of every move he made, every breath he took. When they were thrown together again later, her throat felt raw and tight as she reached for the champagne he offered. Then, to avoid a scene, she ate the bit of toast smeared with caviar that Logan nudged against her lips. He made her fearful and fascinated, all at the same time.

✧   ✧   ✧

HE WATCHED HER stand dutifully beside him accepting congratulations for the award, arms crossed tight over her chest, which, to his delight, only accentuated those wonderful mounds of womanly flesh. He wanted to tell all the guests to leave, go away and leave them alone, alone where he could touch her, taste her, savor her in private with no interruptions but his breeding raised its ugly head demanding he be polite, cordial, and so he smiled and was. While his lascivious nature sighed and stomped off to pout.

She smiled, waiting for the last of the reporters to leave, tension rolling off her in waves. He knew even before she spoke that she had questions he might not want to answer.

"Enough, Mr. Kincaid. What's going on? Why did that woman's rant bother you? Don't deny it didn't."

"This isn't the first time she's intruded on an event connected to me."

"Why did she say those things about you?"

"I haven't a clue, perhaps she has dementia."

Allyson's arms dropped to her sides. Logan's moment of hope Allyson believed him vanished when just as quickly, they came back up to hug her middle. Damn.

"Why did you give me the scholarship? If you think it's a way to get me in bed, you're sadly mistaken. Because, that's not going to happen."

Her seeing right through his tactic galled him, though it shouldn't since it was blatant. His masculine pride pricked, he could do only one thing, turn the tables back on her. "I won't deny the thought of you in my bed isn't intriguing, Allyson, but did you consider I might believe in your talent? Your artistic talent, although I do wonder if your other talents are as good?"

"Damn you, Logan Kincaid. I have to accept the scholarship, but I don't have to accept you." Allyson moved to turn and then rounded on him. "Maybe the crazy old woman is correct, maybe you are a monster." Her words stinging him more than he'd ever let her see or know.

✧   ✧   ✧

BODY FLUSH FROM all the eyes she supposed on her, Allyson avoided contact with all, trying her best to blend in with the wall behind her. She bid her time until the crowd thinned, when it did, she saw her chance to escape. Limbs stiff from embarrassment like a marionette on strings, she made it to her car sure all eyes were on her and judging. In contrast to those feelings, the whole ride home she couldn't get thoughts of Kincaid's strange effect on her from her mind. Sitting in her garage with palms so sweaty they nearly slid off the steering wheel, she realized the weird buzzing had stopped. It stopped the moment she left Kincaid's side. What was it about him?

✧   ✧   ✧

LOGAN NOTICED MICHAEL watching him all evening. The man's attention to him exceeded polite interest. His employee waited for the crowd to trickle down before making a B-line straight for him. Great. All he needed was Michael adding to tonight's problems.

First the old woman, why did she have to pick this event to show up? Just when he was hoping to make headway with Allyson.

Allyson. What a screw up. Why couldn't she just accept the scholarship and be done with it? *Maybe because she was right and you want in her pants.* No, there was more to it. The sight of her. The smell of her. She disturbed him to his core, and not in a terrible way. That hadn't happen before with any woman. Yes, he wanted her, but he didn't have a clue as to the why.

He'd been celibate for several decades after the last fiasco.

Gods, if that was all there was to this infatuation. Maybe he should go and get laid. Maybe then this obsession with her would leave. A little voice in his head laughed uproariously.

Michael standing in front of him drew his attention back to the present.

"Kincaid." Michael's voice carried a hint of demand that died on his lips when Logan locked his gaze on him. Michael licked his lower lip nervously. "Mr. Kincaid, may I have a word with you?"

Michael was an annoyance, much like finding dog crap on the bottom of his expensive shoes. But, this annoyance might be harder to clean off; it might pay to listen to what he had to say.

"Yes?" Logan replied in a tone hovering on annoyed boredom.

"Who's the crazy?"

Well, points for the pest, he had the balls to bring up the other nuisance. "I have no idea."

"Not any one you know?" Michael challenged.

Logan ground his teeth, "Exactly what I said." This little piss-ant was really starting to bug the hell out of him.

"She acted like you two were acquainted."

"Drop it." Logan barely suppressed a snarl.

Michael stupidly pressed on, changing tactics. "Funny how Allyson won the scholarship."

"Ms. Weston topped another list which made her eligible," Logan added.

"Right. Your personal list?"

"You're cross, Michael." Now he really was angry. "What do you want?"

"Oh, I don't know. Peace on earth, good will towards men, fifty grand in an off-shore account."

Logan gave a short bark of a laugh and arched a brow before leaning into Michael's face. "Smaller minded men than you have tried this kind of stunt."

"Really? Well, they must not have had the info I do." Michael sneered.

Logan returned the sneer. "You think you have incriminating information concerning me?"

Michael swallowed hard. "Yes, and I've got friends who have a lot more dirt on you."

"Really? And if I refuse to facilitate this pathetic attempt at extortion?" Logan watched Michael squirm, enjoying the man's torment. Could blackmail be all there was to this spy thing?

"You'll help facilitate," Michael said with a lisp, "because, I can help keep you from enemies you don't know about. Don't mess with me."

Enemies? So Michael was working with someone.

"Mess with you?" Logan let a smile that made many a man back off creep across his face. "I don't have to. My attorneys can handle it for me. They have the confidentiality form you signed with Kincaid Enterprises."

From the way Michael paled, he was just remembering it, too.

Logan let the smile on his lips widen as he leaned closer to Michael. "Breaking it, I believe, means the loss of your job and being blackballed in your line of work, which is tantamount to a death sentence career wise." He decided to push Michael a little further and stepped toe-to-toe with him. Michael clenched his fist and Logan hoped he would lash out. Then he could release the fury bubbling under his controlled façade. Much to his disgust, Michael whined.

"You're good with words, aren't you? You like playing word games, mind games, with people, don't you?" Michael's lisp thickened. "Well, you sanctimonious leech, there's a fine line between consent and advised consent. And you didn't cross it, you took a flying leap over it!"

Logan made his gaze hard and arctic, letting the

scorn for this worm slowly spread across his face.

Michael tossed back the rest of his drink, no doubt for courage, and then went past pale to flush with rage at Logan's next words.

"I'm curious about a couple of things, things your lovely wife might find interesting, perhaps helpful to her in the divorce."

"What?" Michael choked out.

"How are Simona and the baby?"

The muscles in Michael's face went slack.

Mockingly Logan said, "You're not corrupt enough to swim with the sharks, Michael. Get back in the kiddy pool while you still can."

Logan turned to leave and then glanced over his shoulder. "Go home or wherever you're living and I'll forget this entire episode ever happened."

He left Michael standing there shaking with rage.

✧   ✧   ✧

MICHAEL HURRIED TO his car, pulling out his cell phone along the way. "Hey, I found info to blackmail Kincaid with."

The voice on the other end sighed. "You didn't try, did you?" it asked.

"No, I'm not brainless." Michael clenched his jaw tight, no way would he admit to being wrong. That was a sign of weakness and he wasn't weak. "I planned to check with you first."

"Good, meet me at the usual place. We'll discuss this further," said the voice.

"I'll be right over."

"No, not now wait a couple of hours then come over."

"Sure, no problem, I've got other places I need to be first anyway." Michael snapped the cell phone closed.

Now that Kincaid had reminded him, a little time with his mistress would be a good way to work off his tension. The woman did have a magical mouth, which was all he got to use now that the baby was growing in her belly. Kincaid and his soon to be ex-slut-of-a-wife would pay later.

Chapter Six

H E'D BEEN BUSY since Michael's call earlier. He flicked his thick auburn ponytail over his shoulder. His eyes closed in bliss the moment his butt hit the chair's malformed cushion. A soft rap at the door beckoned him. Michael had arrived sooner than expected, good thing he hadn't dawdled over dinner.

"Michael." He opened the door. "Welcome, please enter." He observed Michael linger in front of the closed door, hands hidden in his suite's pockets. "You're early. I barely had time to clean up." It amused him when Michael took in the shabby-chic, heavy on the shabby, miniscule on the chic, room. He'd deliberately chosen the seedy motel far off the beaten path because it sat at the end of a long, weed-choked lane. The interior didn't present much better.

Nondescript carpet that once may have held a pattern lay worn to near threads along the room's heavy traffic areas. Any disturbance to the carpet's remains released a musty, dry, moldy smell reminiscent of a wet dog. He watched Michael glance nervously around and give a shudder at the CSI paradise.

"Little dark in here, isn't it, Mr. Arnaud?" Michael licked his lips several times before trapping his lower lip between his teeth.

"It's Frank, Michael, remember?" Frank Arnaud was only one of his many aliases. "I apologize, I've a bit of a migraine and the light hurts my eyes." Frank sat again in the same large chair, back straight; legs spread wide, elbows resting on the arms of the chair and fingers steepled in a façade of relaxed elegance. "Turn on the table light if you must."

"Yeah, um, sure. No problem. We can leave the bathroom light on." Hesitantly, Michael perched on the bed, the only other place to sit.

"Thank you for your understanding. Would you like a drink?" He could tell Michael was already several sheets to the wind when he walked in the room. A little more to prime him wouldn't hurt. "Now, tell me about Kincaid."

"You missed all the fun," blurted Michael.

Frank tilted his head to one side, feigning interest. "Really, what happened?"

Michael squirmed in his seat. "A crazy old broad came in yelling about monsters and stuff."

"Fascinating."

"Yeah, she went straight for Kincaid. I think she shook him up." Michael wiped his hand over his lower lip and switched subjects. "He's a sanctimonious leech; he thinks he's frigging better than everyone else. Tried to order me around like a lackey!"

"He didn't!" Frank tapped his fingertips together. The old woman must've been Daisy. She and George had finally arrived and were already harassing Logan. He should call on them. Frank tsked then said to Michael, "But then again, Logan always believed himself better than those around him."

Michael abysmally mimicked Logan's voice. "Go fetch me and the lovely lady a fresh glass of champagne. Kincaid tried to threaten me with his lawyers," Michael spat out. "He's nothing but a prick. Besides our usual work load, which is horrendous enough, he had us slaving for weeks, choosing candidates for his frigging scholarships." Michael spoke quickly, his speech developing a heavy lisp.

"We had over two hundred applications for those artsy scholarships." Michael ran his tongue around the inside of his mouth. "Bunch of pansy ass bleed'n heart, tree-hugging artists."

The poor boy must be developing cottonmouth from all the alcohol, Franchot mused. Graciously, he pointed to the bottle beside Michael, indicating he should help himself, and Michael did.

"Painting pictures, poetry writing, what careers are those?" Michael shuddered in disgust. "They need to get their heads out of their asses and find an occupation that will get them a good paying job." Michael filled his glass.

Frank let the man ramble and drink. Michael gave a dismissive wave of his hand.

"We go to all the trouble of finding Kincaid good candidates, and he doesn't go with who we chose. He chose my wife!"

"Aren't you two divorced?" he interrupted. Poking an already agitated bear could be fun.

"Separated," Michael snapped.

"Sorry." He didn't care in the least.

"What were you saying?"

"I, oh yeah, Allyson's name made the first batch."

"Wouldn't that be a conflict of interest?"

"It was a blind judging. No one on the committee knew who did what, but I recognized her pathetic attempt. I've seen monkeys slinging shit make better art than her stuff."

"What a colorful description." This com became more of a complete imbecile with each passing minute. "If I may ask, then how did she receive the scholarship?" God, it was hard to keep a straight face while listening to this baboon.

"Allyson's work was marked for special consideration, which is code for the boss wants this person to win."

"Didn't the committee think this was prejudicial?"

Michael took another gulp of his drink and snickered. "Hey, he's the boss. He signs our checks. Who's going to argue with him? If he wants to give it to someone who can't find their way around a canvas, it's his business." He scrubbed his hand over his face then shook his head.

"He's screwing her. I know he is." Michael stared into the now empty glass. "The slut spreads her legs for everyone but me."

"Well, Kincaid always did have an eye for the ladies." His nostrils flared, and one specific woman sprang to mind. Flora Rainey. Such a pretty name for such a horse-faced woman. Of course, Kincaid's late flower did have a thorn or two. He rubbed the flesh, between his thumb and forefinger where the little weed had left her teeth marks for all eternity. Oops. Michael wanted his attention again.

"Lady, yeah, right, more like from a kennel."

He laughed at Michael's pathetic attempt at a joke. After all, he could do that for a condemned man.

"I taught her everything she knows." Michael filled his glass again.

"About art?"

"Hell no. Sex." Michael rubbed the knuckles of one hand over his mouth. "She was a virgin when I met her. My fraternity brothers were all jealous."

Michael's face lit up. "She'd dated jocks; everyone knows the type of woman they like. I happily perpetuated the idea she slept around." Michael drained his glass. "I let them all think I was banging her six ways to Sunday and back." Michael began to giggle, caught himself, and coughed instead. "She's lucky I didn't take after my old man. He used his big, old beefy hands to make a point. Me, I use words, the mark of an intelligent, educated man." Michael slammed his empty glass down. "Blobs and slashes of colors." Michael peered around.

"I need to use the bathroom." Michael urgently rubbed his palms back and forth over his thighs.

"You know where it is. If you please, leave the door open a bit." Michael gave him a quizzical stare.

"For the light," Frank explained then watched Michael go into the tiny room.

He listened while Michael relieved himself and waited.

"Boy, you need to call the front desk. There's a real disgusting smell in here. Smells like a dead thing."

"Yes, I'll have to do that." Amazing. Could the man be denser than he originally believed?

"It's coming from the tub." He continued listening when Michael pulled the shower curtain aside, the metal fasteners screeching loudly over the metal rod. He inspected his manicure and counted to five, three more than he expected to reach before Michael came stumbling out of the bathroom.

"There's, there's, a woman, I think it is, was, a woman. In the tub. She's dead."

"Yes." His reply came icy like the woman in the tub.

Michael's voice rose in a strangled scream of horror.

"You know! How? Why?"

It took several more seconds for the answer to form in Michael's alcohol soaked-mind. "You?" A small mewing sound slid from Michael's mouth.

"Yes." He grinned and let his feeder teeth slip into

place. "Me."

In the split second it took Michael's body to freeze, he crossed the room and grabbed his throat, cutting off any other sound Michael might utter.

Then, much to his dismay, Michael went limp in his grasp.

The man had passed out, or worse, fainted.

How utterly unmanly.

"Well, this is certainly a disappointment." He gazed at the limp body in his grip. "Michael," he chastised. "I had a higher opinion of you."

He shook the body once in disgust. "Is a little bit of struggle too much to ask?" he asked in exasperation then let Michael's body fall to the floor. Next, he bent over the prone form and placed his hands on the sides of Michael's head.

A quick jerk. A loud pop.

Then the hum of the central air kicking on filled the now silent room.

"Well, don't lay there my boy." He stared down at Michael on the floor. "We have places to go and people to see." He laughed then hefted the body over one shoulder toward the room's door.

"Don't worry sweetheart, I'll be back before you miss me." He called out to the corpse in the tub before shutting the door behind him.

The lack of guests negated interference, which suited him fine. He dumped the body into the trunk of Michael's car. He'd use Michael's car for this trip, gas being ridiculously high and all.

Waste not, want not.

Chapter Seven

SLEEP ELUDED ALLYSON. She tossed and turned. Her body thrummed with desire and frustration. Images of Logan Kincaid and she…naked, entwined, haunted her. Finally, she gave up, rising to spend most of the morning cleaning. Physical activity helped clear her clouded mind and ease the tension dancing through her. Toward mid-afternoon, her stomach growled. Last night's champagne and caviar didn't make for a lasting meal. Checking the refrigerator, she found it lacking and decided to go the store.

She was placing groceries in the trunk, when a voice from behind startled her.

"You must cast the demon aside. You must let us help you! You must be saved, child!"

Allyson whirled, her hand going over her heart, gasping, as adrenalin surged quick and sharp through her. The religious zealot from the party last night stood in front of her. The woman, still disheveled, eyes wild and darting, advanced on Allyson, who stepped back, trapped between the woman and the car, leaving her wondering how to make an escape.

"Daisy, this is not the way." An elderly man spoke to the zealot. "You're frightening the child." His face was gentle, serene, so different from the woman beside him. He placed a comforting arm around her shoulders.

"My name is George Kingston, and this is Lennabelle, my wife, my sweet Daisy. Forgive her please. She is a passionate woman who has suffered greatly. Her mother lost her life to the demon. We have traveled many miles into many countries, for many years to hunt this fiend. We wanted to warn you."

"Warn me about what?" Why were they confronting her?

"The demon vampire," they replied.

"Demon? Vampire? You're kidding right?" The couple gave her a sincere stare. "Okay, I'll bite. Who or what is supposed to be this monster?"

They each made the sign of the cross and Allyson refrained the urge to roll her eyes in disrespect at the gesture.

"It is a creature spewed and vomited from the bowels of the earth. It has walked the earth since the dawn of time." The man's eyes bulged with horrific splendor.

"It feeds on the blood of mortals as though they were its cattle. The fiend turns them into coffin-sleeping creatures!" Angry blotches of spidery crimson spilled across his face.

"This devil-spawned monster walks among us now. He uses the name Logan VonKruger Kincaid!" Spittle formed on his lips as his tirade reached a fevered pitch and his face shone with vengeance and righteousness.

Allyson's jaw dropped. "Let me get this straight. You're saying Mr. Kincaid of Kincaid Enterprises, who yes, is dashing in a tux, is a bat-changing, coffin-sleeping, blood-sucking vampire?"

They both nodded. "Yes, my child, you do understand."

She never meant to be rude, but the emotional turmoil of last night and little, if no sleep, took its toll. Allyson commenced to laugh. She laughed until tears streamed down her face. From the expression on their faces, they didn't bargain for such a reaction. Still laughing, she made her getaway. Once home, she put the groceries away, fixed a light meal, and decided to lie down, hoping to rid herself of a headache.

She awoke to pounding at her front door. Allyson wondered who that could possibly be.

The couple from the grocery stood there. *Great. How did they find where I lived?*

"Yes, what do you want now?" she asked, a little creeped out to find them on her doorstep.

"We have followed the demon here. Leave this house, and we will burn him out!" The woman, Daisy, held out a large cross.

Allyson threw up her hands. "Folks, you've gone too far. I may not like Mr. Kincaid, but to say he is a vampire and you're going to burn down my house is crazy!"

She nearly shut the door, but then paused. "Besides I've seen the man in broad daylight. Last night he drank champagne and ate caviar and a lot more at a dinner. Vampires are not supposed to be able to do those things!" She slammed the door and reached for the phone to call the sheriff's department.

Allyson watched the couple from the window. The Kingston's exchanged what appeared to be a heated conversation for a few minutes, then got in their car and left. Minutes later, a deputy drove up. She went down the walk to meet him. The officer listened to what she said then gave a brief wave before driving off to patrol for the crazies.

"Allyson?"

✧   ✧   ✧

SHE JUMPED, SPINNING towards the sound of her name and Logan saw the stark fear on her face.

"Logan, it's only you."

Perhaps she wouldn't be relieved to see him if she had any idea he'd spent the pre-dawn hours sitting on a log in the woods outside her house. He'd lost his mind; it was the only explanation. How else could he, the powerful head of several companies, have turned into a demented stalker? A sane man didn't tramp through the woods in the dead of night to sit on a log until the first light hours outside a woman's dwelling, in a tux no less.

He'd planned her seduction well, or so he thought. Her rejection of the painting amused him; the scholarship problem pricked his ego royally.

He was wealthy, handsome, charming, and sexy; well, other women had told him that, so what was wrong with her? Yet, he was the one who sat in the woods, soaking wet from the morning dew while she was cozy, warm, and dry in her home.

His driver, dedicated man he was, hadn't even questioned him when he'd been instructed to let him out along a desolate stretch of interstate.

Logan could only imagine what the man thought of him when he set out deep into the forest.

Shortly after tramping through the woods, Logan arrived in the sleepy neighborhood and then circled her house in bored curiosity. The feeling that Allyson was in danger tugged at him. The trees surrounding the dwelling disguised its deceptively large size. He learned from the public records that Allyson had inherited the house from the maiden aunt who raised her. As the morning wore on, he nestled himself deeper in the shadows. At one point, he heard the whine of a vacuum cleaner. It cheered him to think Allyson might be restless too. When she left the house a short time later and drove off, he was really questioning his actions.

Allyson, returning shortly with groceries, relieved him.

As dusk began to creep in, uneasiness began to

nag him. When he saw the light-colored car with the driver's side fender in dull gray primer slowly coast down the road, he understood why. The car rolled up to her house. When Daisy and George exited, his gut clenched tightly. Great, now they were hounding Allyson. Were they the danger?

He tried to listen to the conversation, but since they were tucked in the front porch, he could only hear raised voices. Relief washed over him when Allyson slammed the front door on the two and they retreated back to their car.

When a sheriff's car drove up, Logan noted that Allyson didn't even wait for the deputy to come all the way to the house. She hurried out to meet him halfway. Since she was out in the open, Logan could hear most of the conversation, and unashamedly, he listened.

As the deputy went back to his car, got in, and slowly drove off, Allyson moved closer to her front porch. Logan reflected on her conversation with the deputy and agreed with her comment about Daisy and George being persistent in their cause if nothing else. Hadn't his driver spent time dodging them before dropping him off? Friends, family, hell, even instinct told Logan he should do something about the couple's constant interfering. But he wouldn't, couldn't raise a hand against Daisy. He owed it to her late mother. He realized his past wasn't as far behind him as he'd hoped.

From the corner of his vision, Logan noted George and Daisy's car slowly entering the street again and he slid back towards the shadows. Allyson turned to follow his gaze.

"Allyson, please, they're back. May I come in?"

She let her gaze roam over him, probably noting the foliage that had adhered itself to parts of his tux and hair, and no doubt thinking he seemed like a crazy wild man. Well, at the moment, he wondered about his own sanity.

"All right, but only until they leave. They make me nervous, too," she said opening the door. "I'm not throwing you to the wolves, or in this case zealots, who want to burn my house down and stake you."

Allyson crossed in front of him to pick up the phone and seemed to make a point of placing herself in front of the window. She called the sheriff's office again. After explaining the situation, Allyson hung up and turned to face him.

She caught him admiring her work. He noticed the play of emotions flitter across her face. If he'd been in her place, his first thought, no doubt, was that he was only being condescending towards her paintings as a way to entice her into his bed. A consideration he wished he'd come to first, damn, he was losing his touch. But no, instead he noted the moment she realized he had given her work the appreciative study and respect one would give a well-known artist's work. He observed Allyson blinked several times, pulled herself together to return to the problem at hand, him.

"Well, Mr. Kincaid."

Interesting, he thought. Did she think using a title would place her back on formal terms with him?

"I really like your…" he paused midsentence when she shot him a look which shouted don't go there.

"I take it you've met the religious zealots. Do you have any idea what they're accusing you of?"

"Yes, I am fully aware of Daisy and George Kingston and their crusade." The damn buzzing clamored back, but Logan had set in motion an idea of why. "Since I last saw you, I've spent most of my time avoiding them."

A frosty, ghostly hand plunged inside his chest, squeezing the breath from him. He choked back a gasp as beads of sweat glistened on his forehead. Logan tried to shake it off. "I'd hoped I lost them coming here."

Seeing his distress, Allyson quickly guided him to the couch but he didn't sit. "Logan, have you eaten or slept since last night?"

He doubted she had a clue that when her voice filled with concern, it took on a lower pitch, throaty and seductive as hell. And, she'd used his first name again.

"No."

"Can I get you toast, tea, or perhaps a sandwich?" Allyson asked. "An aspirin?"

"No food, no drugs." He reached out to brush his fingertips across her forearm. "What I need is…I…I need to feed." He cursed himself, hearing his voice tremble with the craving, for her.

"The Kingston's are correct. My nutritional requirements are a little different."

Logan watched her process this information. She opened her mouth and shut it several times, guppy-like, and then gaped at him. Her eyes glanced up and down his body repeatedly. The emotions playing across her face screamed disbelief and this had to be some type of outrageous joke.

"There isn't any reason for you to be troubled, Allyson. If you're still offering, I could use a bite. By the way, I'm Tarczal, not vampire."

He watched while she digested the information and the moment when the pieces became a whole, for her. "A bite. Real funny. What the hell is the difference between a vamp and a Tarczal?" she snapped then pulled away from him. She ran a hand through her hair sending the locks tumbling down her back. "What's a Tarczal?"

It stung when she stepped back from him. "We're just members of the human race."

"I've never heard of you. Wait a minute you said we, there's more of you?"

"Yes, our numbers are limited, we're an extremely private people, but we're much like you."

"I don't drink blood and I don't know of anyone

else who does except weirdoes who believe they're vampires."

"I can assure you, I'm not a weirdo and I certainly don't think I'm vampire. And, for your information, the Maasai drink blood, well, cow's blood mixed with the milk for extra protein, but it's still blood."

"Right, cow's blood, not human."

"So our dietary needs differ slightly, but it's the same principle." Brow wrinkled, he sighed. "Allyson, I can show you a kiss more powerful than you've ever known." The words tumbled from his mouth like a ghastly cliché, and he cringed.

She laughed. "Do you really get women with that line?"

"It's not a line," he balked. "It's the truth."

"Oh, please," she snorted. "It's a line if I've ever heard one. Vampire, really, is this part of some type of offbeat reality show?" Allyson glanced around. "Where are the cameras? Are you wearing one? Is your sorry looking boutonnière a camera?" She stormed over to the window. "Is the old couple in on this? If this is Michael's idea of a joke and you're in on it I'll…"

She let the sentence hang. She wouldn't be the butt of some tasteless joke like so many times before. Crossing her arms over her chest, she straightened to her full height and actually stomped one foot in frustration before storming over to pick up the phone and begin dialing. In one swift, smooth motion, Logan advanced on her, snatching the device from her hands. Infuriated, she tried to grab it back. Logan effortlessly held it high over her head. Twice, three times she jumped up to retrieve the phone, each time he easily eluded her. Finally aggravated beyond words she gave a hard shove against his chest, and to her surprise he stumbled back. Pain etched his features. "Logan? I didn't hurt you did I?"

LOGAN GAVE A harsh laugh. "No, you didn't, you couldn't actually, no like a foolish diabetic, I've disregarded my health and put off ingesting the nourishment my body requires." He set the phone back in its cradle. Shoulders slumped, he closed his eyes. "Call the authorities, if you must. I'm too tired to care." A chill washed over him, nauseating him. The buzzing turned to a roar.

He could tell the moment she knew he wasn't playing some macabre joke on her.

"You're telling the truth." Allyson cocked her head to one side. "You're really a vampire."

"Tarczal, not vampire. Vampires are only in legends. I have an extra set of teeth, which slide into place when needed. That's the closest to the myths I come." He swayed, and tiny spots danced before his eyes.

"Vampires aren't real."

"No, they're not."

"But you said, the whole blood thing, vampires do those things!" Her feeble protest sounded whinny even to her.

"I'm Tarczal."

"A vampire."

He corrected. "Tarczal."

"And the difference is?"

"Tarczal's are real, I'm real. Vampires aren't."

"But you need…"

"Nourishment."

"Potato. Potăto."

"There is a difference, I assure you."

"Logan, you don't look so good." Allyson reached out to touch him but stopped short of actually doing so.

"I'm less than you fear and more than is known." Logan moved closer to her. "Allyson, let me hold you, let yourself give me the nourishment I need. It is a simple thing to do. I promise you, there will be no pain. No danger."

Allyson's gaze ran over him. Indecision marred her face.

"I want to give you more…."

"You mean sex?"

"No, I want to make love to you."

"Isn't that sex?"

"No, they are two separate things and I want to show you the difference between them. Let me give you much more than the physical of two bodies joining. I want to give you not only my body, yes, but and my heart and soul as well."

"Oh… I want to, really I do…"

"But you're anxious, I understand. You were raised to be a good girl and you don't want to disappoint any one."

"There's no one left to disapprove of me."

"Just yourself."

"Yes."

"You won't be disappointing anyone, especially yourself. You're a grown woman, with a woman's wants and needs."

There was pounding, from his head, from his heart, he didn't know or care which. Only she existed for him. The scent of her, the feel of her, he had to know the taste of her. Like a drug, she tempted him.

"Let me taste you, Allyson." Logan stepped forward lightly running his hands over her arms, keeping his voice low, soothing.

"What are you trying to do?" she whispered.

"Seduce you." Gooseflesh danced over her skin at the words.

"Please."

He watched, fascinated as her tongue darted out to moisten her lips. The simple action nearly brought him to his knees with desire.

"Yes, I'll please you," he whispered and stroked her face in a feathery caress.

"I can't think,"

"You don't have to." He heard the urgency in his own voice.

Pain, white-hot, searing, shot through his head. He sank to the couch rubbing his forehead. "Incredible, I'd never suspected. You don't have to be fearful of me, Allyson. I am too weak and wouldn't force you if I wasn't."

He struggled for control. "Could we reach a compromise?"

"Suspected? Compromise? What do you mean?" With his eyes closed, he felt her move away from him.

"How can I be sure you're not lying to me to get what you want?" she croaked.

"Because I come from a society where one's word is still their bond and I give mine to you freely. Your wrist, give it to me. If I feed from there, you will have complete control of the process."

She trembled. "I won't be hurt?"

Logan shook his head.

Allyson hurried over to close the drapes, coming back to sit down beside him. Logan reached for her left arm to pull her closer. He unbuttoned the cuff of her blouse, rolled it up, and held her hand palm up.

"Relax, this won't hurt a bit. I promise." The delicate hue of her skin, the pale blue lines of life under it and its softness tantalized him.

Allyson laughed. "My dentist's exact words."

"And?" he slyly asked.

"It hurt like hell when the numbness wore off."

"I promise you it won't hurt, now or later." He chuckled when she mumbled, "We'll see."

Slowly, sensually, he trailed a path with his tongue to where her pulse beat. Passing the racing throb, he trailed his mouth, nibbling kisses along the way then began a slower path back to where he'd started. Lust, hot and fast, rocketed through him, spellbinding him when Allyson closed her eyes, giving into the seductive nature of his actions. Since their first encounter, this woman's presence had sung a siren's song, entangling him in a silken sea of erotic emotions he'd gladly drown in.

Quickly, he sank his teeth into her wrist. A rush, like an ocean wave washed over him, around him, pulling him into its depths and taking with it the buzzing. His hand lightly brushed her face. Then he gasped.

"Allyson?" He said her name as though it burned his tongue. "Relax, I won't harm you. May I please continue?"

Confusion seemed to cloud her face, mirroring his, no doubt, but she nodded yes, and he began again. Logan felt the fear abandon her and contentment replace it. Strange, it gave him a feeling of coming home. One, two, then three minutes passed. Logan pulled her closer with his left arm.

A murmured moan filled his ears. Had it come from her or him? Logan removed his arm from her waist, rolled down her sleeve, and buttoned it.

Through half-closed eyes, she watched him. "Are you going to be all right now? What happened earlier?" Worry laced her words.

It pleased him she was concerned enough to care, and her caring caused pleasure to shoot straight to his groin. He closed his eyes, letting the sensation engulf him like a downy mattress.

"I'll explain later."

It felt good, when like a mother checking a child for fever, she placed a hand to his cheek. "I'll be all right, for a time, just need some sleep." He smiled weakly and shivered. He felt more than saw Allyson reach for an afghan on the next chair and cover him.

Chapter Eight

H E ARRIVED IN the quiet, picturesque neighborhood in time to see Kincaid's late ladylove's offspring, Daisy, and her husband leaving. How interesting.

If Daisy and George were here, then Kincaid couldn't be too far away. Then he caught sight of the sheriff's vehicle. Quickly, he cut the headlights and drove down a side street. Pulling into a carport beside a darkened house, he turned off the engine.

All the players were here. Now, to set the stage for the next act. He slouched in the front seat and considered how to proceed. Reaching up to disable the dome light, he silently slipped from the car.

He made his way through the sedate neighborhood lawns. Night shadows smudged sharp edges of manicured lawns, while walk lights softly muted buildings' edges. Remains of children's daytime play lay scattered like the first leaves of autumn. Bicycles leaned against their stands, while swings creaked in a breeze. A wolf stalking wicked sheep.

Creeping up to Allyson's front window, he peered through a crack in the drapery. There, he saw Logan feeding from her wrist. He rolled his eyes and shook his head in disgust. Kincaid was always the gentleman while dining. He, on the other hand, appreciated a meal where a man could roll up his sleeves and dig right in.

✧   ✧   ✧

ALLYSON'S MIND REELED from what had happened. This couldn't be real. This only happened in terrible B-movies. She unbuttoned her sleeve to inspect her wrist. There were two tiny puncture marks, smaller than those shown in the movies. If she hadn't witnessed the procedure, she would have thought they were insect bites.

Why hadn't he taken all he'd needed? She barely felt the loss, and yet understood he had needed much more. Why in the world did she let him drink from her? Why did he find it important that she trust him? Why had the buzzing stopped? Too many questions, not enough answers, and yet strangely, she trusted him. Why? She swallowed a laugh. It was another question to add to a long list. Trust him, an inner voice echoed. The voice's command oddly soothed her.

She commenced to doze herself when a moan awakened her. Quickly, she rose and sat beside him on the couch. Speaking softly, she touched his face.

"Logan, Logan, it's all right you're here with me, Allyson. You're safe." He woke; half rose, and searched the room with his gaze. Then he placed both arms around her waist to draw her down onto the couch and he whispered her name. Several minutes ticked by and he shifted for a more comfortable position. Allyson tried to rise, not wanting to disturb him. Her back cramped in the uncomfortable arrangement, and quickly she froze, feeling an unusual vibration on her left breast.

"Logan, do Tarczals have a weird muscle problem or is your cell phone in your pocket?" she whispered, sliding into a sitting position. He released his hold on her.

He withdrew a cell from his jacket pocket. "Hello," he said, and she knew he studied her for any reaction to his taking the call. "Yes, it's a good idea. I'm at…, of course you know."

She wondered who he was talking to, not caring if her face gave her away.

"In ten minutes? I'll be ready." Logan pressed a button on the phone and put it back in his pocket.

"It appears a friend has taken it upon themselves to come pick me up."

Allyson stepped back, making room for him to stand while he spoke.

"Brunette or redhead?" she blurted out before she could stop herself.

"Jealous?" The wolfish grin ran across his mouth again.

"No."

She could tell her indignant denial thrilled him.

"Call this number," Logan reached into his wallet and withdrew a business card pointing to a number, "Anytime. If I am not there, you can leave a message."

"I won't call." Nevertheless, she took the card.

Allyson followed him to the door. A sleek, dark car pulled into the driveway, catching her eye. He hesitated at the door. He was stalling and, she suspected, having second thoughts. She was. Second, third, heck she was having a couple of hundred thoughts. Less than four hours ago she'd given a pint of her best to a vampire, no, a Tarczal, she corrected herself.

"How can you trust me?" she blurted. "How do you know I won't tell the world about you?"

To her dismay, he flashed that fantastic smile of his. "I don't know. I shouldn't, but I do. Trust you."

"Just like that?" In disbelief, she raised her arms up then let them fall against her sides.

"Exactly."

"This is crazy." Her brow furrowed.

Hand on the doorknob, he still hesitated to leave. Strangely, his reluctance warmed her, frightened her, and confused the hell out of her. His hand slid from the doorknob. His gaze pinned her where she stood.

"You were married for over ten years. College sweethearts, I've been told." He glanced around the room. "You live in a nice house, nice neighborhood. Your husband just began a new job with a six-figure salary. But, instead of riding the gravy train, you initiate a divorce." His eyes searched her face. "What made you decide to end it? Another woman?"

Allyson shifted uncomfortably beneath his gaze.

She didn't owe him any explanations, her life—her past, was her own, but the words spilled from her before she realized she spoke.

"Part of me almost wishes it was another woman."

She nearly laughed at the thought, but the truth was too sobering.

"I could've handled it."

A chill slipped up her spine at the memory. She didn't want to explain about the rest, but his intense gaze held her in place.

The truth would come out eventually. She took a deep breath.

"I grew up in this neighborhood and you're right it's wonderful if you live with loving people. I didn't."

Turning away, she ran her fingers over an empty vase on the entry table. Empty.

A testament to the quality of her life since Michael showed his true character. Was she now so desperate in her bid to change her life, to believe in vampires? She was.

"The house belonged to my aunt. She raised me, saw to my education and made sure I married well. She'd seen to her duty."

A sarcastic laugh bubbled to her lips. "That's what I was to her—a duty. When she died, she left the house to me." Raising her chin, she squared her shoulders.

"Not Michael. Not Michael and me. Just me. If I believed she was a forgiving woman, I'd thought she'd left it to me as a form of an apology."

"Apology?"

"For convincing me to give up college, my dreams, and marry Michael."

"Was it? An apology?"

"No. I doubt it." Frustrated, she ran her hand through her already tousled hair. "She believed my talent was a curse. She believed women shouldn't have careers other than being the wife of a successful man."

He cocked his head to one side. "Is there something wrong with being a wife?"

"No, of course not, but when you can't be yourself, explore or develop who you are, when you're ridiculed for wanting to be more than arm candy for a self-absorbed chauvinist pig, then there's something wrong."

"This was the reason you filed for the divorce?"

"No, and it should have been enough, but it wasn't the reason. In the beginning, Michael was kind, considerate; perhaps you could say even loving. The beginning didn't last long. Michael eventually had a nasty comment about anything and everything I did."

"It was only verbal abuse?"

Appalled, she gasped at him. "Only? Like it wasn't enough?"

"No," he snapped. "You twist what I meant. Abuse of any type is never acceptable." His answer was full of disgust.

"No, he only commanded in the soft whisper he used when he was displeased, but it was only a matter of time before he'd have done more." Logan raised a brow.

"Our neighbor, an elderly woman with only a small, yappy poodle to keep her company, found her pet dead one morning on the edge of the road."

"The animal strayed into the road and was hit?"

Fear curled in her stomach as she remembered. "Many believed so."

"But you didn't."

"No. The dog barked at everything and anything, annoying but harmless. If you stomped your foot, the tiny bundle of black fur ran for her owner's front door. It wasn't a threat to anyone, probably not even to a flea living on it. Michael hated the dog and complained about it constantly. I told him to ignore it, but he muttered someone should do something about it."

Allyson watched the anger darken his face. "And you think he did?"

"I helped the old woman bury her pet and even said a few words over the grave for her. A car didn't hit the thing. It was a tiny dog smaller than a cat; damage from a car would've been great."

"I see."

"The dog didn't have a mark on it. But, its neck was broken. He was barking when Michael went out the front door. I remember it clearly. The yapping stopped several long moments before the car engine roared to life. I remember hearing the barking, the barking stop, Michael singing gaily as he passed our front window, and then the car roared to life. I didn't see him do anything to the dog, couldn't prove he harmed the animal, but in my heart, I know he did."

"And, if he could harm a defenseless animal,"

"My gut told me I could be next."

"I believe you made the right decision."

A weight slid from her, a lifeless skin waiting for the right catalyst to shed it from her, and Logan was the catalyst it seemed.

"I know I did." Allyson shook her head, a wisp of a smile on her lips. "You know, since you've come into my life it's been one thing after another." Giddiness from finally being able to rid her terrible secrets from her soul tickled her flesh.

"Funny, the same thing just popped into my head about you." Logan reached out and tapped the card in her hand. "If you need me for any reason, any, you call and I'll come." He strolled out the door with the proclamation.

Allyson watched him get into the car on the passenger side and ride away. She watched until the car turned out of sight. She clutched the card in her hand to her heart. She tried to deny and accept all at the same time the curious emotions she was beginning to feel for a man she barely knew, with a secret so bizarre she didn't still comprehend what it encompassed.

She'd only met the man, and yet, the thought of a future without him astounded her. "Can a vampire and a human find happiness together?"

SLIDING INTO THE shadows, he didn't have long to wait. A nondescript black sedan pulled in front of the house. Aha, his darling sister Salina's car. Idiot Kincaid couldn't hang around long enough to bang the piece Michael bragged about all evening. Well, it made his job easier. He waited until the car pulled away with Logan and Salina before heading back to the carport and Michael. Once behind the wheel again he eased the vehicle down the road.

Since his Tarczal vision gave him a perfect view, there was no need to turn on the headlights. Turning off the engine, he let the car glide silently into the driveway. No need to wipe his fingerprints away since they weren't on file anywhere in the world.

He debated whether to leave Michael in the trunk or put him in the front seat. He enjoyed leaving surprises. He left Michael where he put him. Too bad he couldn't be there when Allyson found him.

Walking briskly away, he chuckled to himself, and then sped up into a jog, making his way out of the neighborhood. He arrived back at the motel feeling exhilarated. To keep the feeling he went in to gather up the girl in the tub. From there he slipped into the check-in area and arranged the body on a nearby chair.

"Really my dear you must rid yourself of such a un-lady like stench." He shooed a small group of gnats away. "I'm afraid we must part," he whispered and left.

He went straight to his car. There was no reason to stay longer. Leaving the body, he concluded, would give the lazy owner a reason to get off his enormous ass. He drove away, peals of laughter ringing out of the car.

Chapter Nine

SHE WOKE REFRESHED despite the previous night's events and her donation. Nothing remained of the tiny wounds from his bite. No telltale signs, at least outwardly, of her experience. She blew out a deep breath. Vampires. Oh, boy.

On a whim, Allyson added extra honey to her morning tea, justifying the indulgence with the fact blood donors ate cookies afterward. She sat, treating herself to a second cup of tea enjoying the warm sunlight pouring in the kitchen window. The shrill ring from the phone broke the idyllic morning.

"Hello."

"Hey, Allyson. How's it going? Big congrats on the scholarship." The false, cheerful voice of her divorce attorney warned Allyson of what was coming. Phil oozed charm and warm salutations; it meant one thing, bad news.

"What's the problem, Phil?"

"No problem, I need you to come in and sign a few things. I really hate to ask since I know money's tight, but I'll need another $300 for filing fees before the end of the month."

"And where am I suppose to get those funds," she

muttered more to herself than Phil. "Okay, I'll be in. Anything else?"

"Um, Allyson."

Here it comes. The news he didn't want to tell her. She shut her eyes and pinched the bridge of her nose in an attempt to release the gathering tension.

"I think Michael's attorney is trying to pull a fast one on us."

"Now what?" She pressed a hand to one temple trying to force out the stressing ache throbbing there.

She heard Phil take a breath before he rushed the words out his mouth. "They're trying to say the house should be part of the settlement."

Allyson exploded from the table, the teacup sending hot liquid to drip on the wood floor below. Seconds later, the cup slid from the table to shatter on the hard surface like her peaceful morning. "Its bull and you know it, Phil." The house was her sanctuary, losing it wasn't an option. She paced the tiny kitchen, ignoring the mess. "The house is mine, free and clear. My aunt left it to me, and there are no mortgages or liens on it."

"Well, not exactly," whined Phil, something she found irritating in a supposedly educated man. Maybe the rumors about Phil getting his diploma from a candy box were true.

"Oh, yes it is," snapped Allyson. Damn, why couldn't she afford an attorney with a brain and a backbone?

"Well, it seems Michael obtained a loan and used the house and property as collateral."

She fumed. "Just how did the piece of snail slime accomplish it?"

Phil continued to drone. "Well, I'm trying to sort it out. You didn't sign any papers without reading them did you?"

"Of course not, why?" Oh, when she got her hands on Michael, he was gonna pay for this!

"Well, I've got a copy of the papers here in front of me and the signature looks like yours."

Allyson forced her shoulders to relax and breathed deeply. "It's a forgery. I never sign anything without reading it first. Believe me, there is no way I'd ever agree to jeopardize this house. Give me a half hour and I'll be at your office to straighten this out." She clicked the phone off, frowned at the mess on the floor, and went to get the broom.

Putting away the cleaning tools, she glanced at herself in the mirror. A change of clothes for the meeting would be a good idea, something more conservative than jeans and a T-shirt. Especially this one from her favorite author, Dianne Castell, a T-shirt screaming, 'Hot and Irresistible', across the front of it.

✦   ✦   ✦

ENTERING THE GARAGE, she hit the door opener, its grating screech reminding her to put one more thing on her ever-growing to-do list. Seated behind the wheel, her fingers beat a rapid cadence while waiting for the door to complete its journey upward. Only, instead of an open space on the other side of the door, a car blocked her exit. Allyson yanked off her seatbelt, shoved open the car door, and stomped back to the vehicle.

Michael's car. She peered inside the windows thinking he might have driven to the house by mistake in a drunken stupor, then decided to sleep it off in the car. It wouldn't be the first time.

Empty seats met her gaze.

Hand on the driver's door Allyson thought to open it, when a second car pulled in behind Michaels. A sheriff's car with two of the town's finest inside, sporting scowls and plenty of attitude. The driver got out wearing a sneer she'd learned to hate in high school. Bertward Mitchell, better known as Bubba. He had a toothpick clenched between his teeth, mirrored sunglass, and a hand resting on his weapon.

Bubba had been a bully in school, and now he was a bully with a badge. She'd been shy in school and ended up more than once being the victim of Bubba's cruel practical jokes. Her heart sank at the sight of him. Then she remembered seeing him at their last pep rally and raised her hand to cover a giggle. Hard to have respect for someone you've seen covered in blue paint over most of his body, wearing only under-wear, while running and screaming down the school's halls.

He walked toward her, his permanently injured knee making a wet, popping sound with every step, the damage a result of the last game. Bubba's dreams of college, pro ball, fame, and fortune died that night.

Bubba didn't even bother to remove the toothpick when he spoke. "Mrs. Weston."

"Bubba."

"Deputy Mitchell to you."

She refrained from rolling her eyes. "Deputy Mitchell, why are you here?"

Bubba hooked his thumbs in his utility belt, his leg making him jut out a hip for balance. "Step away from the vehicle, Mrs. Weston."

The second deputy now stood alongside the patrol car, too. He wore the same reflective sunglass and his pants sported a crease sharp enough to cut day-old biscotti. Fear pricked her skin as she eyed the two men and warning bells echoed in her head. Allyson took a couple of steps back.

"Heard you had some trouble out here last night." Bubba chewed out the words.

Allyson hoped she could downplay the incident. "Trouble?"

Bubba worried the toothpick. "Bible thumpers, I believe you called them." She watched as he used his tongue to roll the toothpick from one side of his mouth to the other. "You got a problem with the God-fearing people who read the Bible?"

Allyson's scalp tingled. "Of course not, they were just a confused older couple, nothing serious."

Again, she watched fascinated as the toothpick switched sides. It certainly was getting a work out. "They threatened to burn you out. Sounds serious to us."

"I really didn't think they would."

"Then why did you bother us?" The toothpick stopped mid-roll.

What were Bubba and friend up to? "What would you have said if I didn't call you and they did carry out their threat?" Allyson challenged.

Bubba took a step toward her, and Allyson backed up. "You sure have a smart mouth on you, just like you did in school."

"Me?" She scoffed. "You were the one always causing trouble, Bertward." The minute she said his name she regretted it, but she was tired of bullies.

The other officer snickered then cleared his throat when "Bertward" shot him a dirty look.

"What were you going to do with this car, Allyson?"

Now he'd switched to her first name. That couldn't be good. "I was hoping to move it so I could leave."

"You have the keys, for it?"

She purposely opened her eyes wide to look innocent as possible. "No, I thought they might be in the car."

Bubba's hand came up to take the toothpick out of his mouth and toss it on the ground. "How long has the car been here?"

Allyson hesitated, chewing her lower lip. He was playing a cat and mouse game, and she sure wasn't the cat. "I have no idea; it certainly wasn't here last night when I went to bed."

"Before or after your boyfriend left?" Bubba sneered in triumph.

She glanced from one man to the other, her stomach clenched and a wintry shiver rained over her. "Officer, I don't see how my private life is any of your concern." How did they know about Logan? "What's going on? I have an appointment I'm going to be late for."

The two men glanced at each other and grinned. "Who do you need to meet?" Bubba shifted his weight.

Allyson didn't like the smile on Bubba's face. "My attorney, if you must know."

Bubba mocked. "Why do you need to see him? You do something requiring a lawyer?"

She licked her lower lip and crossed her arms over her breasts. "I'm in the middle of a divorce. Now why are you here?"

"Could you open the trunk?" the other deputy asked.

A shiver of determination slithered up her spine. "Since I don't have the keys, no."

"Then we'll ask you to take a seat in our cruiser

while we open it."

"Am I under arrest?" Her mouth went dry.

"Not yet." Bertward pushed his glasses up on his nose.

Her heart raced with panic, bumping her ribs with a painful thud. She wouldn't allow this bully and his friend to have the satisfaction of seeing her scared. She slowed her breathing. "Then why do I need to sit in your car?"

The second man strolled her way taking his handcuffs from his utility belt to slap them against his palm. He'd taken off his glasses and hooked them in his front pocket. She didn't like the glint of glee in his eyes. "Sounds like she's resisting, doesn't it?" He laughed.

Allyson automatically backed away, and Bubba reached out to snag her arm. "Sounds like it to me, too."

The two of them outweighed her by several hundred pounds. Quickly, they cuffed her then plunked her down in their backseat. Allyson fumed as they retrieved a crowbar from their car and began prying open Michael's trunk. It didn't take much. With a quick twist of the tool, the lid popped up. For a moment, the men blocked her view. Allyson strained to see what they did, but from her vantage point, all she saw was the hood of the car. Then they stepped apart to glare at her. Bubba stomped back to where she sat and yanked opened the door. "Get out," he snapped.

Allyson scooted across the seat to the opening. He didn't remove the cuffs. He grabbed her arm above the elbow twisting it upward. She gave a hiss through clenched teeth.

He mumbled, "Sorry."

She really thought his apology was more an automatic response because he kept shoving her towards the front of the sheriff's car, pulling her arm roughly.

"How'd this get in the trunk?" She could only gasp.

Allyson stared at Michael's pale body for what seemed an eternity before the deputies stiffening snapped her attention from the still form. Something behind her drew their focus. She turned to observe a short, balding man with small tuffs of white hair sticking up from above his ears. He wore a rumpled suit that had missed a few cleanings and seen better days. A haphazardly hung tie dangled down his shirt with a voluptuous hula dancer posed seductively, dodging several stains.

He lumbered up the driveway to plop his briefcase on the cruiser hood. "Morning, boys!"

"Sir, you'll have to remove the case, this is an official vehicle."

The man in the suit ignored the deputy, asking, "What's going on here, son?"

Bubba hitched up his pants. "We're investigating a homicide."

"Really?" The older man came over to view the

scene. He harrumphed a couple of times, smacked his lips, and made a sucking noise with his teeth and lips before going back to his briefcase.

"You have any suspects?" he asked.

The men puffed out their chests full of macho pride. "This woman."

"I see, so you've charged her."

"We're about to read her, her rights."

Allyson's chest squeezed tight and she fought for air.

The older man let a slow grin creep across his face and the constriction eased in her. His smile gave her hope. She took in a welcome breath.

"Well, good job, boys. It's not every day two of our finest see a crime first hand."

The two deputies didn't reply.

"Something wrong, boys? I thought you said you saw this woman kill this man." He pointed at her. "Then stuff his body into the trunk with your own eyes."

For some reason, Allyson rejoiced when the man's grin threatened to split his face.

"By the way how much would you say the man weighed alive? 160? 180 pounds?" He studied Allyson then turned to the lawmen. "What do you think she weighs 115? 120, tops?" One arm crossed his chest, the other rested against his cheek. He tapped his pursed lips with one finger.

"She's a little bitty thing. How in the world do you

suppose she could lift that much alive, let alone dead, all by herself?" He leaned toward the trunk, peering inside, harrumphed a couple of times, and loudly cleared his throat. "Then how do you suppose she hoisted him into this trunk?" Rounding on both men, he pinned Bubba with a shrewd look. "You haven't answered my question, son. Did either of you witness my client kill this man?"

Allyson's heart raced. Client? Did he mean her?

"Well?" the elder man demanded.

"No, sir. But, the car is in her driveway." The officer actually bleated.

"Yours is in the driveway, son. How do I know you didn't kill the man and stuff the body in there? The two of you are pretty fit looking."

The officers actually squirmed.

"From where I stand, boys, it's nothing but conjecture and circumstantial evidence. Both are pretty thin."

The officers put their heads close together. There were raised whispers, several scowls, and wild, intense hand gestures.

✧   ✧   ✧

ALLYSON STOOD RUBBING her wrists from where the cuffs chaffed her skin pink. She watched the lawmen tape off her driveway and stand guard over Michael and his car while they waited for the detectives and coroner to arrive.

"Mrs. Weston?"

"I prefer Ms."

"Right, Ms. Weston, I'm Harry Butcher."

She bit her lip as nervous laughter bubbled up her throat.

He held up one hand. "Please, I'm an old man and I've heard it all."

Allyson's eyes sparkled with mirth. "I didn't say a thing, did I?"

"No, ma'am you didn't." He chuckled, then turned serious. "And we're going to keep it this way when the detectives show up. They're going to want to question you. They can ask what they want, but I'll be doing the answering as your legal representative."

She gently rubbed her wrists. "Mr. Butcher, why, and I'm eternally in your debt for it, and I do mean debt, are you here?"

Again, his hand came up. "A mutual friend of ours asked me to come to your rescue. It's been a long time since I got to be a knight in shining armor. A long time."

"How?"

"Did he know? Seems someone reported, anonymously of course, they'd seen a body put in the trunk of a car. A car now sitting in your driveway." He moved her closer to the house and away from the eager ears of the deputies. "The same anonymous caller also reported the victim had heated words and was even threatened earlier in the evening by a man seen leaving your house last night."

Allyson paled. "Logan didn't do this. Someone is trying to set us up." She worried her lower lip between her teeth.

Harry patted her shoulder. "He's aware of the problem and is in the process of finding out who and why."

"I can't afford another attorney, Mr. Butcher."

"My fee is already paid, dear lady." Mr. Butcher pursed his lips, drawing them thin with a Mona Lisa smile. "Let's go inside, you can make me a cup of coffee or tea, and you should call your divorce attorney to tell him you won't need his services anymore."

They were walking up to her front step as he spoke and she abruptly stopped. "But what about my divorce? I…?"

Harry gave a quick jerk of his head toward the driveway. "What about your divorce?"

Allyson stared at him for a heartbeat before the realization of Michael's death, and what it meant, caught her like a blow to the gut. She staggered then sagged against Harry. He caught her under the elbows and for an older man, he was surprisingly strong. He directed her onto the porch and through the front door, finally seating her at the kitchen table.

He gave a little chuckle. "Congratulations, you've just become a widow, Mrs. Weston."

Chapter Ten

LOGAN GRUMBLED AT daybreak. "Someone answer the bloody phone."

The item tormenting him lay beside his bed, ringing persistently. He opened one eye to stare at it. Too late, he remembered Salina and he were the only residents in the house. He snarled at the modern day convenience, snatching it up and resisting the urge to do violence to the high-tech black and silver object. Sitting up, he rubbed his face with one hand. A two-minute conversation with their Janissary planted in the local sheriff's office snapped him wide-awake. Next, he called Harry Butcher, his old friend from law school.

Waiting for Harry's all-clear call during the day drove him to distraction. Logan tried working in his town office but couldn't stay focused and prowled the corridors. He then drove the local streets for a while before giving up and deciding to go home. Thanks to Harry, Allyson was out of harm's way for now. She was safely at home with no charges filed at present.

Logan walked down the hallway of his home as tentacles of the sun's last rays burned a robust tangerine in the interior of the house. Deep pockets of shadows woke from their slumber to reclaim their rightful places. The night reminded him of the two of them curled on her sofa.

Allyson. He swirled his tongue in his mouth remembering how the tiny taste of her blood nourished his body. His soul. Until he'd met her, he'd blissfully buried any feelings of consequence.

Consequences. What part of his past seemed to run head-on to catch up with him?

Logan shrugged off the questions, unwilling to deal with the answers. Striding down the hallway to the room he and Salina shared as their private living room, he resisted the urge to turn on every light he passed, knowing the shadows he wished to expel resided not in these rooms and hallways, but in his soul. There were things refusing to stay buried it seemed.

Hearing voices from the sitting room and thinking Salina to be taking nourishment, he entered the room only to find her sharing a glass of wine with his Uncle André.

André Delacroix rose to embrace him. "Here is my nephew."

"Uncle." Logan kissed the elder man on each cheek in greeting asking, "Is Aunt Maryse with you?"

André held up his hands and then dropped them with a tsk. "My beautiful wife is still in our home."

"Is there something wrong? I'm sure you didn't decide out of the blue to travel from France to the U.S.

to use up your frequent flier miles." Logan cocked his head.

"Your cellar didn't have a decent bottle of wine in it." André picked up a wine glass from the end table. "Now it does. I brought several cases." André turned to Salina asking, "How can I hold my head up knowing my own nephew didn't carry his family's wine in his cellar?"

Salina, smiled, picked up her glass, finished the contents, and kissing André on the cheek, sailed past Logan. "I'll leave you two alone."

"Did you speak to Nairn before he left?" Logan asked her retreating figure.

Ignoring him was her answer. "Always a pleasure to see you, André." Salina waved goodbye, gliding out the door.

With a shrug of his shoulders, Logan accepted the fact he was on Salina's hit list, too.

André asked upon her exit. "Those two still arguing?"

Logan shook his head then warily eyed his uncle. "They live to torment each other. You came all the way from France to properly stock my wine cellar?"

André evaded the question. "Your aunt misses you."

"I call her. Send gifts."

"Those are not the same." André scolded and Logan accepted the chastisement as being a concerned parent's love and nothing more.

"I will visit soon," he said in attempt to make amends.

Logan watched André smile approvingly at his answer before he spoke, abruptly changing the subject. "You're doing a good thing with Nairn and the school."

"I'm donating the use of a few buildings." Logan tried to brush off the compliment.

"A few buildings?" André gave a dismissive snort. "That's what you call it? You've opened your home and in the process helped a friend achieve a dream," André admonished.

"Nairn came up with the ideas because security must have a place to develop if his men are expected to do their job." Logan didn't like being given credit for what he deemed only natural and right.

"You could have offered him any structure but you offered him your home. Why? Is it because a certain titian-haired beauty lives here, too?"

"The house." Logan saw his uncle roll his eyes at his choice of words. "My home is large and empty." Logan grinned. "Yes, I'm hoping being in close proximity, those two might finally realize they deserve each other."

"I wish you luck with such a union." André laughed.

"Why are you here, Uncle?" Exhausted after last night, he didn't need any more head games.

André's eyes warmed with love. "I can't visit because I miss you?"

Logan knew his uncle too well to buy the man's innocent act. "You don't leave Aunt Maryse or your vineyards unless, well, there is no unless. You never leave either. What grave matter draws you to my doorstep?"

Logan watched the man who raised him after his parent's death. André filled his glass and went back to the overstuffed chair he sat in when Logan first entered the room, but he didn't sit.

"Thomas came to me." He swirled the wine, staring at the golden liquid.

"Thomas? Aha, the Alliance. I'm surprised they didn't contact me. What exactly are their concerns?" Logan replied, not caring if his words were blatantly flippant or sarcastic.

"Don't mock our ruling counsel, young man," André snapped before dropping to his chair. "They're your elders, our law, and the men who sign your paycheck."

Logan's jaw clenched and he chose his words carefully. "Since I'm aware who they are, being their attorney and whipping boy, I know what they do. As for my Alliance paycheck, it wouldn't feed a starving mouse."

His uncle sighed. "They have concerns. The Alliance is made up of anxious old men who remember the past and worry about the future." His uncle ran his tongue over his lips.

Logan thrust his hands in his pockets, an old habit from his childhood when uneasy with a situation. He noticed his uncle's eyes widen in surprise before André schooled his features. Logan removed his hands and unexpectedly felt twelve again.

André burst from his chair to pace the room's length, his jaw ground as though the words he wanted to speak required tenderizing first.

Logan watched his usually calm uncle prowl the room and waited. It didn't take long before André abruptly stopped.

"The repository's been breached."

"Why didn't they inform me?" Logan straightened. "What's missing?"

André gave an age-old Gaelic shrug meaning nothing and everything. "Nothing is gone, but files were disturbed. One of which was the report on your parent's death." He pursed his lips. "Other files have old men brusquely terrified of their own shadows. Why they haven't told you, I have no idea." André then collapsed into his chair. Logan watched his uncle choose his next words. "Thomas said the past is fast catching up to the present."

"Well, isn't that cryptic and worthless as hell." Logan ran his hand over his hair as an eerie déjà vu tingled his scalp. "Thomas has been a cherished friend and mentor. You'd think he'd give me a little more to go on. Any idea on whom or why they broke in?"

"No. That's why I came to you."

"Why would my parent's file be of concern?" Logan felt the pull for movement and rose to take his turn at pacing the room. "The report states that I saw them trapped in a burning lodge by idiot, superstitious villagers." Logan chose the moment to rub his forehead. "Of course those records could be some of the incomplete files; the files the Alliance assures me are intact. I'm their attorney, but the coterie keeps secrets from me."

"You must be mistaken. I'm sure they give you all the pertinent information. Now, let us speak of different matters. Salina tells me you are seeing a woman outside our circle."

Logan couldn't hide his surprise and quickly sat down. His uncle words stunned him. "I'm surprised at you, Uncle; I thought you were above petty prejudice."

"Prejudice, no. Relief, my nephew, relief. You haven't found a woman in our circle of Tarczal or com women. Your aunt and I were beginning to worry."

"I've dated." Logan sought to vindicate himself.

André chuckled. "Yes, but never seriously. Tell me of this woman."

"She's an artist."

"Fascinating. Tell me more; is she imaginative in other areas?"

"Uncle!"

"Oh, posh." André tsked. "We are men of the world; we may speak of such things."

"Does Aunt Maryse know you talk about other

women this way?"

André pulled a cheroot from his jacket pocket and pointed to Logan, silently asking if he wanted one or minded him smoking. Logan shook his head. He didn't want one or care if his uncle smoked. André inhaled deeply before releasing the smoke. "What my darling wife doesn't know keeps me alive. Now, more about your woman."

"Originally, Nairn suggested I meet her to gain information about her husband."

In the middle of another puff, André swallowed instead of exhaling when Logan uttered the word husband. He coughed and sputtered. "Husband?"

"This is different. Allyson was in the middle of a messy divorce when we met. You don't have to worry about an aggrieved spouse and child hunting me for decades."

André relaxed back into the chair cushion taking a cautious puff of his cheroot. "How is your Daisy?"

"She and George are in town, as you already know since you spoke to Thomas and Salina. They've stuck to their normal routine of dogging most of my waking hours."

André cleared his throat. "I understand you feel responsible for her because of the complications which arose from your association with her mother and father but –"

"I swore to protect Daisy after her mother died. Why won't anyone believe me? Daisy and George are harmless, incredibly annoying at times, but harmless," Logan grumbled.

André nodded his head then twirled his index finger indicating Logan to continue.

"Avoiding Daisy and George is how I came to arrive at Allyson's house late last night." Logan hated mentioning what happened afterward, but he suspected André knew the rest thanks to Salina. When she picked him up she'd had several colorful words in as many languages about him being with a woman outside their cultural circle. "I told Allyson I'm Tarczal and asked for a donation."

His uncle waited a moment before replying. "I see, and how did it go?"

"Not unpleasant."

André ground out his cheroot. "She accepted you without any questions or hysteria?"

"Pretty much." Logan bit the inside of his mouth waiting.

André held his gaze with the stare a parent gives a child that says *you're not telling me the whole story.* Logan flinched first. "We've been experiencing headaches in the proximity of each other. She hasn't confirmed it, but I see the pain and confusion in her face."

André pursed his lips. "It mirrors yours?"

"Yes."

"You have pain?"

"A headache from time to time."

"We don't have headaches."

"And dreams."

"Dreams? Like when you confided in Lucian St. Clair, Nairn's father, that you witnessed your parent's death?"

Logan bit out. "I saw them clearly as I see you now."

André held up one hand in truce. "Tell me the rest about this Allyson. Salina hinted of trouble this morning?"

"Her husband ended up dead in the trunk of his own car."

"Impatient one is she, couldn't wait for the divorce? Offed him herself, did she?"

Logan sputtered. "No, she didn't kill him, someone else did."

His uncle slapped his hands together in a dusting off motion. "Not the type to soil her hands?"

Logan grimaced. "I had a spy in my company."

"You had the spy kill him?"

Frustrated, Logan's mouth dropped open, a gasp of exasperation blowing out. "Uncle, please."

"I've never seen you this flustered, not even when you were young and caught the exhilarating whiff which is unmistakably woman." His uncle laughed until tears shined in his eyes. "This woman must be a sorceress like the Blood Witch Alaza to have you twisted into a babbling bundle of manhood. You remember from your elementary lessons the legend keepers claim Alaza bewitched the Warrior Kharzarin much the same way. Poor man didn't know what way to turn. I must meet your Allyson." André sobered. "Who killed this husband of hers?"

Logan chewed on it. "I'm guessing whoever he was working with."

"Do you or Nairn have any leads?" André tapped his glass in thought.

"Nairn first believed the trail of crumbs carried signs similar to Franchot. For obvious reasons, we quickly dismissed the idea."

His uncle held out his glass. Logan took it over to refill it, turning sharply when André spoke.

"You never recovered a body."

Logan's stomach clenched, "Franchot gave some alligator heart burn."

Logan placed the refilled glass on the table beside his uncle who murmured. "If you're sure."

Then André quickly switched topics again. "These dreams you have, tell me of them. Are they anything similar to the vision of your parents?"

Logan knew his uncle didn't believe he'd seen their death. "Nairn's father went over it with me and he never doubted what I saw. Why do you?"

"No one in our family, to my knowledge, has the ability. It's passed on from two like parents to off-spring. Your Grandpère bragged, never around Grandmère, of course, we were direct descendants of the warrior Kharzarin who had the skill."

Logan raised an eyebrow. "What did Grandmère have to say on the subject?"

His uncle chuckled. "The Delacroix pedigree is too civilized to have a barbarian in it."

They both laughed.

Logan ventured. "Lucian St. Clair shared speech with me, mind to mind. He assured me it's rare, but not unheard of in some Tarczal's to communicate with each other this way. He's shared the link with several of his children." Logan sank back into his chair. "The dreams. I've considered calling Auntie. I know she loves to decipher images, but I didn't want to make a big deal out of possible nothing."

"Yet, you have pain and disturbing dreams."

"None of this makes sense." Logan's shoulders slumped.

André lifted his chin. "I've lived too long with your aunt and her beliefs to dismiss anything."

"She still clings to the old ways?"

"Each equinox and every phase of the moon is given its own respect."

Logan gave a half grin and shook his head. "Things have happened to make me believe in those old ways."

André waited.

"The dreams began about the same time I met Allyson. I did see my parents." Logan couldn't help but interject. He'd never told his uncle and aunt, only Lucian, that he'd also spoken with his parents on the fateful night.

André said nothing to him and only raised an eyebrow, a telling family trait.

Logan studied his empty glass. "The legend of Kharzarin and Alaza is a tale, a myth, stories for children's bedtime and wishful lovers. Aren't they?" He searched his uncle's face for reassurance.

"Each fable has a true beginning," André said quietly, carefully.

"Yes, they were real people, but the rest is too…"

Logan raised one hand only to let it drop on the armrest.

"Magical?"

Logan snorted. "Incredible. Unbelievable."

"Why do you doubt it? Our historians credit Kharzarin's life story for being the catalyst for the Slavic legend of Volkh."

"My argument exactly. The story's been embellished to the point no one knows what fact is and what isn't." Logan shook his head. "According to the Kharzarin legend, both Kharzarin and Volkh were said to be powerful wizards who were adept at shape shifting into a gray wolf, no less. Both were supposedly born the night of a month with two full moons and a terrible earthquake." Logan gave a dry laugh. "I guess myths and legends are never given a mundane birth."

André challenged. "You don't believe Kharzarin's life changed when he met Alaza? You don't think she wove her magic around him and tamed the mighty warrior?"

"I think Kharzarin, a man before his time, finally accepted the fact that if they kept killing their food supply, they would soon starve to death. He wisely began the practice of paying coms, in coin or trade, for nourishment. He took Alaza, a com, a half-blood gypsy, the woman he reported to have a telepathic link with, to be his wife. Magic had nothing to do with the decision."

André chuckled, shaking his head. "For all your years, you know little about women and their influence upon men."

"But the rest, Uncle, the part about her being a Blood Witch and Kharzarin only had to sup from her to heal him. Or take in enough nourishment to last several days, even weeks, is preposterous." Logan held up his hand to stave off André from speaking. "Don't think to remind me many of our people wait for a second rising of their union."

"Are you asking me or yourself?"

Logan sat, unable to answer as the emotions swirled violently in him.

André leaned forward to place his hand on Logan's. "When you supped from this woman, did you take the normal amount?"

"No."

"And?"

"I felt like I'd gorged." Logan sank wearily back in his chair. "I felt energized beyond belief. Her blood had the sweetest under notes of cinnamon. It lingers on my tongue yet." He let his head drop his chin rested on his chest, then quickly he brought his head back up. "Now, thanks to my involvement with her, Allyson's in danger."

"Could Daisy be involved?"

Logan leaned his head back against the chair's comforting cushion. "Daisy and George wouldn't kill an innocent man and blame his wife to get back at me."

André interpolated. "They're getting older and have gathered followers."

Logan tried to dismiss the importance of the problem. "Fanatics and fringe elements, not anyone of consequence."

"Perhaps, but they could've reached the point where they've become desperate. Or a member of their flock is out to prove themselves to them. Either way, if this is true, the Alliance is correct you should handle the matter soon."

"If you're referring to Daisy, she has a few years left at best. I won't be forced into harming her and I'll protect her from anyone who tries," Logan said with rage.

"You carry her life like a penance; the fault is not yours to bear."

Logan slammed his glass down, cracking the stem. "The fault lies at my feet. You forget, Uncle, I swore on her mother's grave to protect her."

Softly, André said, "There are rumors she is receiving help from a person who knows entirely too much about us."

Logan rose, and strode to the bar. "Daisy is my responsibility and mine alone. I'll take care of it." Logan wearily placed the damaged glass on the bar to exchange it with another, something he wished he could do with his life.

The last twenty-four hours had been excessively long. Logan turned to find André staring at him, sadness shadowed his uncle's face, and then André cleared his throat, adding quietly, "Like Kharzarin you too were born during an earthquake in a month with two full moons."

Chapter Eleven

A LLYSON DROVE DOWN the road. She had questions and Logan Kincaid held the answers. The scholarship was hers, but at what price? Her reputation and Michael's life?

She turned off the main drag into his lane. The guard gave her unquestioned passage. Gray night shadows inquisitively spread across the driveway. Winding up the elegant path, she wondered how Logan knew she was in trouble. Thank goodness, he'd sent Mr. Butcher. Someone set her up. Someone knew Logan and she were together last night, had spied on them. The thought made her skin crawl. Parking her car, she hurried up the front steps. Arm up, fist clenched to knock, she hesitated.

✧　✧　✧

THE ATTENDANT ALERTED him to her arrival. He watched her park and sweep up the steps, determination clearly fueling each stride. Logan stood on the other side of the door waiting for her to knock, hoping she would and hoping she wouldn't. His life turned from a blissful daily grind to bizarre upon meeting her. Spies. Dead employees. The gods awful buzzing in his head. Legends and their implications. For nearly a hundred years his life had been ecstatically quiet, organized, and even dull. He missed his quiet life. A little voice snickered in his head with his last thought. He quickly told it to shut up.

✧   ✧   ✧

ALLYSON INHALED DEEPLY and reached up to knock, only to jump back as the door opened. Logan stood there.

"Hi," she blurted out.

"Hi, yourself." The corners of his mouth twitched almost into a smile, and for some reason, it ticked her off.

When he just stood there, she asked, "May I come in?" Allyson glanced at his face. Was he laughing at her? "We need to talk."

Logan moved back, inviting her in. They stood in his entranceway apparently neither sure what to do next. Finally, Logan cleared his throat. "Maybe we should continue this in the parlor."

"Parlor? I haven't heard that word since my aunt died." Died. Oh, great, could she have chosen a worse word to use? She closed her eyes, cringing and counting to twenty in an attempt not to do something else stupid.

Logan shrugged her comment off. "The living

room is this way."

She followed him down a long corridor past the door she remembered leading to his office. The suit he wore today accentuated his broad shoulders. Did the man wear anything besides suits? She imagined him in jeans, tight jeans, and a white shirt, open at the collar with the sleeves rolled up to the elbows. Yum. No, she needed to stop thinking about him.

Dark woodwork, deep burgundy leather sofas faced one another, gold accents in lamps and accessories dotted the room they entered. Her feet sank in the lush carpet. Heavy drapes hid the night from the room.

"Michael's dead."

Too calmly, he answered, "Yes, I know."

"Of course you do, you sent Mr. Butcher. By the way, thanks." Chewing on her lower lip, she asked, "Did you kill Michael or have him killed?" She squirmed under his hooded gaze. "Well, did you?"

"It wouldn't be prudent for you to be here if I did either, would it?" He appeared annoyed but not surprised she asked.

"I guess not." Allyson ran her hand through her hair spilling the locks down her back. "I know you didn't do it."

"But?" Logan rocked back on his heels. She waved his question off with her hand and then wandered over to the bar. For a moment, she toyed with a glass.

"I need some answers."

Logan glanced down at the floor then back to her. "Yes, you do."

"If I hadn't met you, I wouldn't be in all this trouble; it's all your fault."

Logan bristled. "Do you know how childish you sound?" he ground out. "Before you, my life had order and tranquility."

Allyson jabbed her finger in his chest triumphantly. "See, it is all your fault! You spoke to me first."

Logan closed the small space between them until air couldn't slip past them. His hand shot out. Startled, Allyson backed up, but his hand tangled the hair at the back of her neck pulling her closer. "You impertinent little grimalkin." Logan brought his mouth down on hers, brutal, possessive and controlled.

Allyson pushed back from him breaking the kiss; his fervid breath fanned her face, his eyes glared down at her. Logan stilled under her touch, his body vibrated with the effort. The decision hers to do with him what she wanted. Her instincts pushed her forward. *Trust.* This man will never hurt you, body or soul. *Trust.* Seconds ticked still he waited. She trembled from the wait, the desire burning over her and then muttered, "Oh, what the hell."

Allyson grabbed the front of his shirt bringing his face back down to hers in an attempt to resume and deepen the kiss. His solid chest crushed her breasts; her arms crept up around his neck. His hands ran over her back and lower. She felt him smile into the kiss, while filling his hands with her ass, appreciatively squeezing each mound. He plunged on, deepening the kiss as passion ignited. She gasped, and then teased his tongue into a duel with hers. Allyson tugged his hair and nipped at his lips wanting more. He yanked at her blouse dispatching it with ease.

She pulled at his jacket freeing him from it and tossed it to the floor. Each tugged at the others waist-bands, buttons popping to bounce on the hardwood below and zippers snaked downward with a sharp hiss.

Breathless, they clung to each other. They rained frantic little kisses on each other's face.

A burst of light flashed in her head. Allyson staggered back, faintly hearing Logan's urgent plea in her head. *Allyson stop, you'll hurt us both. Pain!*

Blinding, white-hot agony encased and filled her mind. There was no escape, no release from it. She clutched her head, slowly sinking to her knees, mouth open in a silent scream and darkness engulfed her.

✧   ✧   ✧

A COOL CLOTH pressed against her forehead, covering her eyes. The pounding ebbed into a dull roar. She went to lift her hand, intending to remove the moist material.

"Keep your eyes closed until the pounding subsides." Logan grasped her hand pressing it to his chest.

"The curtains are drawn. You need to stay in the dark awhile longer, try not to move and keep the cloth on." He kissed her fingertips laying her hand on her stomach. After kissing her cheek, the bed dipped as he straightened.

"Lucien, thanks for holding. Yes, she's awake." She listened to Logan, guessing he spoke to this Lucien by phone. "Now? But is she okay? Give me a minute."

Allyson? Soft and cautious, he whispered her name mind to mind.

Aloud Allyson replied, "I hear you."

Grimalkin. She heard the word the minute it popped into his head and heard him admonish himself with *I shouldn't have called her an alley cat.*

Allyson cautiously lifted a corner of the cloth to gaze into those onyx eyes of his. *Who you calling an alley cat?*

The smile that broke over his face warmed her heart. *Not you, never you, my love, you definitely lean more to vixen.*

She listened to him finish his phone call with Lucien. Allyson struggled to sit up. Logan helped her, placing a pillow at her back.

"What happened?" She accepted the glass of water he offered. "And who's Lucien?" She sipped the cooling liquid.

"Lucien St. Clair is the father of a friend, and he's an amateur historian of the Tarczal people." Logan took the glass back. "As to why you collapsed, you understand how feedback works with electronics?"

"In theory, but not the technical stuff."

"I have found, curiously enough, your telepathic ability has linked us. It is strong, but unskilled."

Allyson was curious. "Telepathic? I can read people's minds?"

"I'm not sure about other people, but you and I are connected. When you and I joined, the first time," he kissed the wrist he'd first fed from, "we started then to have the ability to feel and read each other."

"How is it possible?"

"Lucien believes you have the bloodline of Alaza in your veins."

"Who is Alaza?"

"She's considered the mother of the Tarczal civilization. Long story short, she's the first of your kind to marry one of us. To carry her genealogy is rare. For a com outside of our race's circle, it's extremely atypical."

"So somewhere in my past, I have a Tarczal ancestor?"

"It would have to be a relative of Alaza's, before she changed."

"Changed into what?"

"Ah, a complicated answer, maybe you could ask something simpler?"

Allyson squirmed. "Okay, I've noticed you eat, drink, and have a great tan with no tan lines, which, by the way is pretty nice, so it's safe to say those facts are null and void."

"Facts?" Logan was tickling her ribs.

She playfully slapped at his hands. "About vampires, Tarczals."

"Oh, *those* questions. I thought you wanted to know about my stamina."

"Ha, ha, funny." Allyson paused. "Is your prowess part of Tarczal physiology?"

For an answer Logan flashed his incredible smile.

Allyson shook her head and chuckled. "What about coffins, flying through the air, or the mirror and the reflection thing?"

"No coffins, oh, heavens, no. I prefer a comfortable, roomy bed to a hard cramped surface anytime, and as to aversion to mirrors, no we don't, unless you count Salina's reaction to mirrors first thing in the morning sans makeup." He laughed heartily and then tilted his head. "As to the flying, not without at least a plane."

"Right. What about religious symbols?" she asked.

Logan laughed shaking his head no. "Much of which has been perceived about my people is inaccurate."

"Myths and legends…," she began.

His smile again interrupted her.

"Myths and legends," he said, "are like burial ceremonies. They each accomplish their precise intent—to grant solace without revealing what man cannot confront." He paused. "Myths and legends are constructed to set forth their own blend of horror and since these falsehoods help protect us, we encourage them." He brushed her face with his fingertips. "We are as you are, with our own subtle differences. We take nourishment at regular intervals. We age much slower. Diseases cannot be acquired or imparted by us. Though not immortal, we heal quicker and have a longer life span than you have. Your race and mine are kinsmen, superior in some ways, inferior in others, but in the balance of life, equal. Our ancestors learned long ago we could exist without violence between our two races."

"You mean this Kharzarin and Alaza?"

"Yes. We have learned to raise our families alongside the commons as best we can. They are paid a wage and benefits so we don't have to unjustly take."

She realized he'd just told her more than most people knew about his race. "Considering what has happened, can you at least tell me if the fact about the three feedings is true?" Logan looked puzzled, for a minute unsure what she was asking, and then laughed heartily. "No, it is not true. You can't become a Tarczal in such a manner, it's more complicated. A metamorphosis or change is much more intricate. You must have certain genes."

"Like Alaza."

"Yes."

Allyson watched a multitude of emotions pass over his face. Logan closed his eyes and a serious note crept into his voice. "Once, in a moment of desperation, I offered to do so. The person I wanted to help didn't react positively to the offer." She held him tight as he buried his face in her hair, inhaling its scent.

"Why can't I stop thinking about you?" Loving you. The words popped into her head before she could stop them, and she could feel them settle in her heart.

"You think about me?"

"Oh, don't get all manly and smug on me. I've noticed the way you look at me."

"I don't deny, I want you."

"So this connection we have is what? Chemical? Magical?"

"Magical?" croaked Logan and then he mumbled, "I hope not."

"Excuse me?"

"Nothing. I haven't a clue why we're drawn to each other. It could be nothing more than the age old attraction of man to woman."

Allyson traced his jaw with her fingertips.

"I've never felt this way before." She held his gaze. "I want you and I don't care the rhyme or reason."

Swiftly he moved, capturing her hand and kissing the tips. "I feel the same."

"What's wrong?"

"My friend suggests we take things slow, and I agree."

"But."

"No 'buts,' unless we're talking about your spectacular one." Logan tapped the tip of her nose with a finger.

Allyson rolled her eyes.

"I don't know who is trying to implicate us in Michael's murder, and until I do, we should limit our contact." When she would speak, he placed a finger to her lips. "I'm sending you home with a twenty-four hour guard. You'll be safe and I can pursue the leads I have."

"I could stay here with you."

"I'd like to, but this connection we have is a distraction I can't afford right now."

"I suppose you're right. When I'm near you I start thinking, with shall we say, the wrong part of my anatomy, too." Allyson sighed. "Ok, you know more about this than I do."

"Thank you. Give me a couple of minutes to make the arrangements." Logan picked up his phone.

✧   ✧   ✧

STANDING IN THE driveway, Logan watched Allyson and a Janissary named Gideon disappear down the lane in her car. Logan was grateful Nairn had sent Gideon, his right-hand man, ahead of schedule. Gideon, while young, if you could call two hundred and fifty young, would lay down his life for Allyson if necessary. Logan hoped it wouldn't be.

Chapter Twelve

L OGAN KINCAID WASN'T a happy man. The damn conversation with his uncle about Logan's birth kept haunting him. They'd talked, argued, deep into the night and early morning. André's travel plans were the one thing cutting the discussion short. Logan sat at his desk rehashing the discussion.

✧   ✧   ✧

LOGAN DRUMMED HIS fingers on the chair's armrest leaning forward. "An earth quake and a full moon. Why is this the first I've heard about this?"

"Two full moons. Your parents and the rest of the family thought it best not to publicize the circumstances surrounding your birth." The muscles in André's jaw clenched and unclenched. "They thought it wise to stop any rumors or implications before they could spread. Your father had already announced his revolutionary ideas about our people. Ideas not accepted in polite society or by the Alliance. Announcing the Tarczal existence to the world was an idea feared by many. Then there was your birth. Later, after my brother and his bride perished, rumors circulated that his death, perhaps, was not because of his beliefs, but because your parents might be connected to the Kharzarin and Alaza legend."

"Nonsense." Logan slammed his palm on the arm of the chair, rising to pace the room.

André shrugged. "Perhaps, but it was a belief many had."

"And you and Auntie, why were you not considered for this exaltation?" Logan tsked.

"Strangely your auntie and I were born in the middle of the day. Many suspected, I suspected, your parents could speak mind to mind, though no one ever witnessed such an act." His uncle sighed. "I took you to Lucien because of his talents and work in the field. He could be counted on to keep things quiet. Because if the telepathy was the reason, not your father's political beliefs, or just a happenstance angry mob that killed them, you were in danger, too."

Logan's pacing stopped as a finger, frosty as the grave trailed down his spine. "You never told me you believed my parents' deaths was anything other than ignorant people and their misguided faith."

André's mouth tightened. "You were but a child, terrified, grieving, and later, your auntie and I didn't see the benefit of filling you with supposition and gossip." André sat, legs crossed at the knee, for all outward appearances an example of calm, parental wisdom, only the hint of awe and fear in his gaze the clues to the turmoil inside the man. "It appears your involvement with this woman Allyson gives some credence to our reservations."

"Aren't there any other explanations that can account for the buzzing, headaches, and the rest?" Logan rubbed the back of his neck.

"I suppose anything is possible, but there is the telepathic connection and you mention she tasted of cinnamon. There is only one documented explanation for these things."

"The Kharzarin and Alaza legend." Logan sighed.

"Exactly."

Logan gave a dry, humorless laugh. "Lately, I can't even manage my own life, how does anyone expect me to be the next step of our people's evolution?"

André shrugged noncommittally. "It will all fall into place, the legend predicts."

✧   ✧   ✧

LOGAN MADE SURE the following morning André's return travel plans included Kincaid Enterprises private jet, shuddering at the thought of a commercial flight, despite his uncle's, assurance the trip over had been quite enlightening and delightful, mingling with the unknowing coms.

Once his uncle departed, Logan hunkered down in his office calling in every favor owed and bargaining ruthlessly for the tiny bits of information now in front of him. None of which gave Logan a name or face to go with the elusive man hunting him. *He's a coward*, sneered an inward voice, why else would this person hide in the shadows and not face him?

Pulled back to the here and now, Logan listened to the slamming of a door, really, doors. The sounds reverberated eerily through the house as Salina swore colorfully in several languages while exiting the building. The reverberations died and he could hear the clock ticking in the hallway. How loud it sounded. In a few days when everyone arrived, its cadence would be lost in the day-to-day activities.

The conversation he and Salina just had. He gave a self-disgusted laugh, it hadn't been a conversation per say. Salina had done most of the talking, or shouting, before he had rebuffed her attempts again, with cruel cutting remarks, to get him to feed. Normally, such behavior was beneath him, and yet he'd done it anyway. Why had he treated her like that? He gave a self-loathing snort. Because he was miserable, and he wanted her to be too, selfish prick he'd become. Deep down he knew her nagging came from their long-time friendship.

Logan let his thoughts turn back to Allyson. Ah, Allyson, sweet Allyson, he sighed longingly at the thought of her. He let a little fantasy of them play in his head. They were alone in this room, a fire in the fireplace the only light, and she lay on the ornate rug beneath him. He imagined how she'd look in the throes of passion.

Swiftly, a pain of hunger caught his attention, shoving the fantasy aside. Salina's words of concern returned to him. He knew she was pissed at him, and right now, he couldn't care less. She'd harped at him that he needed to feed. He'd argued he was too damn busy. Besides, he'd feed when he damn well wanted to, not when she, or it, demanded. Being older than her, he could go without longer.

The hunger in him flared and blinded Logan with its need. Logan fought back, and with an angry motion, cleared the desktop with a swipe of his arm. Papers flew into the air to waft to the floor while heavy objects bounced and rolled to a stop. The painting still on the sofa taunted him. Rising from his chair, he stomped over to the painting and with a roar, punched his fist through the canvas. Snatching up the frame, he brought it down over one knee, snapping the fragile wood. With a heave, he tossed the broken bits into the fire, his sudden rage catching him by surprise. The flames caught the oils, igniting them with a flash. Sparks dotted the oriental carpet like scattered tears winking in the last evening light before twinkling out.

Logan strode out into the hallway, pausing and listening. The clock ticked, and the tick echoed.

"Salina! Salina!" he shouted and waited on the off chance she hadn't left. Only the ricochet of his own voice answered him. Logan shrugged. She'd gone to feed, no doubt. He was restless and went through the kitchen, out the backdoor into the garage. Their driver, a member of Salina's small staff, and one of the cars were gone. Just as well, he felt like driving. He reached for one of the keys, a sharp, brief stabbing pain made him pause. The hunger didn't like being ignored. Taking a breath, he let it out slowly. He was master here, not the hunger, he would decide, not it, when he would feed.

Backing the car out of the garage, he did a quick "J" turn and roared down the long drive for town. He headed to the nearest retired feeder's home.

The small town held several retirees. A feeder's donation span was usually twenty-five years, though many went as long as thirty. Those extra five years meant a generous bonus in a unique retirement plan.

Normally, Logan enjoyed visiting with the retirees to reminisce about days gone by and catch up on the family's growth. He knew many from the days their great-grandparents had immigrated to this country. Lately though, he'd only stayed long enough to conduct his business at hand. Then he moved on. Staying to chat brought on too many questions, questions he didn't want to answer. It was a close-knit community, no doubt the gossip of Allyson and he rampaged like wildfire.

Coming to a retiree's home he pulled to the curb, a light-colored car with the driver side fender in dull gray primer slid into a spot several spaces back from his. George and Daisy had found him. Logan pulled back into the street not wanting to endanger the feeders. For the next several hours, he traveled through town trying to lose the Kingstons, but as Logan drove, he noticed something disturbing. The active feeders in the area didn't have their normal watch lights on glowing with their welcoming amber, indication they would make a donation to any Tarczal in need. No, they glowed blue, for danger. Could George and Daisy have stepped up their harassment that much?

Logan continued to drive. Finally coming to an older section of town, he pulled the car over in a vacant parking lot and turned it off while he considered his next move. Meanwhile, the hunger was now beyond tantrums, it was becoming a howling, gnashing, and violent thing inside him. It tightened his chest, making each breath an effort and his stomach clenched as though fed ground glass. He glanced at the clock on the dash, startled to find two hours had passed. He'd begun losing bits of time, not a good sign. Sleep called to him, and he curled up on the front seat, silently damning his self-important machismo and self-pity.

He'd stupidly let himself go too long between feedings like some foolish adolescent. Briefly, he considered grabbing a passer-by for a quick meal, but his childhood training reminded him one doesn't foul one's nest. A small voice laughed at his misery, mercilessly taunting him. *You've gone and done it again. You let your guard down. You let her form a crack in your armor. It was just enough to let me gather in the one thing you fear more than anything. The one thing you swore you'd never do again. You've gone and fallen in love.* The voice laughed long and hard, the sound echoing in his head before fading away leaving him alone, stripped raw with emotions and the stifling stillness in the car. Logan knew it was his heart that spoke to him.

Curling tighter, he hoped for sleep, and prayed it would pacify the hunger. Later, as he dozed, noises too close for comfort in his surroundings drew him from his slumber. A mindless self-preservation drew him out of the safety of the car to stumble into the icy night, hunting, for sanctuary…and food.

Chapter Thirteen

SHE CRADLED THE half forgotten tea mug in both hands. The dark, strong, black tea sweetened with more than just one dollop of honey had turned chilly and bitter. She gulped it down not wanting for some unknown reason to leave any. Staring out the front window she noted in spite of the cold, the lawn was still green. The lingering shades of green appeared as if someone had added a darker tint to the varying hues then smudged their edges to soften them.

It was early evening and the night sky held a gentle light. Allyson drew the curtains closed against the darkness and chill. A small lamp softly lit the living room, giving the area a warm and cozy feeling as if being in a cocoon. Gideon had made his rounds outside and now double-checked the inside. She wandered the house, ticking off several items she could busy herself with and rejected them all. Never before had she felt such restlessness, it weighed on her and more than once, she stopped, struggling for breath as the rooms seemed to close in on her. Until Logan, she'd dreaded the nights when the loneliness crept into her soul. She prowled the living room and jumped, startled, when she heard a knock at the door.

Gideon came down the hallway, signaling her to stay put while he answered the door.

"Ms. DeBois?" he announced in surprise.

Salina DeBois stood there in the muted glow of the porch light, glancing around nervously.

Allyson came up behind him blurting, "What are you doing here?" Then as a blast of icy air darted in the door, Allyson moved him aside. "I am sorry, where are my manners? Come in, it's freezing out there." Salina stepped in and Gideon shut the door.

Allyson noticed Salina fidgeting with the belt on her coat, wondering briefly, where the confident sophisticated woman she'd met the first time had gone. Tonight, Salina reminded her of a frightened child.

"Is Logan here?" Salina asked, sounding hopeful.

"No, he isn't."

Allyson and Gideon answered in unison.

Gideon spoke up. "Why would you think he was here?"

"I was hoping he was hiding out here, or you might know where he was."

Instantly on alert, Gideon asked. "Who's Mr. Kincaid hiding from? Not saying Mr. K would hide from a challenge or anything. Did he find the killer?"

Salina wrapped her arms close to her body in an effort to center herself. "Killer? No, I don't believe he did. He would've said something." She fidgeted more. "We had a stupid argument. I stormed out and when I came back he was gone. He's been gone for a long time. I've searched everywhere I know of, even the off-the-beaten-path places he haunts. I've talked to others, but no one has seen him or knows where he might be." Salina snatched off her coat and threw it onto a chair. "I tried to contact Nairn, but his phone goes to voice-mail. I even put in a call to Thomas, but Zilvia says he's en route to the States and can't be reached as yet."

"Mr. St. Clair's phone never goes to voice when you call, its set up for emergency notification." Gideon rubbed his chin. "And you can't get through to Mr. Rothwell, this isn't good." He moved off, flipping his own phone open and placing a call himself.

"Who are Thomas and Zilvia?" Allyson interrupted. "Can't either one of you just call to him? You know with the telepathy thing?"

Salina chewed her lower lip. "We can't do what you do. We're not telepathic, like you."

"She's… Mr. Kincaid… are telepathic?" Gideon rocked back and forth from heels to toes. "Wow, that would make them…"

Salina turned on him. "You'll do well to forget what you heard just now."

"But, Ms. DeBois, she'd be a T'yhiél."

"Gideon, shut up." Salina stood, staring Gideon down and the air vibrated around them. Allyson figured it prudent to let one of them make the next move, literally. What the heck was a T'yhiél?

"Yes, ma'am. Now do either of you have any suggestions on how I can find the boss's BFF? I can't get through on my phone either."

Salina pointed to Allyson. "We have her. She can find him."

"Whoa, wait a minute the last time Logan and I connected, I blacked out. Logan said someone named Lucien told him we needed more training before we tried it again."

Allyson's utterance of the man's name had Salina snatching up her purse, digging out her cell phone. "I'm calling Lucien." Minutes later, Salina spoke with him snapping her fingers for paper and pen, which Gideon quickly gave her.

"Thanks, Lucien, yes, I'll let you know as soon as I do." Salina stared at the carpet, not seeing, and then whispered quietly as she raised her eyes. "Allyson, Logan's only fed enough the past week to just barely keep himself going. I'm not even sure he's fed at all in the last few days. I haven't seen much of him. He's stayed glued to his desk and on the phone or computer."

"Salina, I'll do what I can." Allyson had listened to Salina's side of the phone call. Anticipation skittered down her spine at what she was about to do. Salina tapped a manicured nail on the small table beside her. "We don't have our regular stable of feeders in place yet. I found out from a feeder family the Kingstons interrupted Logan when he tried to meet with them.

We can only live on supplement, for so long before needing fresh. Logan hasn't consumed either." Salina chewed her lip. "Allyson, please help me find him."

Logan was only a few short feet away from her each time she had reached out to him. How did Salina think she could find him over any great distance? Yet, what would be the consequence if she didn't even try?

"I'm not sure, Salina. I may have the ability, but not the training or skill."

Salina interrupted. "I can help you, talk you through the procedure and be a guide. Lucien was pretty clear on his instructions."

"If you're sure. When this is all over, I have to meet this Lucien. What do we do first?" Allyson resigned herself to the unknown.

Salina walked into the living room, paused, and then pointed to the recliner. "Sit here and try to get comfortable." Allyson sat down, pulling out the footrest. Salina gracefully arranged herself on the ottoman while Gideon hovered nearby. "Allyson, I want you to relax, clear your mind of everything. Take a deep breath and slowly exhale. Try to release any tension from your body. I want you to think of Logan."

Closing her eyes, Allyson listened to the hypnotic lilt of Salina's voice. "You're attracted to Logan, right"

Allyson nodded. "Yes."

"You've slept together?"

"It's really none of anyone's business." Allyson's cheeks flamed.

"Your response indicates a no. I'll have to go with how you're drawn to him. Remember his face, the shape of it. His eyes, their color, and how they blaze when he stares at you. I'm sure he's at least kissed you, so remember his mouth, how it felt against yours, hard, demanding, gentle, and soft. How it felt pressed against your body."

Allyson sat straight up. "Is this a joke?" Allyson's face burned with embarrassment, glancing from Salina and Gideon, neither showed any signs of unease.

"No." Salina hesitated.

"You're serious." Allyson arched an elegantly plucked brow.

Salina straightened. "Completely."

"Ah, listening to you talk is making me extremely uncomfortable." Allyson averted her gaze, unexpectedly feeling awkward.

"Sorry. I forget coms can be prudish at times." Salina brusquely seemed offended. Allyson watched as she straightened in her seat and brushed a nonexistent speck of lint from her skirt. Gideon shrugged his shoulders, as if to say, whatever.

"Is there some other way we can do this?" Allyson tried to smooth things over.

Allyson watched Salina think, for a moment. "I suppose, if you just let yourself relax and concentrated on Logan it should work without a voice prompt."

"Ladies, if you don't need me for a couple of minutes, I'm going to check the grounds." Gideon tossed on his coat.

The women sent him a look telling him to get on with it.

Salina locked the door after Gideon went out. Allyson leaned back in the chair, took a deep breath and slowly let it out and imagined Logan standing before her. Memories flooded in like a dam bursting. Allyson screamed, terrified, not knowing she did it, the noise a distant resonance to her ears.

"Allyson, push aside the pain, feel as Logan does, and see as he does now." Salina's voice was urgent, guiding her.

An endless sea of blackness, emptiness, stretched before Allyson as she searched to connect with Logan's mind. She lay foundering in darkness, no buoy to set course from, until a wave hurled her onto jagged rocks of excruciating loneliness and overwhelming sadness. A frigid, painful cold seeping into the marrow of her soul left her gasping as though the air had been sucked from her. Allyson grabbed blindly, frantically, for an anchor and latched onto Salina's hand, not noticing Salina winced as Allyson's nails dug into her arm. Then Allyson cried out.

"Oh my God, Salina! The pain, the burning, the hunger, the need!"

Faintly, Allyson heard Salina instructing her to push past the pain as a groan of anguish escaped her.

She was feeling the thing demanding to be fed. She wondered if this was the price they must pay to live as they did, drinking other human blood.

Then slowly she felt her mind brush Logan's and his presence surrounded her.

"He doesn't realize I've reached him." She sat bolted upright, still clutching Salina's hand. "I'm there with him. He's so weak, distant, and empty."

She felt something wet on her face. Tears? His or hers? "He's too weak to move, too weak to feed or hunt. Part of him knows what he needs is nearby, but it's as though part of him has given up."

"Concentrate, Allyson. Open your eyes look around at your surroundings," Salina whispered anxiously.

"How do you expect me to see anything if it's dark where he is?" Allyson snapped.

"Oh, Allyson, see with his eyes!"

Like a curtain slowly parting, Allyson blinked, trying to clear away the film obscuring her vision. No, not her vision, Logan's!

Allyson relaxed, letting Logan's body work for her. She stared, amazed at what he was capable of doing. It made perfect sense, Tarczals having the capacity of night-vision. Scanning the area was her next priority. Old machinery parts, dust, cobwebs, and dilapidated cardboard containers littered the floor. The building smelled of non-use, stale and musty, a storage place used only infrequently. A place remembered in another time past, now different to Logan, yet, something vaguely familiar to her.

The room, the shape of it, the windows placed high on the walls. Lights from a passing car ricocheted off one window and far wall to dance out another window. Shadows flickered flame-like to disappear, engulfed by others of its kind. The height of the car lights nagged at Allyson. They came from too far above. They would seem to have been coming across a bridge. Yes! She knew where Logan was!

Allyson turned, laughing, crying, blinking rapidly, clearing her eyes of Logan's images. "Salina, I know where he is. He's in the warehouse beside the old train depot."

The women held each other, hugging, laughing and crying. Salina stood, hauling Allyson up with her while reaching for her coat and telling Gideon, who'd come back in, that they had to hurry.

Gideon stepped in front of them, hands up, palms out. "Wait a minute ladies, I can't let you go traipsing off into the dark."

Salina patted his cheek with her hand. "Don't worry, you're not going to, you're going with us." She slipped her arm through his.

"Oh, crap," muttered Gideon.

Allyson paused to grab an afghan from the sofa, rubbing her arms as she remembered the emptiness she'd felt in Logan.

"This isn't a good idea," Gideon muttered again minutes later after they pulled up near the warehouse. Salina reached out to stop Allyson from exiting the car. She stared into the night and then running her tongue over dry lips, turned to Allyson. "Maybe you should stay in the car while Gideon and I check this out." She licked her lips again. "Logan might have let his *civilization* slip."

Allyson whispered her voice flat. "I can feel how weak he is and we'll need all of us to get him out of here." Allyson gave a faint smile and held Salina's gaze. "We know why I'm here, after all fresh is best, isn't it?"

"Yes he'll need to feed, but you're more important to him than just a warm body for food. I'm worried what will happen when he does take nourishment. He'll have to feed from the carotid and Allyson; he may not realize who you are until its too late." Salina then looked past her.

Allyson's throat clogged the words thick in her throat. "We can't sit here and debate this. He's slipping away, I can sense it."

Gideon slammed his fist down on the back of the front seat. "Damn it, this is not going to end well. I'll go in first and you two follow close." He glanced at both women. "Understand?"

They nodded yes.

Allyson took the flashlight Salina dug out of the glove compartment and the afghan she'd grabbed from home. Silently, the trio made for the building's backside.

Gideon found Logan's point of entry, a side door,

its knob now a twisted bit of metal. They stepped into the building, Gideon first, Salina next, with Allyson trailing.

They'd begun traversing the labyrinth of forgotten boxes and equipment when Allyson heard a noise.

The sound, too low for normal hearing, softly brushed against her mind, halting Allyson. Eyes closed, clearing her psyche, she tried to locate Logan.

A tug, a word she didn't understand beckoned her forward.

Logan?

Closer.

Where are you? It sounded like his voice, but different.

Closer.

Forgetting the others and listening to the voice, Allyson rounded a corner; she found Logan slumped along a wall. Stunned, she froze then stumbled forward.

"Allyson, no!" Gideon yelled and ran to intercept her.

Logan, silent as death, sprang up slamming into the young Janissary's midsection sending him into a structure support. The old wood cracked like a gunshot, but stayed true.

Gideon, the wind knocked from his lungs, grunted rising to his feet. "Mr. K., its Gideon, stop."

Logan's answer was a feral growl as he charged again, the two men grappled, each trying for a better hold. Gideon had youth on his side, but Logan had years of experience from when men's lives depended on brute strength and cunning. Logan slid behind the young man, wrapping his arms around Gideon's neck in a chokehold.

The Janissary fought him tooth and nail, but slowly deprived of oxygen could only do so much.

Allyson ran forward dropping the afghan. "Logan, no, you'll kill him."

Salina, seconds ahead of her, reached Logan first; grasping his arm she yanked hard trying to break his hold on Gideon. Logan snarled and flicked her off him like a bug. Salina slammed into a wall and then crumpled to the floor. Logan dropped the unconscious man like a sack of feed to the planks underfoot. Turning his attention to Allyson, he stalked her in the small space.

"You want blood?" Allyson tugged off the turtleneck sweater she wore. "I've got plenty, come on big boy, come and get it." She walked backwards away from the two on the floor, wishing a silent hope they were only stunned and not dead. Bare from the waist up, she held out her arms welcoming him.

Prey! Logan's mind flashed the word and it echoed in her. His survival instincts were strong and raw. One hand snaked out to grasp her by the nape, snapping her head back painfully as he exposed her throat. Allyson went, still registering these facts when he punctured the artery, smoothly, effortlessly.

She clung to him as he pulled her closer, securing

his hold and drank deeper. She felt her strength flow into him and hers ebb. As her body relaxed, so did the grasp Logan held on her neck.

Arms…his…hers…circled each other's waist. The darkness, quiet and cold, stealthily wrapped itself around her, coaxing her to join with it. It would be so comforting, so easy to give in to. If only someone wasn't shouting her name, someone who wouldn't let the darkness complete its task.

✧   ✧   ✧

LIKE HIS ANCESTORS, his instincts took over when he sensed food close. As the life-giving substance flowed into him, so did awareness. Recognition brought with it curious facts, no struggle and no resistance from the body he held. It gave in complete willingness. Strange? Usually captured prey resisted at this point, even if only a little.

More senses returned. A fragrance. He inhaled the scent. Not fragrance, an essence like Allyson's. His fingers wrapped in long silken stands. Like Allyson's hair. The body against his chest was soft, rounded like Allyson's. Pausing in his feeding, he opened his eyes to inspect this willing victim. He jolted at the sight of whom he held. "Allyson? Allyson! Please hear me. Hear me! Oh Goddess, don't let me have gone too far. Allyson, please, Allyson, please hear me. Please answer me," Logan cried.

✧   ✧   ✧

SALINA BOLTED UPRIGHT a scant minute after the anguished animalistic cry shook the warehouse. Still stunned, she scanned the room to get her bearings. From the farthest shadows, she caught a muffled moan and she hurried to the back of the room. She had hoped not to see the scene before her. Logan held the limp body of Allyson in his arms. He brushed the hair from her face, rocking back and forth, calling her name repeatedly. Logan pleaded with the Goddess she live. He begged Allyson to wake up, to answer him.

Salina stepped carefully towards them, not wanting to startle Logan. He could, in his present confused state, view her as a threat and inadvertently hurt her, worse than last time.

"Logan?" she said calmly.

"Salina?" His head shot up. Tracks of wetness streaked his face.

"Yes, Logan, it's me," she answered gently, watching him.

"I can't tell." He bent over the still body, cradled it to him as he rocked back and forth. "I can't tell if she's alive. She won't answer. When I reach, I feel darkness. Why, why did she do it?"

"Let me help you." Salina held her hands out, palms up in an ancient gesture of no harm. She picked up the discarded afghan to arrange it over their shoulders. Logan hugged Allyson closer to his chest. Salina wrapped her arms around both of them.

Gideon stumbled into the small area. The threat of Logan had passed. Salina pulled, pushed, and prodded Logan into a stand. He ignored her and Gideon's attempt to help him carry Allyson. They would have to be content keeping him on his feet moving towards the car. Once they reached the safety of the car, Gideon raced for the estate. Salina watched from the front seat as her friend cradled the limp form of the woman he loved.

✧   ✧   ✧

"ALLYSON, PLEASE DON'T leave me." Logan drew in a sharp breath, "Come back to me. Please, Allyson, please. I didn't know it was you, my sweet Allyson."

Logan? A mind's faint whisper brushed against him, the voice thick with the darkness' sleep, *Logan all right?*

I am all right. Logan's voice echoed throughout the darkness around her. *Please come back, I need you Allyson.*

Allyson shivered mentally and physically. *I am so frozen Logan, come keep me warm.*

I'll keep you warm, but you must come to me. He wrapped the afghan snugly around her, and then spoke aloud. "You must wake up. I can't keep you warm where you are, come to me now, Allyson!" She stirred, tried to focus her mind as she fought through the tangle grasping at her, struggling to find an anchor. She found it in the light of Logan's face.

Chapter Fourteen

ALLYSON WOKE TO find herself looking at a thin, elderly man who bent, placing a tray with juice on the nightstand. The man gave her a brief nod and a warm, friendly smile before he slipped out the bedroom door.

She felt a body, large and warm, behind her. One strong arm snuggly wrapped around her waist. She twisted a bit to confirm that Logan indeed held her. He tightened his embrace in a sleepy hug. Save for a small lamp softly glowing in a far corner, she could tell it was still dark. Or was it dark again? She wondered. She'd lost all track of time.

Her eyes focused on the pitcher of juice. To lessen his hold, she patted Logan's arm reassuringly then sat up and poured a tall glass of the liquid. Her mouth was dry, the juice chilly, never had anything tasted so good. She listened to the soft, low hum of the central heating, poured another glass of juice, and sat to gawk at the room.

It was a man's bedroom. A masculine man's room. The bed was a dark wood, mahogany, large and heavy. Carved in the footboard panel were words, a phrase, perhaps in the Tarczal language. The rest of the furniture matched the bed, a desk, armoire, and two chairs. One constructed for a man's form and the other strangely feminine. A set meant to complement each other. Each piece was old and made with loving care and artisanship.

Logan reached for her in his sleep. Allyson smiled, placed the empty glass on the nightstand, and slid down to lay facing him. She thought briefly of a shower, but the bed and Logan were so warm and enticing. A short nap would do her good. Before she dozed, she wondered who the man was that brought the juice.

When she came to, she found herself draped over Logan, who lay still fast asleep. As she watched, he woke, stretched, scrubbed a hand over his face, and then let out a breath.

"I should apologize or at least explain my previous behavior."

"Salina mentioned your 'civilization' might have slipped, whatever that means. Is that what happened?"

"An accurate enough description, but it wouldn't have happened if I hadn't been an idiot, acting like an unruly child, and eaten when I should." Logan slid closer to her. "I nearly killed you."

Allyson cupped his cheek in her hand. "But you didn't."

He cocked his head. "I didn't frighten you?"

"Maybe a little." She shrugged. "But I knew, and I don't know how, so don't ask me to explain, but I knew you wouldn't."

Logan growled in disgust. "So you can forgive me for attacking you like an animal?

"Yes, I can." She brushed her mouth across his. "Just don't let it happen again," she said teasingly.

"How do you feel?" Logan asked.

Allyson leaned forward and kissed his cheek. "I think I feel pretty good, but you tell me." She smiled, he was alive and all right, and she felt excited to be alive, too. Sliding a leg over his, she sat up and straddled him. She ran her hands over his chest, he in turn ran his over her hips, up her back, then down.

"I think you feel pretty good, too." Logan pulled her down to him, kissing her lazily, deeply, exploring with his tongue. She felt him harden beneath her. She rested on her knees, reaching between them to guide him into her. Logan thrust his hips upward to imbed himself deeply. Leisurely, she rode him, rising and descending, building painstakingly to the pinnacle they each desired. Hands on her hips urged her to quicken the pace. Two people locked in one of nature's most basic rhythms, sensations building, ebbing, and building. Jagged gasps of breath mingled with cries of longing, nearer to the apex, finally, shuddering over its brink and collapsing in its glory.

The wind scraped a tree branch against the window. No one else existed save for the two of them.

Later, as they snuggled under down covers, Logan stroked her hair absentmindedly. "You have questions?"

"Did you just read my mind?"

"No, you're an intelligent woman, and intelligent people always have questions."

"Who was the guy who brought in the juice?"

"Tall, thin, elderly, dressed like a major-domo?"

"Major what?"

"Majordomo, head of the staff, a super butler. The man who really runs this place." Logan chuckled.

"Oh, I didn't realize anyone else was here. I thought you lived alone or with Salina"

"No, Thomas and I own the house together. We have a rather large staff working here when we're in residence. Some live in the house or on the premises, others just come and go as their schedule's dictate. Thomas and his entourage must have arrived while I was out."

"Salina mentioned someone named Thomas. Who is he? If you don't mind me asking."

"Thomas is…" He took a deep breath. "Surrogate father, best friend, business partner, and sometimes, father confessor. You'll meet him and the others later."

"If you want me to, I will." She tapped his chest with a fingernail. "By the way, where is Salina?"

"She's here in the house. It's a big house, we have lots of spare rooms for guests, and the others live here." He cocked his head. "Any other questions?"

They cuddled for a moment. Allyson wanted to chase the cloud over them away. Pulling back to look at him. "How old are you anyway?"

Amusement twinkled in his eyes, "My driver's license says I'll be forty-five on my next birthday."

She tugged on his beard. "I have ways of getting the truth from you mister, talk."

He flashed his snow-white grin. "Hope you like older men. I was born in 1564." He waited for her reaction.

Taken aback only a moment, she tickled him. "For an old geezer, you sure can get it up quickly." She could feel his hardness pressing against her.

His hands were causing shivers to form all over her body as he spoke. They were side by side now. Closing her eyes, she enjoyed the sensations; her nipples hardened and ached for his touch.

"Do we stop here?" Logan ceased his caresses, gazing at her. "My people are sensuous by nature. A male or female Tarczal, upon the point of orgasm, for themselves and their partner, can puncture here," Logan placed his index finger left above her collarbone where the carotid artery was, "and taste. Both partners will climax in a heightened state humans cannot reach alone."

Allyson trembled from desire and the unknown. Logan was stroking, caressing, kissing, nibbling, his mouth and hands on an erotic exploration, kneading one breast as he ran his tongue from an ear lobe down her neck. "In my arms you need not fear, only feel. I wish to show you pleasure. I know the superficial things about you. I want to know the intimate secret things. Where you like to be touched, how you like to be touched in your secret spot. I want to know how to kiss you to make the butterflies flutter in your stomach and how to make your toes curl in passion. I want to make you shudder in desire. Laugh in joy and weep from the intimacy of two bodies joined in lovemaking. I want you with every breath I take. Tell me Allyson, tell me what you want." His voice was husky, raw with desire.

When she spoke, she was surprised at the sound of her own voice bursting with the same exposed longing as Logan's. "You could have any woman in the world."

"Can I?"

"Yes, and you know it, too."

"Then I want you."

"You're crazy."

"Yes, crazy in love with you."

"Love me; show me how to love you." She nibbled at his neck.

Logan soon had her moaning his name, only this time before she lost all control she knew she must taste what he had to offer, as he had tasted her. Allyson slid down his chest to lay her head on his hip. She inhaled his musky maleness. Slowly she circled the tip of his manhood, delighting in how it twitched when her tongue flicked over it. Down the shaft and back up she dragged her mouth, nibbling now and then, caressing the firm delicate pouch beneath it. Taking the entire thing deep into her mouth, she was pleased when he groaned from the searing pleasure-fire of her touch on his skin. He moaned her name in the same ragged gasp she had once called to him. Wrapping her long hair around the base, she let it slide over its length.

Strong hands pulled her towards him. Logan was over her, she reached to guide him into her. They both were swollen and ready. When he would pull to leave, she could feel her muscles tighten to pull him back. Logan bent his head to take an aching nipple between his teeth. His eager hands squeezed and plumped each breast in turn, pinching the stiffened pebbles straining at their peaks. Shocks of excitement sprang from each tweak to join the ones between her legs. Her breath caught and turned into ragged gasps with each rise and fall of her chest. Breathing became harder, more labored for each. She was trying to pull him closer. What had been caresses with her nails now turned into raking.

"Harder," he commanded her. Allyson's nails dug deeper, and he gave a satisfied masculine growl of approval. Just when she was about to beg him to end her torture, Logan thrust deeply. Allyson locked her legs around his waist as he bent his head. She tried to hold off one more climax but her body wouldn't be denied. Hot feminine liquid soaked the V of her sex. Her back bowed and her legs tightened their grip on Logan's waist. Her release finally found its liberation like a floodgate opened wide.

A fire raced through her veins, and just as sudden, a cool, calm serenity replaced it. She listened to the lulling sound of her heart beat mixing with the rushing of her blood through her veins as they joined with the sounds of Logan's to form an orchestra of peacefulness. Once more, she nestled in strong, loving arms. She heard Logan whisper her name and speak something in a language she didn't recognize before drifting off to sleep.

✧   ✧   ✧

HE LAY WATCHING her. Everything about her felt right, like a missing piece completing a puzzle. When they made love, the hunger grew, not as it usually did, maybe it's why he was unprepared for what happened. Allyson locking her long, shapely legs around his waist, her hand pressing his head, instinctively almost, to her neck, wanting him to feed at the moment of their combined climax. His teeth buried deep, his cock deeper, and she pulled him closer still, a silent plea, for him to drink, to consummate their lovemaking as only a mated pair of his kind could. Even educated feeders seldom welcomed their first time, okay, technically her second time, as willing as Allyson did. She'd responded as any female of his race would have and it puzzled, scared, and delighted him. Allyson wasn't one of his kind, not even a half-breed. He murmured ancient Tarczal words of love. He watched her sleeping and eagerly waited for her to awaken.

Chapter Fifteen

FRANCHOT REALIZED HE'D have recognized the old woman anywhere. Much of her mother resided in Daisy's face. His mouth twitched at one corner. The half-light of first evening shone through the windows into the abandoned factory leaving deep pockets of shadows. He watched from one such pocket while the elderly couple shuffled into the building. The cooling air ruffled his recently shortened auburn hair, tickling the exposed skin on the back of his neck like an electric charge. Waiting until they were deep inside, he stepped into a dwindling shaft of light. His sudden appearance startled the couple. The woman thrust a large, glittering cross and worn Bible unsteadily at him.

She cried out. "Stop demon! We command you!"

"Madam," holding his arms wide, "you, a person of great faith, can see I am no more than a mere man. If you are the Mr. and Mrs. Kingston I spoke to on the phone, I believe I may know where we can find the bait to finally capture and rid this earth of the one who has caused us tremendous grief."

The elderly man circled her shoulders with one arm. "Is he, Daisy? You have the sight, is he one of us or one of them?" Protectively, he squeezed her to him.

"I must let the goodness touch him, it will tell us, for sure. His aura is of a color I've never seen before."

"You go ahead, dear." The elderly man raised the sawed-off shotgun he'd hidden behind him, leveling it on the young man. "I'll make sure he doesn't try anything funny. Human or not, a twelve-gauge at this distance will take care of any problems."

Daisy, back poker-straight and quoting scripture, strode toward him. He stood still while she recited a prayer under her breath, finally placing the cross against his forehead. It took all his concentration not to laugh in her face.

"He is one of us, George!" she decreed over her shoulder. George lowered the gun and walked toward them. Daisy clapped her hands like a schoolgirl dancing to an internal tune. George laughed, too, and coming up, slapped his back in a good will gesture.

"It's good to finally meet you, Mr. Dunard."

Fools believe what fools believe. "Please, call me Frank."

They exchanged pleasantries with Daisy chatting on about how their quest would soon be ending now they were to have his help.

"You mentioned in your letters, Mr. Dunard, that the beast took a loved one from you." Daisy touched him gently on the arm. "If I may ask, who it was?"

He swallowed hard, turning his head to brush an imaginary tear away. "The monster took a woman I knew and my…" he sniffed. "Forgive me; it's still difficult to talk about. He took my mother, also." *Actually, I took great pleasure in killing the woman myself, she who'd given birth to me and abandoned me.*

"Oh, my. Oh, goodness gracious." Daisy took his hand in hers. "You poor dear, was it recent?"

He bit the inside of his mouth to keep from laughing. "It seems like a lifetime, ago. Tell me who did he take from you?"

Daisy blindly reached out and George clasped her hand. "My mother, and eventually, my father. He didn't kill him, my father, but he may as well have. Father pursued him 'til his last dying breath."

He choked back a chuckle smothering it. "I'm so sorry for your loss."

"I was only a child when my mother died but I'll never forget finding the fiend bending over her dead body."

He reached out to pat her hand. "You must have been terrified."

"I remember vividly running to her rescue and beating my tiny hands on his back. Of course, I was too little to do any damage to him."

"It sounds like you bravely defended your mother with no regard for your own safety. I don't believe many children would've been so courageous."

"It was too late. She was already past saving." Daisy dabbed her handkerchief to the tears forming at the corner of her eyes. "The monster grabbed me. I suppose he intended to kill me, too. Luckily, my father arrived just in time to save me." Her face glowed with righteousness. "The monster fled at the sight of the truly religious man of faith my father was."

He laughed to himself at their blind trusting naivety. They were lambs being led to slaughter and he enjoyed being the butcher. These innocents wanted him to come up with a plan to capture their demon. Oh, he had a plan all right, one he'd had close to a century to design.

"Frank, how do you propose to capture the demon? IIe's always eluded us."

"We're lucky to be in this time and this place. We now know what he holds dear to him, the woman. If he knows you hold the woman he craves, he will try to rescue her, especially if he believes she is in mortal danger. A man who fears for a loved one is a man who becomes careless, and in turn, is prone to mistakes and recklessness. This is a man who will be easy to capture and destroy," Dunard proclaimed solemnly.

"What about the woman? What shall we do with her?" asked Daisy and George nervously.

"She has allowed herself to turn her back on her faith and her fellow mankind. She has shared pleasures of the flesh with this demon. She may have committed a more heinous sin against mortal man. Perhaps this devil's spawn grows in her womb." Frank smiled inwardly hearing Daisy's gasp at his words and he pressed on. "My friends, we have no choice. Our faith demands we do what is righteous. We must destroy her, too!" He smiled to himself as he watched the Kingstons nod their heads in agreement.

"Why don't we go back to my hotel room and get Mrs. Kinston out of this cold, drafty building? I'd hate for her to catch a chill." *Before I have a chance to taste her blood.*

"Mighty thoughtful of you, young man. Most of your generation don't give a mind to the elderly now days." George hugged Daisy to him.

My generation, ha, I was born before your great-grandfather was a twinkle in his father's eye. Franchot stopped the smirk from reaching his lips. "Guess it makes me a throwback to another time and place. Shall we go?" He ushered them back to their car.

He led and they followed him to his new residence; it proved a wise decision, moving to a better class of dump.

"Please excuse the odor of the last tenant, this is all I could afford and it reeks of a harlot's stench."

George, using his handkerchief, dusted off a chair for Daisy. "Don't you never mind, son, we've stayed in worse places. In this line of work, you make do." He walked over to sit on the bed. "This warehouse you found, you really believe we can lure the monster to it?"

"I've done a bit of reconnaissance work on the demon and the area and yes, with the right bait, he'll come. This woman, Allyson Weston, he's drawn to her for some reason. He can't leave her alone as you've discovered."

The pair shook their heads.

"She was with him the night of the party. I saw her there hanging all over him." Daisy's body trembled with age.

"We didn't see them together at her house but we're sure he was lurking nearby. The area held the stench of evil." George stroked the bedspread absent-mindedly.

He shuddered. "He was there, I saw them doing despicable things. I won't elaborate since there is a lady present."

"Mighty respectable of you, young man." George patted the bed and glanced at his watch. "I best be warming up the car for my Daisy. I'll be right back."

He sat watching Daisy, his hooded gaze belying his thoughts. She hummed to herself, lost in her own world, completely unaware of the danger. Minutes ticked by, the urge to taste her grew strong. He stirred to move forward when the door of the motel room opened, staying him, as George Kingston slipped inside. He nodded to Frank, picked up Daisy's coat from a nearby chair, and carried it to her. "The car's all nice and warm the way you like it, sweetheart." Daisy stood and George helped her put on the coat.

"Now." Frank reached out and reassuringly squeezed Daisy's hand and she smiled, "you and George go get some rest and we'll meet at the agreed place later. I've phone calls to make which will set our plan in motion. Then I'll join you straight away."

"And then the monster and his Jezebel will come? We'll vanquish them from this earth?" Daisy glanced from man to man.

"Yes, Daisy, yes. We will vanquish the monster and his succubus from this earth." Frank patted her hand comfortingly, and then glanced at George. "The building will be ready in time?"

"Yes, I'll handle it myself. I'm not fast, but I get the job done."

"I'll see you have all the explosives you need. Your experience as a demolition supervisor on construction sites is coming in handy."

"Just get me what we discussed and it'll do the damage you want." George turned to his wife. "Come sweetheart, we better go." He coaxed his wife out the door.

Frank waited until their car pulled away before his went to his, removing the cell phone from the glove compartment. He flipped the phone open, punched a key, and placed it to his ear, checking if it still worked. It had taken quite a pounding in his procurement of it. The phone still reeked of the cheap perfume of its previous owner. The smell distracted him. Pausing, he ran his tongue over his lower lip, remembering the prostitute and her outlandishly dyed hair. Tresses nearly matched the color of her blood, he recalled. Happily, he whistled an old tune and dialed the first phone number.

Chapter Sixteen

"YOU'RE SUCH A stunning creature."

"Why do men do that?"

"Do what?"

"That, call us…women…creatures?"

"Because you are."

"Like form the Black Lagoon?"

"Depends on that time of the month." He muttered under his breath, wondering how the conversation had taken this turn.

"Excuse me?"

He smiled, "I said you're elusive and exotic like the light from the moon, silver and slippery."

"Aha huh, that's pretty but do you really believe I'm buying all that?"

"It was worth a shot."

"Oh, by the way, I heard that time of the month remark."

"Women are a mystery to us, mere mankind, give us a break."

Logan gathered her in his arms and gave her a lingering kiss. "How would you like to go to a night club?" He'd showered and wore dress slacks and half-buttoned, tailored shirt. Feeling satiated, Allyson sighed, reaching to tease the dark curls peeking from his shirt. Her attire entailed little else besides one of his shirts; she'd been sitting on the bed brushing out her hair.

"A night club?" She seemed surprised. "Why, yes, but do you think we should be seen out in public? Besides." She pulled at the shirt she wore. "I don't have anything to wear. My other clothes took a beating getting you here."

"I like what you're wearing, but you're right, you can't go out wearing nothing but my shirt." Playfully, he tugged her hair. "I don't need any more men than necessary lusting after you. I can have Jovy bring over some things for you."

"Jovy?"

"Madame Jovialis, known to most, they would call her a couturier, but she'll tell you she's a simple dressmaker." Logan stroked her back.

"Have you known her long?" She twisted a lock of hair around one finger.

"Is that what you're asking or are you asking if she's striking, and how well do I know her?" He lifted her chin with his finger as he looked into her face.

"It really isn't any of my business." Allyson turned away, but he brought her gaze back to him.

"Madame Jacquetta Raissa Jovialis knew and liked my mother." He wrapped his arms around her. "So I've known her all my life. She favors me, which means she usually charges me slightly less than her other clientele, which irks Thomas to no end since Zilvia has her clothing bills sent to him. Is she attractive? Yes, she is. She is a tiny thing with the deepest violet-colored eyes I have ever seen, and considering her age, has jet black hair."

"How old is she?"

Logan leaned forward, glanced around as though guarding a secret and making her laugh, "Because Madame will never tell, rumor has it she is at least 1,500 years old."

Allyson gasped. "1,500? You're kidding me, aren't you?"

"No, and I think maybe a conservatively young guess."

Allyson shook her head, smiling.

"It's also rumored her family tree has the Rroma of Machavaya Gypsies in it and they're reported to know things."

She gave him a conspiratorial look. "Like what?"

"Like how to keep herself fit, for one thing."

Allyson burst out laughing. "Anything else?"

"Things even I find farfetched." Logan rose to answer a knock at the door. Logan's majordomo, Seabrook, stood at the thresh hold.

"Perfect timing, Seabrook. I would like you to reach Madame Jovialis and put it through to my room."

"Certainly, sir. Will there be anything else?"

"Yes. Seabrook, I'd like you to meet Allyson. Allyson, this is Seabrook." They nodded to each other. "Seabrook and his family have been with me since…"

"The first Seabrook claimed the title of major-domo for the Delacroix Kincaid household, sir, in the 1500s."

"A while, yes, thank you, Seabrook. Please inform the staff she is to be permitted access to me and the house any time day or night."

Seabrook flicked a moment's longer gaze over her then raised an eyebrow and turned to meet Logan's eyes. "It's about time, sir."

Logan stifled a chuckle until Seabrook left the room then burst out laughing. Allyson tilted her head, one eyebrow raised.

"I've known Seabrook since he was born and he's forever been after me to, in his words, 'Find a good woman and settle down'."

"Oh, certainly you've been with, ah, well, you have been around for a long time. I am sure there have been…what I mean is. I don't imagine you've been without female companionship for any long periods of time."

He brushed the back of his hand along her reddened cheek. "Let's just say it's been a while since I was serious about anyone, long before Seabrook was born."

Allyson's eyes opened wide. "Before he was born? Is Seabrook a com or Tarczal? I can't tell the difference."

"Com."

"Oh, ok, then he'd be at least sixty or seventy years old!"

"He turned sixty-seven last month and we can't convince him or his wife, Helena, our cook, to retire." Logan reached over to pick up his watch off the nightstand and snapped it on.

"Why did he say Delacroix Kincaid household?"

"Jean-Pierre Delacroix is actually my birth name." Seeing her confusion. "When I came to the new world, I wanted a new start and took the name of Logan Kincaid."

"So do I call you Logan or Jean-Pierre?"

"I prefer Logan but, sweetheart, you can call me anything you want." Logan leaned in to nibble on her mouth, then swooped in, for a more satisfying plunder before pulling back leaving her breathless. "Getting back to the club, Rothwell's is owned by Thomas and me. It's private; a place where others like us can go and relax."

"You mean, Tarczals?"

"Yes."

"Will everyone there be Tarczal?"

"No, there are feeders and other coms who work there."

"Coms? Feeders?"

"Coms are like you and feeders are coms, too. But, feeders have been raised since birth to supply nourishment for us."

"Like cattle?" Allyson sat up, seemingly alarmed.

"Good grief, no. We're their benefactors and they're ours. Some families have been with a single or family of Tarczals for generations."

"Oh, right, you told me there are whole families who supply you with…"

"Nourishment. Yes."

"Wow! Why? I mean what's in it for them? The feeders. You once mentioned something about supporting them?"

"Tarczals have a knack for amassing wealth; money is not a problem for us. We use it to better the lives of those in our care." Another knock at the door interrupted them.

"Come in," commanded Logan and nothing happened. He shook his head and went to the door. He paused and Allyson watched as he backed into the room while a petite, elegantly dressed woman, all in black, furiously grumbling in French, poked his chest with an impeccably manicured finger. She backed him all the way to the edge of the bed. Then the woman noticed Allyson. She took Allyson's hand, stood her up, and guided her to the middle of the floor. With a tsk here and a cluck there, she then began circling Allyson, inspecting her like a drill sergeant with his troops. The woman made comments, seemingly to herself. Until she noticed she was alone.

"Claudette!" she shouted in a heavy French accent and threw up her hands in disgust when no one responded. A birdlike woman peered through the door from behind thick-rimmed glasses pinching a too thin nose. Of indistinguishable age, her mousy brown hair caught in a ragged bun with trailed wispy tendrils, she hurried to the summons. The birdlike woman crept baby-steps into the room before glancing nervously around, then she turned and bolted back toward the door. The elegantly dressed woman grabbed her before she could take flight.

A battle of words and frantic gestures ensued and ended when Logan cleared his throat. He spoke in a language Allyson didn't understand, addressing the women. The bird woman gasped and the elegant one eyed Allyson. The first woman straightened her back even more than Allyson thought possible. The woman smiled and dabbed at her eyes with the lace handkerchief pulled from her sleeve.

"Bonjour, mademoiselle."

Logan addressed her in the other language again, she responded with an, "Ah-ha," then she turned to Allyson again, this time in English. "Hello, Allyson. I hope you are the answer to this old woman's, and many others', prayers."

"Allyson," Logan chuckled and shook his head. "I would like to present to you the esteemed couturier, and dear friend, Madame Jacquetta Raissa Jovialis."

"How do you do?" Allyson was able to say before the woman hugged her tightly. Madame Jovialis turned to the bird woman.

"Please call me Jovy, as only my personal friends are permitted, as I hope we too will become friends. This is my assistant, Claudette, who does not speak any English and refuses to learn anything but her native French. She is an excellent assistant and a good friend for far too many years." Madame Jovialis spoke again in French to Claudette, who shot Madame a nasty look before she smiled and gave a nod to Allyson. Logan whispered in Allyson's ear saying Madame had repeated everything except the part about Claudette being an excellent worker and friend. Allyson turned her head to hide a smile.

Jovy made a short call and thirty minutes later Logan's bedroom took on the appearance of an exploding boutique. Logan proved to be a braver man than most. Not only did he stay, he consulted with Madame on each article of clothing.

Three hours later, Jovy and crew departed and Allyson wore one of the many purchases Logan made for her. A V-neck, black, silk-nylon, angora knit sweater trimmed with gold sequins and beads and a black, short georgette skirt of all around pleats that clung to her like a second skin. Allyson moved her hips and received a sensuous shimmy from the material. She turned and shivered in anticipation at Logan's attire.

Allyson always admired the way he dressed but tonight he looked exceptionally handsome in a charcoal gray, double-breasted suit. The jacket had a six-button front with peak lapels, two front pockets and

one upper welt pocket held a burgundy silk handkerchief. The shirt, she noted, was an Oxford solid white
with a burgundy stripe. She was impressed he sported
an Edwardian Jacquard tie in a black floral print.

Logan watched her watching him. "Now, just what
are you smiling about?" he asked.

"I am not sure if I want to share you. You're ex-
traordinarily handsome tonight." She ran her hands
over the front of his suit.

"I know how you feel." He trailed a finger up one
silk clad leg of hers. "On the other hand, I have a
passionate desire to show you off."

"Let's go so we can get back." She stood on tiptoes
and kissed the tip of his nose. They made their way
down to the main floor while passing household staff
in their crisp black and white uniforms efficiently and
quietly going about their work. The house that had
been mausoleum quiet on her first two visits was now
awash in a constant hum. It was as though a sleeping
giant had come to life and the people were its life-
blood, coursing through its corridors.

✧   ✧   ✧

NOT FAR AWAY in a room dimly lit and smoked filled,
sat seven men without Logan Kincaid, their legal
watchdog, present. They were making a decision
without him, because he was the reason they were
there. The past, their past, had come back to haunt

them.

"He's resurfaced."

"His timing couldn't be worse."

"We should have stopped this at the beginning."

"How could we? He's in possession of the original documents."

"And who's fault was it he found those documents?"

"Whose fault was it those documents exist in the first place?"

"All these years, the best security in the world, and we couldn't find where he hid them."

"What are we going to do?"

"We're already doing it. Thomas left last week to try and negotiate with him."

"Negotiate? He doesn't bargain, don't you remember last time?"

"We all remember, you fool. Thomas has controlled him for these past years. I'm sure he can again."

"And, if he can't?"

"Where has he been?"

"Thomas wouldn't say and frankly I couldn't care less where he went to ground."

"I heard Thomas had him locked up."

"I've heard Thomas was supplying him with women and money to do with as he wanted."

"I've heard he's responsible for the wars in the east."

"Enough! It doesn't matter where he's been or what he's been doing. What matters is he's back and already interfering in The Kincaid's life."

"What do you think he'll do?"

"You mean when he finds out we've lied to him for most of his life?" The magistrate gave a bitter laugh. "He'll probably come and kill us. It's what I'd do."

"We have to destroy the son first."

"Of which son do you speak? The son of the innocent man or the one with hands soiled because of us."

"One leads to the other."

"If this isn't atrocious enough, the rumors of the legend have begun again."

"Damn legend."

Seven men sat arguing when the doors to their private sanctum opened permitting a petite, chicly dressed woman all in black, from her elegantly coiffed hair in a face-lifting tight bun, to her impeccably manicured fingernails, to enter. Stunned, the men remained seated until they remembered their manners and all but one rose.

"Madame Jovialis, while we're honored by your visit, this is a closed session."

"Yes, this is no place for a dressmaker, leave now before you are removed."

Jovy's violet eyes flashed at the man who'd spoken; she directed her words to him. "Your family always has had a lack of good manners and better judgment starting with the not so great granddame of your line. Shall we discuss the unpleasant beginnings of your lineage before we dwell into recent events of Kincaid and his chosen?"

Jovy raised one eyebrow and many on The Alliance coterie shifted uneasily in their seats. The anger rolled from her tiny frame hitting them like a vicious slap.

"You foolish, pathetic men. You only think of yourselves and your positions. You're frightened of a woman and you should be. Your interference between the Kincaid and the turned half-bred DeBois has nearly cost our people much."

"The Delacroix and the DeBois' petty squabble isn't our concern."

"Call him by the name he's chosen, Kincaid. You dare to call what conspired between them a squabble! The DeBois is deranged! Even before he became one of us, his mind was horribly twisted. He never should have been changed."

"It was within our rights."

"And it was within your rights to correct the mistake but you chose not take responsibility and ignored the damage he caused. For this alone, you cannot be forgiven."

"Yet you defend the Delacroix, the Kincaid, who now seeks to taint us with an outsider."

"You stupid, stupid men, the Rroma of Machavaya foretold the births of the great warrior and the blood witch. Since those times, they have waited for the bloodline to breed true again. The young Kincaid is a direct descendant of Kharzarin."

"Many claim this, it doesn't make it so."

"He doesn't claim it, its fact proven by the keepers of such knowledge. I'm the oldest of those keepers." Jovy lifted her chin to stare down at the men.

"And the woman?"

"Yes, what of her?"

"She is nothing."

"Just, when I think this Alliance might have a brain, I'm proven wrong." Jovy pinched the bridge of her nose with the thumb and forefinger of her right hand.

"Here now."

She fixed him with a stare that closed his mouth. "The Rroma sent one of their own, again, to a chosen, this time a woman of Alaza's line. She chose the *gaujos* name of Permelia and he was a com of the name Jacob. She was sent to her for one purpose, to be impregnated by this Jacob."

"The woman Permelia."

"Was Allyson's mother."

"So you claim this woman is kin to the Blood Witch Alaza and ask us to believe this nonsense?"

"Take the wax of stupidity from your ears, man. My family has been given the responsibility of guarding the secret; yes it is true! Allyson is a direct descendant of the first Blood Witch Alaza before her change to Tarczal. She is the woman who saved our race. She is the one who taught our mighty warrior Kharzarin that strength is nothing without wisdom, power or compassion. To be without these three then we are no more than a prowling animal. Without her teachings, we'd still be mindless drinkers, roaming the world for nourishment. Or worse, condemned so vile by the cosmos, hunted nearly into extinction."

"And where are this Jacob and Permelia now, who gave us this new savoir?" The Alliance magistrate sneered. "And why did they only have one child, why not a dozen to save our sorry asses?"

Jovy shook her head. "Because it was decreed one child, a girl child, was to be born."

"And, if it had been male?"

"It would have been sacrificed the same as the sire and dam."

"Sacrificed? Completely barbaric!"

"And the petty wars you incite for money, land, and power are not?"

"Those are necessary."

"Necessary? The lives of many are lost for so little and yet, you quibble over three. Perhaps there will be hope for you someday. Until then, the Machavaya will also do what is necessary."

"We are The Alliance! We rule."

"What we allow you to and nothing more. You'd be wise not to forget this again."

"Or?"

Jovy raised one eyebrow. "To deny these two, the Kincaid and his woman, the sanctuary of community, our support, is nothing more than blasphemy to our heritage. Harm them and you will know the wrath of the Rroma of Machavaya." She turned and walked out of the room leaving the men opened mouthed.

Her friend Claudette waited on the other side of the door. "Did they believe you?"

Jovy sighed, "With some threats and arm twisting."

Claudette patted her arm then leaning in close, whispered. "Your family's sacrifice will be rewarded. Your great-great, oh I forget how many greats she is." Tears welled up in Claudette's eyes.

Jovy hugged her. "It's all right, I forget, too."

"Your granddaughter looks so much like your Permelia." Claudette sniffed back more tears. "Allyson will make a fine Tarczal mate for Kincaid."

Jovy touched the linen handkerchief to the corners of her eyes dabbing away the tears hovering there. "Grandmother Tansy would be proud of our family's accomplishments."

Chapter Seventeen

LOGAN DROVE THE car with a practiced ease. Allyson inhaled deeply, sighing contentedly from the interior's aroma of real leather. She tickled her fingertips over the buttery soft feel of the seats enjoying the caress of supple leather against her thighs.

"Tell me about the club." Her left hand rested on his thigh.

Logan reached down to place his hand on hers. "Thomas launched it during prohibition. He built up the area around Rothwell's into a maze of connected dwellings. The outward appearance is of single residences, like townhouses, when in fact the center of the entire four block section is actually the club."

"Why did he do it?"

"Smoke and mirrors. If the police are searching for a speakeasy, all they'd find is homes."

"Wouldn't the fact of no one living in these homes give them away?"

"Who says there aren't people living there?" He raised her hand to kiss her fingertips. "The residents are…"

"Ok, I get it, they're feeders."

"Such a smart woman."

They pulled up to a house with a small brass plac-ard proclaiming one word, 'Private' and a small plaque depicting a single red rose in a thick patch of thistles. The markings, the heraldic sign of the family Roth-well, were the only indication, Logan explained, to what was inside. He turned into one townhouse's garage. Once the door shut, valets hurried out to assist them. Escorting her to an elevator, they descended several floors below ground level. Inside the elevator, he began to explain the club's layout to her.

"On the subterranean ground floor there are sev-eral rooms divided into the main dining area and bar and smaller private rooms for parties. The upper floor holds the main office, Thomas's and his assistants', and then there are the feeder rooms." A hostess es-corted them to a table. Logan ordered a bottle of champagne then continued his description of the club. "Most of the nutritional rooms are decorated as inti-mate sitting rooms."

"Feeding rooms?"

"Yes." Logan shrugged. "Many guests feel more comfortable taking nourishment in a private setting." He noticed her swaying to the music. "Would you like to dance?"

"I'd love to."

Logan and Allyson had just reached the dance floor when a man stepped in front of them. He was as tall as Logan but with a slighter build, lean and wiry like a dancer. Short auburn hair graced his head while his face held the coldest gray eyes, eyes that raked over Allyson. Logan snagged his arm around Allyson's waist, placing himself between the man and her. The man directed his words to Logan without taking his eyes from her.

"Hello, Jean-Pierre, long time, no see. You have a lovely companion for your dinner. Aren't you going to introduce this morsel to me?"

Logan stood stunned, then roared, "Franchot!" Pushing from Allyson, he lunged for Franchot, slamming into his mid-section, crashing them both onto a table, sending silverware and dishes clattering to the floor. The crowd of patrons scattered when Logan and Franchot thumped onto the marble floor. Franchot landed on the bottom. In a matter of seconds, Logan brought his fist back, repeatedly raining blows to his opponents jaw. Franchot lay there enduring each blow and not defending himself.

Music and conversation halted. The clientele circled around the pair. Flesh and bone smashing into flesh and bone, a sickening wet crunching sound. Logan's grunts of fury and effort filled the room. Logan pulled back one more time and felt both his arms being grabbed. He struggled as two men lifted him up and away from his intended victim. The men were the Alliance's Janissary.

"Get your hands off me you damn dirty bastards!" Logan's voice reverberated in a hailstorm of fury. "Let me finish him!"

The Janissary held him tight but Logan fought back, sliding the men forward. The security pulled back, regaining their footholds halting Logan.

"Sir, we can't let you."

Logan's gaze never wavered from Franchot as two other men helped his foe to his feet. Logan directed his words to the Janissary. "Why the hell not? Do you know who he is?"

The representative of the quartet sighed, "Yes sir, we do. We're assigned to protect him."

"*Protect* him?" Logan rounded on the man, clenching and unclenching his fist, they held him tight. "By who's orders?" Logan held a slippery grasp on his volcanic rage.

"Mr. Rothwell." The Janissary's words held an apology in them.

Logan paled, his shoulders slumped, anger leeched from his face, and betrayal drained the light from his eyes. He shrugged the Janissary from him.

The four security men nodded their regret to Logan before directing a smirking Franchot to the bar.

Allyson hurried to him and rose on tiptoe to brush a kiss on his mouth. Blood dripped from Logan's knuckles. Allyson lifted each hand with hers, kissing each torn area, marveling how they healed before the blood dried. Logan held her tightly but his eyes never left Franchot, who was now leaning nonchalantly against the bar, flirting with the woman bartender. Franchot's gaze flickered over them with an amused disinterest.

"Logan, let's go home." She tugged his arm directing him to the exit.

Back in the car, Allyson snuggled into the buttery soft leather of the car seats. She glanced at Logan who insisted on driving. Quiet and distant, he seemed relieved when she suggested they go back to the estate.

✧   ✧   ✧

SEABROOK MET THEM at the door, taking their coats. Logan strode to his office and immediately called Nairn.

Logan listened to the phone ring, on the third chime his friend picked up. Logan growled, "Nairn, what the hell is going on?"

"What do you mean? What's happened? Are you and the woman all right?"

"Franchot is alive and your Janissaries are guarding him per Thomas's orders!" Logan's fury bubbled at the surface. "Your men kept me from killing him."

"Aw, crap. I've no idea what's going on but before I come home you better believe I'll have answers." Nairn paused. "Which of my men?"

"There were four of them; they're usually the escorts for the Alliance members."

"This explains why they're not here."

"Where are you?"

"I'm in Europe. I'm not sure how secure these

lines are so I'm not giving you my location."

"How soon will you be back?"

"Soon, don't ask for specifics." Nairn swore. "Is Salina alright? Does she know her brother is back?"

"No, I don't believe she does. I'll find her and tell her myself."

"Thanks, keep in touch. I should have answers soon."

Nairn hung up. Logan sat for a minute staring into space until Allyson lightly touched his shoulder asking, "Is there anything I can do?"

He pulled her onto his lap and brushed his lips across hers. A fire burned in the hearth, a soft glow of light and heat enfolded them. "Just sit with me." Logan cuddled her to him. "We never got to eat dinner. Are you hungry?"

Allyson slid from his lap and reached for his hand. "Not for food." She pulled him up and led him upstairs. At the door of his room, Logan drew her into his arms, holding her tightly. She kissed him, towing him into the room, playfully nibbling on his mouth. Dancing away, she excused herself to slip into something more comfortable.

He loosened his tie, shed his jacket, and tossed it over a chair. Logan went to the house phone and instructed Seabrook to find Thomas or his location. He hung up the phone and went to sit on the roomy window seat along the big bay window. A few minutes later, Allyson emerged to find him still sitting there.

Wrapping his robe around her, she settled herself between his legs and cuddled up against him.

"Talk to me, please," she pleaded.

"All these years I believed Franchot was dead, believed I'd killed him, avenging a woman I cared about. How did he survive? Where has he been all this time? Where was he hiding? Did someone hide him? Why did the Janissary stop me and protect him?" Logan slammed his fist into the window casement. "Why has Thomas betrayed me? Damn it, he knew about Franchot. He knew about Flora. He knew about everything." Logan ran his hands through his hair, the ends stuck out emphasizing his distress. "The Alliance is responsible for this, only they can give such an order, and I'm going to find out why. I have Seabrook calling around trying to locate Thomas."

"What are his chances of finding Thomas?"

Logan gave the clock on the wall a half glance. "He won't leave a single stone unturned in his search."

She turned, facing him and reached up to run her palm along his jaw. "I think it's time you tell me about this Franchot and Flora."

"It's a long story." Logan took a deep breath.

"We have all night." She kissed his chin.

"I love you," he whispered. They sat in silence for a while, then, with a tired sigh, he began. "Franchot was not first-born a Tarczal. His father, Franchot A. DeBois, Salina's father, had an affair with a woman, a com, while he was married. Her stage name was

D'Arcy Arnaud. We never found out her real name.

Franchot Sr. was an uncommonly handsome man but unfortunately not a strong-willed man. He dearly loved his wife but he had a fondness for the ladies, gambling, and the theater. He was a wine broker for several of the local vineyards, my family included, and his commission was extremely good."

Allyson raised a brow and smiled knowingly. "Let me guess, he was in town, loaded, and decided to celebrate."

"Right on the money."

"He decided to treat himself to dinner and a show. The extraordinary D'Arcy Arnaud was on stage. It was lust at first sight for both of them."

"They had an affair?"

"One-night stand. Unfortunately, Franchot left a little more of himself behind then he planned."

"D'Arcy became pregnant?"

"Yes. For reasons which died with her, she never contacted Franchot about the pregnancy or the birth."

Early in her doomed marriage, Allyson had re-signed herself of never having children, but still dreamed of what if. She couldn't imagine a woman keeping that moment, that knowledge of a pregnancy, from the father of a child that grew inside her a se-cret…unless the father had been Michael. "How strange she didn't tell him he had a son."

"Salina's father doted on her. I'm sure it would've pleased him to have a son. But, he died in a stupid hunting accident, not knowing."

Allyson straightened. "A hunting accident?"

"Yes, he and…" She observed Logan's gaze drift and then his eyes narrowed. The many possibilities, the scenarios of that incident assaulted her before he slammed his mind closed to her.

"What, what is it?" Allyson snapped her fingers in front of his face bringing him back to her.

"Franchot, Sr." Logan captured his lower lip between his teeth; his words were clipped and forced. "Went hunting with Thomas."

"Do you think?"

Logan chose his words carefully. "I don't know."

"What motive would your friend Thomas have to kill Franchot Sr.?"

She could see the wheels turning. "Clarice, Salina's mother. She threw him over for Franchot Sr."

"Some men would find it hard to swallow."

"When it's been brought up, Thomas has always made light of it." Logan let the sentence trail off.

"Okay, so Franchot Sr. is dead and his wife's a widow. Thomas should've made his move then, what stopped him?"

"He'd been appointed as the Alliance's attorney. As his successor, I can tell you those first few years are consuming. Perhaps he placed his feelings for her on the back burner until the time was right."

"Then what happened? What stopped him later? Salina mentioned someone named Zilvia. Did Thomas fall for her?"

"Zilvia would've liked him to, but Thomas always put her off when it came to marriage. I'm guessing Franchot Jr. showing up on Clarice's doorstep, the image of his late father, had something to do with it."

"Bet it was a hard reminder for Thomas."

"No doubt it was especially hard since Clarice moved Franchot in with her and petitioned to have him changed."

"D'Arcy told him about his father? She knew who he was? Tarczal?"

"I find it refreshing you refer to Tarczals as who and not what."

"Of course, a race of people are a who, not a what."

"I'm not sure you're correct but I won't argue the point."

"So, D'Arcy tells Franchot about dear ol' dad."

"No, she didn't. D'Arcy sadly loved the stage more than her son. He was less than a day old when she left him in a Parisian orphanage."

"What year was it? Weren't those places terrible back then?"

"The mid 1700s and the orphanages weren't the models of humanitarian welfare. Franchot and the rest of the children were beaten and worse no doubt. I've always suspected Franchot for his mixed parentage, was singled out more than others."

"Then other people knew back then who Tarczals

were?"

"No, they just knew he was different, unfortunately that's all it would've taken."

"Okay, he's in her home and changed, what happened next?"

He brought his mouth down on hers searching comfort in a kiss, breaking it a minute later, he rested his chin on top of her head.

Allyson twisted in his arms. "Wait a minute how did he get the name Franchot? Did he do what you did, take a new name?"

Logan cleared his throat. "D'Arcy left a note instructing them what to name him. This was something I've always found a bit of a cruel joke on her part."

"A bit bitchy wasn't it? How old was he when he was changed?"

"Mid-thirties by then."

"Okay, he's with Clarice, what happened next?"

"He abused the advantage given to him for years. Franchot nearly left Salina and her mother destitute. The Alliance intervened, froze the accounts, and helped Clarice rebuild her finances. Nairn and I help Salina establish herself. Both women are more than comfortable and secure now." Logan chewed on his lower lip. "Why the Alliance didn't rein Franchot in, I've never known. The situation would usually have The Alliance sending in a Janissary to handle discreetly."

"Seems key people are keeping things from you."

Allyson lay in his arms.

"Yes, doesn't it?" He hugged her tight. "I'm going to have to reach Thomas as soon as possible. I'm hoping he and Nairn can shed some light on all this."

"Nairn? Isn't he the man Salina's involved with?"

Logan gave a sharp bark of a laugh. "Involved with, interesting way of putting it. Yes, they're involved." Logan sobered. "Until I know different, I'll have to say Nairn St. Clair is a man you can trust with your life and the lives of those you love." He gave her a quick hug. "Nairn pioneered a," he paused searching for the right word and the phrase finishing school popped into his head. He laughed inwardly at that choice, "school to expand the knowledge of certain Janissary."

"Like the black ops green berets the military has."

"Yes, exactly. The students that come here will be able to conduct the more delicate aspects of the work all Janissary are trained to manage."

"How many Janissaries are there?"

"Several thousand, I do believe."

"Wow, you need that many?"

"Some work outside the community, military, law enforcement, fire, and the medical profession"

"So they're doing their job and being useful in other areas."

"Yes, and keeping an eye on the world around us."

"So are you, the Tarczals, running the world?"

"Too much work to run the entire planet ourselves… we only make suggestions to those who do."

"Ah, huh, sounds like the old iron fist in the silk glove thing or is it more like you make suggestions that can't be ignored?"

"You watch too many movies."

"You didn't answer the question."

He just smiled.

"Does the government know about you guys?"

"Which one?" he smiled devilishly.

Allyson shook her head, realizing she wouldn't get a straight answer and changed the subject.

"Okay, I'll keep what you say about Nairn in mind. Continue please, about Franchot." Allyson laid her head on his chest.

Logan stroked her hair. "Nairn and I tried for years to befriend him. Nairn was smart, he dropped the friendship, if what you could call what we had, long before I did. When I finally did drop it, I came to America to explore your West, and unbeknownst to me, Franchot followed."

"And?"

"Franchot attacked the woman I was in love with."

"He killed her!" Allyson, reclining against his chest sat straight up.

"No, he didn't kill her. I did," he said softly, and waited, for her reaction.

She cocked her head and eyed him. "Finish your story, Logan. I asked for details, and I want them, the whole story."

"Her name was Flora, Flora Rainey."

"She was married." Allyson smiled sympathetically.

"Yes, I can't seem to break the habit." Allyson snuggled into his arms again. "Flora was married to a man named Isaac Rainey. He was fifteen years her senior, a farmer with no previous wives or children. I believed he cared about Flora in his way but his primary reason for marrying her was because she was young and could provide him with children."

"Which meant more help, more crops, and a bigger farm," Allyson interrupted.

"It wasn't a perfect system." Logan nodded in agreement. "But it was the best they had. Isaac was good to her until I came along. She didn't love him. I doubt he loved her. When I met her, her daughter was close to five years old. A sweet child with a cherub face, a halo of blonde curls, and huge blue eyes." He smiled, remembering. "Flora was shy, gentle, and her laugh made wind chimes envious." He couldn't stop the image of her forming before him, vision of a woman, young and pretty with dull brown hair, large, dark eyes full of wonderment.

Allyson jerked as if exposed to a live wire; she blinked rapidly staring beyond him.

Logan clenched his teeth, air hissed through his teeth. The realization Allyson shared his vision made him swear.

"I apologize. Sometimes it happens this way when

someone is drained. This is why we're careful not to gorge, but to only take enough to sustain. To live with those memories is something too dark for a soul to carry." Logan took a deep breath and slowly let it out.

"Tell me more," she urged.

"Are you sure?"

"Yes."

"I drained her, all, completely, not only her blood but of everything she had seen, felt. It all flashed before me as if it had happened to me. I knew the pain, the torture he'd inflicted on her. I heard her praying for me to come and save her.

"Flora was sweet and innocent of the true cruelties in the world. It sickened me. All I could do was sit there, holding her. She was a broken, empty shell, nothing of her remained and I mourned the loss in my soul. I vowed to kill Franchot, for what he'd done that day on a Kansas farm."

Chapter Eighteen

Kansas 1920

LOGAN MEANT TO stop only long enough in the small, dusty town to purchase more supplies. Why he lingered more than necessary, he'd never know.

He watched her sitting on the buckboard's hard unyielding seat, cradling a small sleeping child across her lap. Unlike most, she held his gaze with her doe brown eyes.

He was accustomed to people casting side glances at him. The presence of strangers in small communities upset a natural balance the inhabitants worked so hard to maintain.

Her eyes immersed his soul. They overflowed with longing, not a longing, Logan was startled to realize, formed from desire, which was something he knew he aroused in com women and used accordingly to his need. No, hers was formed by loneliness, which could be erased only by love or death.

The heat of the day beat down on her and the child as they sat there quietly. The man…her father? No, her husband. The man loaded the wagon either not noticing or not caring of his family's discomfort.

How could he not?

Logan took the canteen from his saddle and walked over to where she sat. He felt the townspeople around him shift uneasily. A few of the older immigrants from the old country would recognize him for what he was, but this man and woman were strangers. Logan wondered why what happened to this woman mattered to him. Still, it did.

Silently, he offered the canteen to her. Her only response was to catch her lower lip between her teeth and look straight ahead as she tried not to give in to the delicious smell of the water. Her husband stopped midway from tossing a grain sack into the wagon bed. Again, Logan offered the woman his canteen and again she made no move to accept it. He kept his eyes on her but directed his words to the man.

"Your woman needs water and you might consider moving them into the shade 'til your done loading."

"It ain't your concern." The farmer glared at the stranger from beneath the brim of his sweat-and-dust-covered hat. He finished heaving the sack into the wagon.

"No, it isn't, but it should be yours."

"Mister, I can and do, take care of my own. You best be minding your own business and moving on." His eyes said he knew Logan was right, but it galled him to have it pointed out by a stranger in front of friends and neighbors.

Logan tossed the canteen to her so quickly that she

caught it without a moment's thought. "Keep it, I can always buy another," he said to her before he walked back to his horse, leading it to the livery stable.

✧　✧　✧

LATER, AGAIN WITHOUT knowing why, he lingered. He made contact with a family of feeders who'd immigrated to this new land. From them, he'd taken nourishment, he'd been feeding from the wild and while it sustained him, it didn't satisfy the hunger within. Logan asked about the woman in town. Yes, they knew her and readily told him where she lived.

Logan took to watching her from a small patch of woods. The first few days, she didn't leave the house except to feed the fowl and hang out yards and yards of laundry. He'd wanted to go to her but the man never left the area long enough for him to do so.

Logan's chance came a few days later. She was in the orchard picking fruit and alone.

✧　✧　✧

"HELLO, AGAIN." HE stepped out from behind one of the trees. She nearly dropped her basket. In three quick strides he was in front of her, grasping the basket and setting it down. She took one step back as though to turn and run.

"Please don't. I only wanted to talk to you, to tell you I am sorry if I caused you any hardship." He'd noticed a fading bruise on her arm that the sleeve of her dress didn't completely cover. He also noted how stiffly she'd moved in the days he'd discretely watched her.

He watched her drink in the sight of him then jerked her head up to gaze into his face. When she looked into his eyes, he saw hope flare and ignite. She gasped, raising her hand to her mouth and turned to flee. He reached out, lightly placing his hand on her shoulder. She turned to him, seeming to enjoy his warm, masculine arms around her. She clung to him trembling.

Logan tilted her head back and covered her mouth with his in a hungry kiss which went on for some time. He asked without words for nothing more than the moment and the kiss.

A crow's cry drew them apart.

"I don't even know your name," she whispered staring down at her skirt, smoothing a wrinkle with trembling hands.

"My name is Logan and yours is Flora, which is Latin for flower."

Her head shot up. "You speak Latin?"

He smiled.

She smiled more.

"Yes and several other languages."

"How do you know my name?" Flora blushed and glanced away.

"I asked someone." He gave her a reassuring hug

when she blanched. "Don't worry. Those I asked are discreet and can be trusted." She relaxed a bit and he wrapped his arms around her.

Logan raised her arm up and kissed the yellowing bruise.

Flora tried to pull away from him and tug at the offending sleeve, but Logan only pulled her closer to him.

"Does he often hurt you?"

"No. It was my fault," Flora said in a near whisper. "I shamed him in town. Isaac has never laid a hand on me in anger or treated me cruelly," she'd said. "Seldom, if hardly ever, has he raised his voice to me or our child."

"Flora." Logan placed a finger under her chin to raise her face to gaze at him. "You did nothing wrong and Isaac never should've hurt you. A man is stronger than a woman and never, never, is there a reason, good or bad, for a man to harm a woman."

They talked and talked. She told him her daughter was at her maternal grandparents visiting for the day and Isaac was seeing to the plowing of a far field.

Logan asked of her family. She told him of her father who had chided her for wasting time reading and for dreaming. She told him of the gallant man she dreamed of on gleaming horses, coming to sweep a girl off her feet and Logan knew he was this man. Her father had told her the only sweeping in her future would be her cleaning a floor of a man's hard day's dust.

Flora explained Isaac had inherited a fine, two-story wood house from his elderly parents. The house had a dining room and kitchen combined; it had a huge wood-burning stove equipped with a reservoir tank which was a consistent source of hot water. The oven interior was large enough to bake several items at once and there was even a warming oven above. An indoor sink with a pump was also the latest in kitchen finery. A large pantry, a room for washing clothes and bodies, and bringing in muddy clothes was just off the kitchen. Facing the front of the house was a bright sunny sitting room.

They even had a parlor with a fireplace sporting a huge oak mantel and a pump organ. In between the parlor and sitting room, a staircase led to three bedrooms, one of which was large enough for half-a-dozen beds. One large barn and a smaller one housed the cattle, horses, geese, and chickens. The latter used for their feathers, meat, and eggs. Isaac now owned the most acreage in the county, which included his prize apple orchard. He was a good man and would make a good husband, so her father had told her.

Flora went on to explain she was the oldest of twelve and considered past her prime at eighteen when Isaac took an interest in her. He agreed to pay a dowry for her. In her future, there could be no matches of the heart if there were younger siblings still at home needing the money an honest dowry could bring to buy food for the table. Flora's mother dutifully reminded her of all the hardships her father endured to raise his family. She had smiled and said she would agree to marry Mr. Rainey and did. Isaac took her to live with him.

She was to become a mother nine months after her wedding.

"Isaac is a good man. I'm grateful, for what he's given me…us. But, when I saw you standing there…."

Then in a near whisper, she told him what happened after he'd given her his water and walked away.

Isaac had glared at him retreating into the distance. Flora quietly laid the canteen down on the buckboard seat. Later, she tried not to notice the harsh way her husband flung it to the ground.

She held the child to her, stealing uneasy glances toward her husband. No, Isaac had seldom raised his voice and never his hand. He treated her like everything else that was his; with the respect of ownership someone gave a useful tool. Nevertheless, there was something about his demeanor telling her this was different.

He kept glancing at her beside him. Finally, he'd spoken and said he thought she should respect him more. Thanks to him, she was married to the most well-to-do man in the county. Because of him, people treated her with a deference they'd not have ordinarily. She shouldn't have looked at the stranger. It drew his attention to her.

Night came, exhausted from the day's work and events, Flora was in their bedroom changing into her nightgown when Isaac came in. He'd gone directly to the large barn after dinner, not giving her a clue as to why. The livestock had been taken care of and as she searched her mind, she could find nothing out of place, just the way Isaac liked things. At first she didn't notice the object he held in his hands. Then he began to advance towards her, quoting scripture of a woman's obedience to her husband. The good book, he'd told her, said a man could discipline his wife. It even gave the dimensions of the rod a man could use. Then his hand came from behind his back.

The next morning she told their daughter when the child asked about the marks on Mommy's arms and why she moved so stiffly, her Mommy had fallen in the dark on her way to the privy.

Isaac didn't meet her eyes for the next few days. He complimented her on the meals and how the hardwood floors, as well as all the woodwork, in the house now shined extra bright. She'd always taken her duties to his home seriously, now she seemed to excel in them. He'd even made a slight joke about being right in showing her the error of her ways. A joke, but she knew he truly felt justified in his actions.

✧   ✧   ✧

LOGAN LISTENED AS Flora marveled at the kiss Logan

had given her. She touched her mouth with her finger-tips at the memory of it. She blushed as she told him, "I shouldn't have let you kiss me." Flora worried her bottom lip between her teeth.

"Then why did you?" Logan raised one eyebrow in question. His eyes danced with amusement.

"Because, I figured I'd never get another chance like this again." She again caught her lip between her teeth.

Logan threw back his head and laughed until Flora giggled too.

There was a need in her he wanted to fill. He leaned forward to rain kisses on her eyes, face, and neck. Soon they stood clutching each other, breathing as though they'd run a great distance. He scooped her up in his arms and went over to sit under a tree with Flora on his lap. Logan began to renew the kiss, cradling her to him.

"Do you know any poetry?"

He grinned and began.

"There is a lady sweet and kind,
Was never a face so pleased my mind,
I did but see her passing by,
And yet I love her till I die!
Her gestures, motions, and her smile,
Her wit, her voice, my heart beguile,
Beguile my heart, I know not why

And yet I love her till I die!
Cupid is winged and doth range
Her country; so my love doth change.
But change the earth or change the sky,
Yet will I love her till I die!"

Flora squealed like a child when he finished and threw her arms around his neck. "Oh, thank you, thank you. It was so delightful, did you write it?"

"No, I don't know who the author was," Logan bent his head to brush her lips with his, "but I'm at this moment I'm grateful to him."

They talked. She said she wanted him to speak of the world, about all the books he had read, all the places he'd been, and where he'd learned to speak so many languages. Logan supplied all the things she was starved to hear.

The day grew late and the shadows long. Flora quickly realized she must head back for the house. Logan offered her a ride but she would take it only as far as the small outcropping of woods by her home. He told her he wanted to see her again and at first, she shook her head no. Logan pulled her into his arms and kissed her then and she had whispered, "Tomorrow, by the small barn."

They met for several days this way, always when the child was napping and the man was in the fields. In the beginning, he felt like a cad insisting she give him, in trade for his knowledge of the world, her sweet kisses and chaste caresses, but he soon grew to know she liked his form of barter. The day came when Isaac was to go back into town and Logan couldn't believe his luck when one of Flora's sisters came to take the child to visit their parents the same day.

❖　❖　❖

IT BEGAN TO rain as he waited in the barn. She came to him. She hovered at the entrance. From farther inside the barn's interior, he smiled and crooked his finger to her.

"Vienir ici, mon joli un."

"It sounded wonderful what did it mean?" Flora, who had started forward, now stopped.

"I said, come here, my pretty one."

Flora laughed and ran into his arms. He lifted her and swung her around before kissing her soundly.

They met like this as often as they could. Logan knew he played a dangerous game, one, if found out, would certainly mean severe punishment, if not death, for them both. These people guarded what was theirs with a swift and lethal protectiveness. Gently, he began coaxing Flora with the idea of leaving Isaac to go away with him and be his wife. She was frightened. She thought he only wanted her and not her child. She could not, would not, leave her daughter with such a man. She would never be able to live happily knowing, when the time came, her child would be used in the same matter-of-fact barter way she had been used. However, when Logan assured her he meant to make a life for the three of them, she let the spark start to grow in her.

✧   ✧   ✧

THE DAY WAS to be a warm one. Logan stopped to pick forest flowers as a surprise for her. Isaac would be in the fields until noon and should be leaving for there now. Shaking the dew from the tender petals, he tucked them inside his shirt and swung up on his mount.

The farm was quiet as he rode across the yard. A quiet that caused the hair on his neck to stand up while a prickle of anxiety coursed down his spine and pooled in the gut. He looked to the house, saw the kitchen curtains billowing out a window and unconsciously made note, even the yard hens were silent and wary.

His gaze shifted between house and barn in indecision. Then, dropping the horse's reins, he instinctively bolted toward the barn.

The first thing to meet his eyes in the cool, dark interior was Flora's rumpled dress lying on the floor.

✧   ✧   ✧

THE CENTRAL HEATING clicked on whirring loudly in the quiet room of the house.

Logan's heart beat beneath Allyson's ear. The moon, striped by dark clouds, rose higher in the sky, bathing the ground in a soft, fairy-blue light. He leaned back, running a hand through his hair and took a deep breath, breaking off into a half sob causing Allyson's heart to ache.

"I'm sorry; I hoped to keep some of it from you."

"I asked. I wanted to know." She took his face in her hands. "I needed to understand the depth of your love—your pain—for her."

"When I found her, she was so near death, the only thing that might have saved her would have been to change her." He gave a dry humorless laugh. "But I didn't even have the time or supplies to do it. Not that she would have agreed to it. I took my shirt off, wrapping her in it and carried her to the house to lay her on the sitting room sofa.

She didn't make a sound and I know it hurt her when I moved her. The look in her eyes, it still haunts me. I kept thinking I had to do something to erase the fear filling them."

Tears left silver paths down his face as he closed his eyes tight. "There was a coverlet lying there; I covered her with it. He'd taken so much from her physically and mentally. He'd told her I was like him, and part of her I know, believed him. For the first time in my life, I cursed who I was. What I am."

Allyson's breath caught as a shudder ran through his body when he remembered Flora's revulsion of him.

"She wouldn't let me hold her; every time I tried, she'd flinch. She sobbed and in a whisper, begged me to end her life; she was terrified of becoming a monster like him and me."

Allyson held Logan as he shook and cried the tears he'd denied himself nearly a century before. The moon disappeared behind the house as he exhausted the last of his grief. His face rose, leaving her breasts damp from his spent pain. He wiped the last of his tears with the back of his hand and took a deep cleansing breath.

"It didn't take much to finish what Franchot had set out to do, just a moment or two. When I did, I saw it all, just as you did, all of it flooding into me with each swallow. She was so still, so pale, lying there against the dark covering of the sofa. I held her, not wanting to let her go. Then I heard a sound. It was Flora's daughter. She took one look at her mother and ran over to beat her small fists against me, screaming her fury at the top of her lungs.

"Unknown to me, Isaac had come home early to fix a broken harness piece. He was in the barn and he'd just found Flora's dress when he heard his daughter's screams. I tried to calm the child, comfort her by pulling her close to me, but I couldn't let go of Flora and the sight of her mother's broken body terrified her.

"Isaac found the three of us, his wife, dead in one

of my arms, his daughter in the other, struggling against me. I fled like a coward.

"I had no wish to harm him. And the child…I could do nothing for her; her mind was shattered by the events. Isaac inaugurated a crusade then to end my life. Who could blame him? I'd taken everything from him. Later, when I outlived him, his daughter took his twisted teachings to heart and continues now to hunt me. Since I am to blame in part for her state of mind, I've never been able to bring myself to harm her, even to this day."

Allyson pulled away from him as she realized the meaning of the last of what he'd just told her. "Flora's daughter was, *is*, Daisy Kingston?"

"Yes."

Logan sighed, a sound so filled with grief that it tore at her soul. He clenched his jaw then snarled out the words. "I went hunting for Franchot. I wanted to kill him, to put him through the same torture and more, much more, for what he'd done to Flora. Finally, the day came. I found him in New Orleans on the docks late one night. He'd just killed a prostitute." He gave a bitter laugh. "One I'd hired to distract him so I could lure him into a trap. We struggled, fought, and I plunged the knife he meant to use on me into his chest. He fell in the murky water, I dove in, I wanted to make sure I'd finished the job but I couldn't find his body. Climbing back on the dock, I saw a gator swim by. I figured if nothing else, the animal would complete the task. I wandered your west for a few years, then Thomas and the Alliance chose me as his replacement and he moved up to a magistrate position." Logan slumped back against the wall, head turned, he stared unseeing into the waning night.

✧   ✧   ✧

ALLYSON COAXED HIM into bed where they lay holding each other until sleep finally claimed them. She woke to the sun casting long shadows in the room, the fragrant, tangy smell of a burning cheroot, and finding herself alone in the bed. Giving a quick look around, she found Logan sitting again at the window seat, one arm rested on a raised, bent knee as he crushed out the remains of the cheroot in a crystal-cut smoking dish. She sat up, smiled, and stretched out one hand invitingly to him. He did not move, only sat watching her with a cold, hard gaze, his jaw set firmly. Her eyes pleaded with him to come to her as something dark flickered in the depths of his.

"You still wish to share a bed with an admitted murderer?" Bitter lines framed his mouth.

"No. I want to share your bed." Allyson slowly lowered her arm. "You are a man who I know to be kind, gentle, and most of all, loving." She raised her hand out to him, watched the hesitation in his eyes, the fear of making the first move, so she slid from the bed to stand before him. He took her hand in his, bringing it up to press his lips to her palm and she gathered him to her breasts, holding him tight. His arms encircled her waist in a desperate hug. Inwardly, he whispered fiercely, the words brushing her mind.

I love you, Allyson.

She closed her eyes and held him tighter to her. *I know. I know.*

Chapter Nineteen

THE BEDSIDE PHONE rang and Logan rolled over to answer it. "Yes?" A commotion and shouting on the other end of line drew his attention.

"Logan, its Salina, can you hear all this?" she snapped.

"Clearly. What's wrong?"

"It's your problem; they've come home to roost."

Calmly he instructed the harried Salina, "Call security and ask them to escort Daisy and George out gently."

He could hear her step away from most of the noise. "It's not so simple; they've brought a news crew with them from one of those trashy tabloids. They're saying you aren't here because you're at home in your coffin."

"Shit."

"Yeah, it's going to hit the fan if you don't get your ass in here and take care of this."

"Hold them off and I'll be in ASAP."

"Your 'A' better get in here quicker."

Logan jerked the phone from his ear as Salina slammed the receiver down.

"Problem?" Allyson inquired.

"Daisy and George are at the office terrorizing Salina."

She gave a clipped laugh. "I didn't think anyone could."

"Smarty, she's probably nervous because her brother's back in town and Nairn has been out of touch more than usual lately." He slid from the bed heading for his closet.

"Do you want me to go with you?"

"No, no sense giving them more fuel for their fire." He came over to the bed wearing slacks and buttoning his shirt. "Why don't you call downstairs and order up breakfast or something and wait here for me."

"In bed?"

"Yes, because when I get back it's where you're going to be."

"I like the sound of that." Allyson grinned.

He finished tying his tie and shrugged on a suit coat. "Good."

LOGAN CHOSE TO use a driver and car to make his entrance. Strolling from the car into his building he was immediately met with bright camera lights and a microphone thrust in his face.

"Mr. Kincaid." A perky, top-heavy woman with hair the color of magenta and too much makeup thrust her microphone in his face. "What do you think of the things these people are saying about you?"

In another time and place, Logan would've found her cartoon character looks comical and her dedication to her job admiral, if not amusing. Today she was a gnat that needed to be swatted away quickly as possible before it could bite.

"Since I only arrived, first I'll have to find out what they said before I can answer any questions." With a smile on his face, he scanned the room assessing the situation.

"These people, the Kingston's, claim you're a vampire."

Logan chuckled. "Vampire, as in a creature of the night or blood-sucking-ambulance-chasing attorney?"

The crowd around him twittered in amusement.

The reported scowled. "They say you're a creature of the night and you suck the blood from innocent women."

"Aren't vampires pale, emaciated, dead things? Have you noticed my tan? The Cayman Islands are quite lovely this time of the year." Logan patted his stomach. "I'm not emaciated in the least. Sadly I admit I could stand to lose a couple of pounds." This received a few chuckles and giggles from the crowd. "As to women, a gentleman doesn't kiss and tell." Playfully he smiled showing off his perfect white teeth, not a point amongst then. "And I can assure you, I'm quite alive, Ms. Templar. Isn't it, Trixie?" He finished, giving her a bemused leer.

With an agitated roll of her eyes, the reporter strode back to where Daisy and George stood behind Kincaid Enterprise guards.

A barely discernible nod of his head to his security allowed Trixie to grab Daisy's arm, pulling her from them.

"Who is this man, Mrs. Kingston?"

Daisy had one hand on her bible and the other clutched the cross hanging from her neck. "He's the demon who killed my parents."

"What do you have to say, Mr. Kincaid?"

It turned his stomach to say the words but there was no other way around it. "When did your mother die, Mrs. Kingston? What year?"

Daisy straightened. "In the year of our Lord nineteen hundred and twenty."

He pushed further. "What year were you born, Mrs. Kingston?"

She glanced back to George for reassurance. "It's a trick! He's trying to trick her!" shouted George. "Be gone, foul demon, leave this place!" George Kingston pulled a large crucifix from his coat pocket, advancing on them but the guards stopped him short.

Logan pinned his gaze on the reporter. "You've done your homework on me, Ms. Templar. How old am I?"

Trixie cleared her throat. "The records claim you're forty-four, you turn forty-five this year."

Logan shook his head. "Daisy, how old are you?"

High-pitched and child-like, Daisy's voice whispered. "I'll be ninety-five, God willing, on my birthday."

Logan captured her confused glances with his gaze. "I'm sorry, Daisy."

The crowd murmured and slowly dissipated. George gave Logan a hard look as he led a softly crying Daisy away. "You'll pay for this, Kincaid."

Logan, heart heavy, already was. He turned to the reporter. "What was the need, Ms. Templar, for you to destroy a poor woman? Ratings?"

She signaled her crew to pack up and stood fluffing her hair. "I don't make the news, I just report it."

"And exactly what did you report? An addled old woman with dementia, still grieving after all these years for a mother who died when she was five, a child, who never came to terms with her death?"

"There are people out there who know what you are, Mr. Kincaid. Someday you'll be exposed." Trixie huffed.

Logan sighed from disgust and weariness. "All I am is a man trying to live his life and run a business."

Trixie Templar gave a harrumph and walked away.

Salina slid up to Logan. "A bit close."

"Trixie is just fishing again but I've made sure she won't catch anything."

"You planted someone in the studio?"

"Well not me exactly, Nairn did, one of his Janis-saries. Trixie won't be breaking any news on us in her lifetime."

A security member came up to the pair. "We've got the zealots over there, what do you want us to do with them, Mr. Kincaid?"

Salina lifted her head and squared her shoulders. "Have harassment, trespassing, and anything else you can, file against them. Also, make sure they do not enter this building again."

"No," Logan said the one word flatly.

"No?" Salina balked.

"They've been through enough. Just let them go."

"Yes, sir." The guard touched his hat and walked off.

"I won today. There's no use hurting Daisy any-more." He ran a finger down the side of Salina's cheek. "We're all under extreme stress. Go, pamper yourself, buy something nice, something you don't really need, hangout at a spa. Whatever you want. Charge it to me."

Salina, hands on her hips, glared at Logan.

"Why? What are you going to do?"

"I'm going back home and spend the day bedding the woman I'm in love with."

✧ ✧ ✧

THE LOVE OF his life rejected the idea of waiting for

him like some harem girl and having people waiting on her. Allyson dressed, made her way down to the kitchen, and sat happily eating French toast while chatting with Gideon, her watchdog Janissary.

"A foal? Which is that? A boy or girl?"

"A colt, they call a boy a colt."

"Have you seen it?" Allyson didn't care who noticed, she licked the delicious syrup off her fork.

"Not yet, I thought I'd stroll down there later and check him out."

"Why don't we do it now?" Allyson dabbed her mouth with a napkin then set it aside. "Thank you for a great breakfast, Mrs. Seabrook." The woman nodded and went about her duties. Allyson stood up. "Let's go see this baby horse."

"Wait a minute. Mr. Kincaid gave strict orders for you to stay put." Gideon shifted from one foot to the other.

"We're only going down to the stables. They're not far. I can see them from Logan's office."

"I don't know."

"Oh, come on, I've got you and we're surround by all the people living here. I'm perfectly safe. What could go wrong?"

Chapter Twenty

LOGAN STOOD OVER the young Janissary torn between sympathy for the man, his wounds, and his own urge to kill the boy. "He'll live?"

"No doubt the wounds will be painful for a day or two but he should heal nicely. I cleaned and flushed them out a couple of extra times. A pitch fork is a nasty choice of weapon with all the added bacteria on it, not that we have to worry about things like germs. It's always good to be cautious." Dr. Legrou patted Gideon's shoulder and discreetly left the two men alone.

Logan leaned against a wall until the doctor left then rounded on the young man. "What the hell were you thinking, taking her down to the stables? Or were you even using the gray matter between your ears?" Logan leaned within inches of the man's face. "You're Nairn's right-hand man, whatever you think I'm going to do to you for your lapse in judgment, I guarantee it'll be nothing compared to what he'll do."

"It was the stables. Here. On the grounds. Other Janissary are here patrolling the place continually. The place is over flowing with people. Who'd have thought he'd try something here?"

"Because he's someone we all thought dead for nearly nine decades. If he could hide this long undetected, then he's capable of anything!" Logan turned away, took two steps, and rammed his fist through the wall. "He's got Allyson. If you can't give me something to find her with, then you've just signed her death warrant."

Gideon held up a thick envelope, stained in one corner with his blood. "He told me to give this to you and you alone."

Logan snatched the package from Gideon, kicked open the room's door, and strode to his office. He tore open the envelope, sending the contents onto the desk, briefly absorbing every gruesome detail. Logan couldn't believe what he saw; he dropped into his chair in disbelief. Everything, every detail, was in print, photos, and sketches of Franchot's life. He'd barely time to glance at the mountain of guilt when his cell phone rang. He flipped it open.

"What!" he demanded.

"Feeling a little stressed out, Jean-Pierre?" Franchot's voice oozed like blood from a putrid wound.

"Franchot," Logan bit out.

"Oh good, you remember. I was anxious you'd forgotten."

"Not hardly."

"Did you get my little package?"

"The one that will sign your death warrant? I can't believe you'd be this careless to send me the evidence

I'd need to finish you."

"Maybe, or not. I thought in the unlikely event I don't make it through our next meeting; let's just say I'm not going down alone." Franchot gave a dry chuckle.

Logan placed both elbows on his desk leaning into it. "I'll make you a deal Franchot. Give me the woman and I'll burn all this."

"You'd give me your word you wouldn't come after me?"

"I said I'd burn all this information."

Peals of laughter rang out of the phone.

"Oh, I do like how you think. You haven't asked about your little playmate."

"If you've harmed a hair on her head…."

"This new woman surprises me. You fell for her without even a decent first tumble in the sheets. By the way, what's with her blood? It has the oddest flavor to it reminds me of fresh cinnamon. Your Allyson put up a much better fight than Flora did, kicked, scratched, bit, and punched me right in the nose." Franchot laughed stiff and sharp. "Your little slugger hit me hard enough to make me bleed; the woman has a nasty right hook, unlike Flora, who just lay there letting me put it to her time and time again." Franchot laughed again, and Logan's stomach clenched and churned. He strained to focus on Franchot's ramblings. "Ever the Boy Scout, Jean-Pierre. I'd have gotten rid of Daisy, her father, and the ever optimistic husband of hers long ago. Did you ever know on the night old man Rainy died, his darling little girl and her husband-to-be George, cut dear old dad's head off? They stuffed his mouth with garlic, sewed it shut, then cut out his heart, and burned it." Franchot chortled wildly. "Momentous night, it was for our girl. She received her first kiss from George, too."

"Daisy is not yours. Will never be yours." Logan snapped then moaned, "Poor Daisy. Rainey filled her with all those lies about us." Logan bit back the bile rising in his throat. "Isaac handpicked George for her, too."

"And you let them chase you to ground like a hounded fox time and time again, never lifting a hand to stop them. You do know what usually happens to the fox don't you?" Franchot sneered.

Logan tried to salvage the situation. "Give me Allyson, unharmed, and you can do what you want with me."

"Oh, what a lovely thought, but, no thanks, I can hurt you more by keeping her. And what a sweet little old lady our Daisy has become."

"Daisy?"

"Yes, she and her beloved should be here anytime now."

"Franchot!"

Uncontrolled laughter ripped through the phone, prickling the hair on the back of Logan's neck.

Franchot wheezed, out of breath from all the effort. "If you'd like to join the party, and please come alone, this is a private party. We'll be at the abandoned factory on Jersey Industrial Boulevard. I think you know the one."

Logan sat gripping the phone until the plastic cracked, listening to silence.

✧   ✧   ✧

IGNORING THE THREAT not to call anyone, Logan tried to reach Nairn. Nairn was in transit so Logan had been forced to leave a message with one of the Janissary's subordinates. He hoped if Nairn got the message, it wouldn't be too late because if Logan couldn't stop Franchot, the task would fall to Nairn.

Logan tried to reach Allyson's mind to let her know he was coming. He reached her, but she blocked him. Something terrified her and she walled him out. Logan grasped a fleeting image of something small and dark, a box, from her mind. Whatever it was, it frightened her to the point of near hysteria.

Chapter Twenty-one

FRANCHOT BROUGHT ALLYSON to the abandoned warehouse after snatching her from right under the Janissary's noses. He'd slipped his own watchdogs, easy enough; they were lax in their duty. They didn't want to associate with him anymore than he did with them. Maybe he'd have a talk with Nairn about the training his men were receiving. Franchot dumped Allyson in a long forgotten broom closet, purposely tying her sloppily, hoping she'd try to escape. Allyson hadn't disappointed him.

High above her on the catwalk, Franchot smiled as he silently followed Allyson around the room and briefly wondered if he'd have time to play with this one as he'd once played with one like her so long ago. Would this woman below him be as innocent as the other? He doubted it; women today read more and watched television.

Allyson had been searching for an escape venue and he was beginning to tire of her wanderings. Cabling hung from machinery high above near the ceiling to ground level, waiting for purposeful usage again. Quietly, he snagged one of the cables and hand over hand, lowered himself to the floor. He came to rest directly behind his quarry.

He grinned as she stopped, frozen, no doubt sensing something amiss, reveling in her terror, watching as her mind and body shrieked danger!

Franchot leaned forward to whisper one word in her ear. "Boo!"

Allyson whirled, the small club she'd fashioned raised to strike. Franchot plucked the weapon from her fingers, tossing it to one side. He pinned her arms behind her forcing her up against his lean, hard body, laughing all the while.

"Hello again, morsel. Aren't you a feisty one? Those who fight, are always much more fun to play with."

Despite her struggles to pull away from him, he leaned forward to run his tongue from her chin to her temple, laughing the entire time. He dragged Allyson back to where he'd tied her the first time. The ropes held no hope of escape a second time. He bound her hands behind her back and her feet at the ankles. Then he stuffed a disgustingly dirty rag into her mouth.

Allyson squirmed. She tried to kick out and make contact with some part of him. Instead, her movements only managed to burn the ropes that bound her wrists and ankles more deeply, drawing blood.

"My, aren't you the spitfire. If looks could kill, as they say, I'd most certainly be a dead man by now, wouldn't I? Fortunately for me, they can't."

Franchot grabbed her by the chin. He brushed the

hair from her face, running a finger along her cheek and jaw. "Don't try it again." He leaned over and swiped one of his fingers over her wrist. He brought the blood-smeared finger to his mouth, stuck his tongue out to lick the finger clean then smacked his lips and grinned at her. "Tasty little thing, aren't you," he mocked. "For the moment, you're of more use to me alive but I can use you just as well dead. It really doesn't matter to me." He bent, picked her up, and tossed her onto his shoulder, ignoring her struggling.

He deposited her in the room prepared just for her then went to sit and make himself comfortable to wait for the next act to unfold in this grand drama of his.

✧   ✧   ✧

LOGAN ARRIVED AT the old road as night settled in. The path already wrapped in deep dark shadows. The once elegantly tamed trees and shrubs that lined the lane now reverted to their more primitive beginnings. Like a slow-spreading virus, grass and various other plants slowly reclaimed the surface that was their domain. The disintegrating road came to an abrupt halt in front of a pair of rusted sagging gates held together with a thick chain. Logan eyed the shackle, grasped the metal, and with a swift jerk snapped the links open. He jogged the half-mile down the road, constantly alert for danger, reaching the small rise up above the warehouse in minutes.

Like a sleeping, prehistoric leviathan, the structure loomed before him.

Logan knelt on one knee, scanning the building's exterior for signs of movement. The edifice, for the most part, appeared locked up tighter than a drum, except for the one conspicuously open door. An opening that screamed trap. So obvious, a flaunting calling card of Franchot's arrogance.

Franchot's game and his rules. To be played by. Or else.

Logan reached out to Allyson with his mind. Her fear slapped back like an ocean wave snatching his breath. Images of her abduction from the stables and a small black box circled her thoughts and terrified her. The irony of Franchot harming both the women Logan loved in a stable wasn't lost on him. He straightened then casually strolled down the path, no use hurrying; he was after all the guest of honor. Franchot couldn't start the party without him.

✧   ✧   ✧

FRANCHOT WAITED IN the shadows, unconsciously rubbing the scar between his forefinger and thumb, a lasting gift from Kincaid's other love. A movement near the edge of the woods snapped him back to the present. Ah, another player was about to make an entrance onto the stage.

Franchot watched Logan make his way to the

building; he also knew the Kingston's had returned. How could they not? Several birds with one stone, he chuckled. They had waited a lifetime to see their quarry captured and destroyed.

✧　✧　✧

LOGAN STEPPED THROUGH the door, partially obscured by the half-light seeping in the tall windows.

One, then two more steps and he stood in plain view for anyone to see.

"I'm here alone, unarmed as you requested. This is between us, Franchot. Let the woman go. She's not part of this," he called out when he didn't see anyone.

Casually, Franchot stepped from the shadows into view.

"Hello Jean-Pierre. Oh, excuse me, Logan. Why the name change? Didn't like the old man's name? Or just couldn't stomach the fact the old man couldn't protect his own from food?"

"Where is she?" Logan refused the bait.

"She? Might you mean Blondie? She's around. I must say, once again, your taste in them is delicious. And speaking of taste, hers is quite unusual. Do you believe in prophecies? Kharzarin the Warrior's beautiful Alaza was said to taste like cinnamon, too."

"If you've harmed Allyson…." Logan clenched his jaw. His breath hissed sharply through his teeth. He changed the topic. "You killed Michael didn't you?

Why?"

A grin spread over Franchot's face. "The world's a better place with him gone, don't you agree?" Logan gave him a hard stare. "No? Oh, if you have to have a reason why I killed him, let's just say because I could. Besides the little piss ant annoyed me and it was great fun leaving him for your paramour to find."

"You're disgusting Franchot, a…" Logan growled, not daring to finish the sentence.

"I didn't catch that, Kincaid, something you wanted to say?" Franchot held up one finger in pause and tilted his head listening. "Thomas, don't hide in the back like a virginal wallflower, come join us."

Thomas Rothwell calmly stepped into the light, a Glock-GmbH in his hand, pointed squarely at Franchot's head.

"Not a good idea. I wouldn't piss me off." Franchot held up a small, black box the size of a TV remote. "If you're wondering, this detonator has a dead man's switch."

Thomas lowered the weapon.

"Put it on the floor and slide it over with your foot." Franchot held the remote close to him.

Thomas did as instructed.

"Why don't you go over and join your prodigy." Franchot watched Thomas step closer to Logan. When the two men were close together, he leaned over, picked up the gun, aimed it at Thomas, and blew out one of his kneecaps.

Thomas screamed, falling to the cold concrete clutching his leg. Logan ran over to him. Together they yanked off Thomas's tie, using it as a tourniquet.

"You should've listened to me about coming alone," Franchot tsked.

"Logan didn't know I was in the area," Thomas said through gritted teeth.

Franchot shrugged. "Ooops, my bad."

Logan pushed his anger deep inside him. It would do him no good if he gave into it now. Hopefully, he'd have time for the anger later, now he opted for a frosty stare at his adversary.

"You're timing sucks," Logan informed Thomas, his gaze not straying from Franchot.

Franchot, oozing confidence, addressed the men. "When will dear ol' Nairn be joining us? I've been meaning to have a word with him about sis. As her brother, it would be my duty to explain to him he really shouldn't string her along like he has." Franchot crossed his arms and tapped a finger to his chin. "On the other hand, I should congratulate him on the control his young Janissary had. He didn't make a peep when I skewed him to the horse stall door with the pitch-fork. I made sure to sink it in deep enough into his leg so he'd really have to work to remove it."

"Enough!" roared Thomas. "This needs to end, Franchot, here and now."

"Oh, I couldn't agree more. It wasn't the first time I'd accessed records in the Alliance archives." Franchot ridiculed Thomas. "It was the first time I let you know I'd been there. Logan has all the documentation he'll need to set things right." His gaze shifted to Logan. "Did you find anything interesting it the records? Granted, I didn't give you much time to do so." He rubbed a finger over the remote.

Franchot rounded on Thomas. "You, set this all in motion, Thomas. Lusting after another man's wife."

He waved the remote at Logan. "Dad didn't know or he wouldn't have gone hunting with Thomas." Franchot snarled at Thomas. "You must've been surprised when D'Arcy showed up on your doorstep heavy with me. Thomas decided my mother wasn't good enough, decided I wasn't good enough."

Franchot's attention snapped to Logan's horrified profile. "Oh, didn't Thomas tell you?"

Again, he rounded on Thomas. "D'Arcy spilled everything about your little talk. I can be quite persuasive. A knife, a little heat, a few shallow cuts, a person will unload every scrap of information you ever wanted to know if they think you'll stop the pain. She babbled all about it, how you convinced her Dad wouldn't want a half-breed bastard, how he'd have her killed if she didn't get rid of me. You even promised to boost her career if she only got rid of me. I've never understood why you didn't kill me yourself. After all, you were the one to actually ditch me in the orphanage."

Thomas winched. "You were an exquisite baby,

helpless, frail, I couldn't harm you."

"But you could kill my father and sic the local fanatics on Logan's parents."

Logan recoiled in shock. The rumors were fact.

"I'm sorry, Logan, so sorry." Thomas flinched when Logan leaned away. "I was young full of myself, drunk on the power of being part of the Alliance. I believed your father heralded the destruction of the Tarczal life as we knew it. I couldn't let him destroy us."

"Did you try reasoning with him?" Logan asked.

"I did, but he wouldn't listen to me or so I believed. We were both speaking, but neither of us communicated to the other clearly. I did what I thought was necessary."

"André suspected there was more to the story than the villagers turning on my parents."

"Yes, I went to the priest, told him about the danger in his parish."

"You deliberately had them killed."

"No, I thought the villagers would frighten them. I believed you father would see the error of his ways."

"Didn't go down like that did it?" Franchot snickered.

"No, oh, gods it didn't, and I had already traveled too far to turn around and help them."

"This is how you came to know precisely their fate." Logan shook his head. "As the Alliance attorney it was your job to make record of the incident."

"Yes."

"The documents."

"I wrote it all down and Franchot Sr. was the keeper of our records."

"He read everything as his duties dictated."

"Read and made copies." Thomas sighed.

"You killed him," Logan said, his voice bitter and flat.

Thomas's expression pleaded for Logan to understand. "He couldn't live with the knowledge; he was going to make the records known to André."

"You went hunting with him before he could." Logan ran his hand over his face in an attempt to wash away the knowledge. "You acted like a god, arrogant with his divine power."

"I did what I thought I had to, to protect the Tarczal race."

Logan turned from Thomas to Franchot. "I know now what he did, but you, why destroy my life, too?" Logan asked.

"Because you were the son Thomas always wanted. He destroyed any chance I could've had with my father so I decided to demolish you," Franchot spat. "Did you know he bragged to the Alliance you were the perfect replacement for him despite what they'd done to you? Thomas convinced them he could train you, keep you in line, mold you into the ideal puppet for them, until his marionette became a real boy and tried to kill me." Franchot jerked towards Logan, halting, scorn washed over his face. "Kind of shattered your golden boy image. You did me proud, the determination you exuded in doing your best to gut me. I really didn't think you had it in you, thought for sure, when you dogged my steps from town to town you'd eventually give up. You hung in there like a trooper."

Logan edged closer to Franchot and froze as Franchot pointed a finger at him in admiration. "I misjudged how much the little brown flower, Flora, meant to you. By the way, it took great effort on my part to find the one button of yours to push. I tried so many things but you were always so damn forgiving. You actually believed putting an ocean and a continent between us would stop me from tormenting you. It only gave me more resolve." Franchot half-turned towards where he held Allyson and Logan lunged.

The control flew out of Franchot's hand and much to Logan's relief, skittered un-detonated across the concert. The dead man's switch had been a lie. They landed hard on the floor, each slightly winded. They rolled and grappled for better holds. Logan's fist connected with Franchot's jaw, snapping his head back. Franchot countered with a head-butt then broke free from Logan. He tried to stand; Logan grabbed his leg, tripping him. Logan attempted to rise, but Franchot lashed out with his foot, catching Logan in the jaw. Franchot scrambled to his feet; Logan right behind him. He spotted the remote and made for it. Logan was just seconds behind him. Franchot's fingertips brushed the control as Logan kneed him in the ribs. The momentum carried both men into a stack of wooden pallets.

Chapter Twenty-two

CARRYING HIS FAVORITE shotgun, George Kingston quietly made his way up to the front of the building to assist his friend Frank with the capture. At first he'd heard murmured voices, still too far away to clearly hear until finally, he came to where the voices were located. He stood in stunned silence. Before him was Frank, the demon Kincaid, and a third man George didn't recognize. George couldn't believe what he'd just heard. Frank had lied to them. Frank was one of them. How could his sweet Daisy have been wrong? Her gift had failed them miserably. She was not to be blamed. George shook his head. They were evil and used trickery like the righteous breathed air. On the other hand, had they pursued the wrong man all these years? No, Kincaid wasn't a man, he was a beast from hell, George reminded himself. A light in an old office caught his eye. Mrs. Weston pleaded with her eyes for help.

George glanced back at the two men grappling with each other. He slipped into the room. "Just stay calm, Mrs. Weston. I'll get you out of here." George removed the gag from Allyson's mouth. He must free the woman. She'd been wronged, too.

"Don't touch anything, please. He has me hooked up to explosives," Allyson whispered.

"Shush now, I used to be a demolition man on construction sites. I know a good bit about things which go boom."

"Are you sure you know what you're doing?" she asked as he released her from the explosives.

"Now, now, don't you worry." George came around in front of her. Gently, he detached the makeshift harness loaded with the C-4. He placed it on the floor in the corner of the room. Next, he untied her, making short work of the ropes with his penknife.

"Can you walk?" George watched as she rubbed the circulation back into her limbs.

"I think so." She took a couple of steps. "I'm fine. Let's go."

✧   ✧   ✧

MOVEMENT AT THE corner of his vision caught Logan's attention. Allyson and George emerged from the office. Logan shouted to them, "He's got the building wired! Get out! Run, Allyson!"

Franchot plunged his fist into Logan's stomach staggering him. He grabbed a broken piece of pallet and brought it down on the back of Logan's skull. Then as Logan fell, Franchot snatched up an old oil drum and threw it at Allyson.

Logan rose to his hands and knees shaking the

nausea and pain from his body. He spied a board. Grabbing it, he charged Franchot, catching him across the back. Franchot went to his knees. Logan clipped him under the chin sending him sprawling backward. Franchot landed hard, but rolled to one side, regaining his footing quickly.

✦   ✦   ✦

ALLYSON DOVE TO avoid the drum, rolled, and abruptly found herself falling. She landed on her back with an oof, the wind knocked from her. She had tumbled into a deserted drainage pit. Slowly, she got up, checking for damage, relieved to find nothing broken. She took a moment to study her surroundings only to find the only way out was straight up. Allyson jumped, trying to reach the pit's ledge. Allyson jumped again, nearly catching hold of the protrusion. Her fingers caught the pit shelf. Using her tennis shoes, she inched herself up the pit wall to place an arm on the building's floor. Half way up, one foot slipped, but she caught the ridge with her other forearm and worked her way out of the pit. Allyson, now on her feet, ran to her lover's aid. She spied a spud bar on the floor, hefted it up and charged Franchot. She swung the metal bar in a deadly ark to bring it down on his head. Franchot snaked his arm out catching the bar and twisting it out of her hands. In the process, the bar clipped the side of Allyson's forehead, stunning her.

George hadn't moved. Now with resolve, he marched forward, the shotgun raised. Advancing on Frank, he cried out, "Though I walk through the valley of the shadow of death, I will fear no evil." He observed Frank pick up a two-foot piece of rebar and then there was a weight and wetness about George's chest. He looked down to see the metal protruding from him. George glanced back at Frank. He fired the gun as he fell dead to the floor. As he toppled, the weight of the gun shifted his aim. The blast caught the left side of Logan's body as he advanced on Franchot.

OUTSIDE, PATIENTLY WAITING in the car, Daisy heard the shotgun go off. With the agility of a twenty-year-old, she scrambled her nearly ninety-five-year-old body quickly from the vehicle. She entered through the side door George had used earlier. Daisy hurriedly shuffled through the building. Her anguished cry of grief echoed in the surroundings, seeing her husband lying on the concrete. She grasped the rebar, ripping the metal from her husband's chest and throwing it aside. Daisy ripped a strip from her skirt pushing it on the wound on George's chest. Habit from years of straightening up after the man in her life, Daisy picked up the weapon, laying it aside without a moment's thought. So automatic the response, her mind didn't identify the gun for what it was, it was just something out of order.

Daisy clasped her hands together and began to pray when the struggles of the two men behind her drew her attention. She placed one hand on the ground beside her to help her stand. It rested on the forgotten shotgun. Daisy saw Logan send the man she knew as Frank sprawling backward. Without thinking, Daisy picked up the first thing close to her, the shotgun beside George's body. Daisy raised the weapon pulling the trigger.

✧   ✧   ✧

THOMAS WATCHED IT all helplessly until Daisy stumbled into the fray. He feared Allyson dead; she hadn't risen since Franchot struck her. Daisy, the last person Logan loved. Thomas did the only thing he could to save both. He struggled to his feet stepping into the path of the gun blast, shielding Logan with his body. A shearing pain ripped through Thomas, thrusting him back, shredding his torso, saving Logan and killing himself.

✧   ✧   ✧

FRANCHOT REGAINING HIS footing rose laughing. "The good die young, don't they Kincaid!" He watched Logan struggle to rise. Franchot turned and swaggered up to Daisy. "Thank you, sweetheart. You saved me from doing it myself." He snatched the gun from her, tossing it aside.

✧   ✧   ✧

"RUN, DAISY, DON'T let him touch you!" Logan roared.

"Ah, come on, Kincaid, I should be allowed to find out if the daughter is as tasty as the mother." Frank reached out with his hand to grip the back of her neck, forcing her closer to him.

"No! Leave her alone!" Logan tried to get up while grasping his side to staunch the flow of blood.

✧   ✧   ✧

LIGHT. BRILLIANT. WHITE. Pure, flashed in Daisy's mind. She focused on Logan and a memory flashed before her. In her mind's eye, Daisy saw Logan bending over her mother, crying saying he was sorry, saying he loved her. A flash of clarity exploded in her mind. The memory, now true and clean from years of muddied repression burst in her. Daisy relived the day in her mind, she saw Logan gathering her up in his arms, trying to comfort and sooth her. Not harm her.

✧   ✧   ✧

A SHARP PAIN tore her from the memory. Franchot was sinking his teeth into her neck. "You, you were the one who killed my momma."

Her voice came out small, high, and childish. She wrapped her fingers around the Glock's handle sticking from Frank's waistband and pulled the trigger.

The man Daisy called Frank yanked free his grip on her neck; staggering to one side away from her, blood poured from his waist. In the next second, a fine mist of crimson exploded from his back. Frank gasped and wobbled. He slowly raised a hand to dab at a fresh hole in his shirt the size of a grapefruit. Blood flowed freely from it.

✧   ✧   ✧

FRANCHOT TOTTERED; ASTOUNDED at his gaping chest, not believing his eyes, eyes which flickered and went dark. He laughed. "Nice shot Jean-Pierre. One usually doesn't get an exit wound…with a brick." Franchot had snatched up the small black box from the floor, now he raised his hand high as he flipped the switch on the detonator.

✧   ✧   ✧

A LOUD RUMBLE launched at the far end of the building and things began to crash. Allyson stood, supporting Logan's weight as he leaned on her, another brick ready in his hands, the only weapon within reach. It wasn't needed. Franchot DeBois II wouldn't rise from the dead a second time.

✧   ✧   ✧

"DAISY, DAISY, COME with us," Logan shouted over the

din, motioning for her to come to them.

The old woman shook her head and ran back the way she'd arrived.

"Daisy!" Logan cried to the retreating figure.

Allyson pulled him with her to the nearest exit. "We have to get out of here. The building is coming down!" she shouted over the sounds of walls crashing and girders snapping. Logan could only nod as they struggled for the exit. He glanced over his should but Daisy had vanished from sight. The floor shook, sending them tumbling. Allyson got up and pulled Logan to his feet. The door was blocked.

"There, over there is a window!" Logan shouted above the din.

It once was a small waist-high window, now minus the glass. Logan pulled her to him kissing her hard. To Allyson's startled expression, he said, "For luck. You go. Get clear of the building. Don't stop running until you reach the main road!"

"No, not without you. I'm not leaving you here!"

"Allyson, don't."

"Argue?" she finished the sentence, for him. "I won't if you shut up and get moving." She struggled to drag him closer to the opening.

"It's too small for me."

"Then I'll just have to make it bigger!" She grabbed the frame and pulled. When it didn't work, she crawled into the opening, placed her back against one side while she pushed with her legs on the other side. The metal groaned and held. She tried again. This time the frame gave way. She hopped down. Logan had passed out. Allyson shook him, stirring him.

She half-walked, half-dragged him to the window, pushing the upper part of him outside. She wrapped her arms around his legs and hoisted the rest of him out. She scrambled out the window after him. Once more, she roused him to his feet, pulled his arm again across the back of her neck and stumbled across the ground.

The building burst here and there, sending debris and shrapnel flying. The ground shook. Fire spewed and set the grasses and trees around them on fire. Smoke was thick, and they stumbled and fell to their knees. Allyson tried again to pull him up, but the smoke left her on hands and knees, coughing. She collapsed but before she lost consciousness, she thought she saw the figure of a man approaching.

Chapter Twenty-three

ALLYSON WOKE WITH a painful headache. She was in a moving car, a souped-up fifty-seven Chevy precisely. Funny what a concussion will do to your perspective. The car was like the one her college roommate's boyfriend owned. Allyson sat in this Chevy beside a man she didn't know.

"So, you're awake." The man gave her a cheery smile. He gave her the once over. "How do you feel? You've a nasty lump on the side of your head."

She reached for the door handle with the thought to bail out. He chuckled. "I wouldn't. At this speed, you'd end up messy and I really don't want to be the one to have to explain what happened." He punctuated his sentence with a jab of his thumb toward the back seat. "To him."

Allyson twisted around to look in the back seat. Logan lay there. He wasn't moving. In the darkness, no streetlights or headlights from the other cars to illuminate the interior, it was impossible for her to see if Logan were alive or not.

"Is he all right? Is he alive?"

"Yeah, he's alive. Lucky for him. It looked worse than it was, it'll take a few days, but he'll heal up. So, you must be Allyson?"

"Yes, I am." Allyson took in the shoulder-length, sun-bleached blonde hair, scruffy jeans, and torn sweater. He looked like a surfer without his board. "Who are you?"

"His best friend." A smile lit up his face. "And, when he gets better I'm gonna beat the crap out of him. He knew I was coming. He should've waited for me."

Allyson looked away as he glanced over towards her. "But, I can understand why he didn't."

He patted her leg. "I probably wouldn't have waited either. By the way, my name's Nairn. Did he ever mention me?"

"Yes, I did. I told her you were a womanizer, and a card cheat, and to stay far, far away from you," the voice came from the back seat.

"Logan!" squealed Allyson scrambling into the back seat.

"Any chance you're up to a little donation, honey?" He smiled and kissed her.

"Just tell me what you want me to do."

"If you'll just lie down here beside me."

"Hey!" Nairn laughed as he adjusted the rearview mirror watching Allyson lie down. "Not in my car! I just had the inside detailed!" He shook his head. "Best friend or not, I'll still beat the crap out of you for nearly getting yourself killed." Nairn laughed harder as he observed an obscene gesture from Logan who had paused from feeding. "Nairn?"

"Yeah?"

"Thanks." Two voices as one replied from the back seat.

"You're welcome." Nairn drove them straight to the estate. He didn't want to, but he had to take the back roads. With lights out, driving at a speed too high on dirt or gravel roads, he drove with controlled urgency. An occasional bump or sharp turn would bring a moan from the back seat and Nairn could only mumble, "Sorry."

NAIRN HAD SEEN some nasty wounds but the ones bleeding like his friend's, those were never good. Close, so close to home, *we're going to make it*, he remembered thinking…right before the doe stepped in front of the car.

Chapter Twenty-four

"**B**LOOD PRESSURE IS nearly nonexistent; chest and abdominal area are heavily bruised." Dr. Dennis Legrou wiped his brow. "Deep lacerations to the right and left lumbar regions and the umbilical region and hypogastric are a mess, too." Dr. Legrou assessed Allyson's injuries calling them out to one nurse who hurriedly made the notations in the computer. Two other nurses scurried to get the equipment needed. "Spleen damage probability is high as well as liver and then there are the minor injuries. Cervical whiplash, fractured feet, knees, and legs, not to mention the havoc the glass from the car has done to almost every inch of her."

Shaking his head, he stared at Logan. "Her only chance of survival is the transformation." Legrou applied more pressure to one of the wounds. "Lucien's positive she's compatible?" the doctor asked Logan, who nodded yes. "We'll have to start the mixture immediately and do a fast drip. I hope she can handle it."

Logan watched the doctor insert the IV into Allyson's vein himself, not trusting, or Logan suspected, not wanting anyone else but himself to take the blame if complications arose.

Dennis adjusted the drip, more a tiny trickle, and stood back to wait. "After this I'd like the chance to study this formula. The combination of the herbs is unique and the procedure is simplicity at its finest. It's the combination of the herbs, the precise timing of boiling, adding, mixing, with the complexity of how they must be applied that's fascinating. One for Tarczals, one for coms, one for female, one for male, how each factor must be contemplated, measured, and mixed. Moreover, it only works with descendants of the Alaza line. A pedigree so rare and hard to detect it makes you wonder how the technique ever came into being in the first place." He went to check the IV, the bag's contents nearly dispensed. "Lucien found the recipe in an old journal of his great-grandmother's and gave it to Nairn?"

"Yes." Logan listened to the doctor voice his nervousness by rambling on about everything and nothing. Logan tuned him out, only acknowledging with a nod here or there when needed.

Logan wouldn't let doubt or fear fester in him. His resolve strong, his beliefs firm. Ironic, his beliefs, a month ago he'd laughed at prayer. Now he prayed to the old gods of the Tarczal's, not asking for their help, but demanding it, willing them to listen. An hour later, Dr. Legrou removed the IV's and other medical equipment attached to Allyson.

Logan hovered, waiting for the doctor to give him

permission to proceed. Dennis raised his head while working on Allyson to hold Logan's gaze. "You drank all of your part of the mixture?"

"Every vile drop." Logan grimaced, remembering the taste but he'd ingest worse if it meant saving Allyson.

Dr. Dennis Legrou stared then nodded. "It's time."

Logan gently turned Allyson's pale face to one side to expose her slender neck. He placed a feather light kiss on the too white skin then brought his mouth down quickly to press against her throat. Minutes ticked by before Logan drew back, caressed his tongue across two tiny naked wounds and leaned forward to place a chaste kiss on her lips. He raised his eyes, cool and dark, to meet Dr. Legrou.

"Now what?" Legrou asked.

"We make her comfortable and we let nature take its course."

Dennis gasped, "Nature?"

Logan gathered Allyson in his arms, lifting her limp form. "I'm not going to call it magic."

"Nature is a good word." Dennis smiled ruefully.

Logan carried her upstairs to nestle her in his bed. He held Allyson tight and hoped the change would begin soon, but in truth he knew it would be several hours if all went right before she would begin to heal and awaken. He brushed a whisper of hair from her cut and bruised face then softly placed a chaste kiss on her cool lips. He called to her with his mind one more time and gasped in anguish as he felt his words echo in bitter dark emptiness.

Earlier, for a brief moment in the back of the pickup truck, he called to her and she responded. Allyson sensed him near and knew she was safe. Now, a silent void emanated from her and she was but a cooling shell. He said an ancient prayer in his native language and settled in for the duration.

Chapter Twenty-five

N AIRN SCRUBBED HIS hands over his face in silent frustration and sighed. After everything Logan and Allyson went through, to have a stupid car accident possibly separate them wasn't acceptable. A wreck he'd caused. He'd trained dozens of Janissary for defensive emergency maneuvers such as a deer, a damn deer. Fighting the steering wheel, he'd done his best to keep the car on the gravel road. The car rolled three times; that he counted, before coming to a crunching halt against a tree. He and Logan crawled from the crumpled metal realizing in seconds, Allyson still lay inside. Thank all the gods they prayed to that Nairn's men arrived on the scene quickly. Of course, he and Logan recovered quickly from their injuries, come to think of it, Logan actually improved faster than usual, but Allyson. So many injuries to one body couldn't be good.

Nairn hoped the formula his father gave him would do the impossible. It was in Logan's and Dr. Legrou's hands, Nairn couldn't do anymore.

Nairn considered getting a drink from the bar in Logan's office and then shook his head. What was the use of alcohol when it couldn't numb a Tarczal body?

Sometimes he envied the coms. Through the study, he went out onto the terrace patio and stopped dead in his tracks.

Salina was there waiting, for him. How did she always know when he needed the sight of her?

"Hi," she said, her mouth curled into the crooked little smile he loved so much, his groin automatically tightening at the sight of her.

"Hi, yourself."

He saw her shiver. "You should have a heavier jacket on." Nairn nodded to the sweater she wore over a dress too short in his opinion.

"I'm okay, are you? You look like you could use a bath. Is any of the blood yours?"

He glanced down at his clothing for the first time since the wreck. His shirt was plastered against his chest, most of the material saturated with blood now drying from a bright red to a dull brown.

"No, not mine. Mostly Logan's and Allyson's."

"Do you think…?" She bit back the last word, her hand covering a moan.

"Hey, he's going to live, I'm sure of it. He has too." Nairn urgently tried to reassure her. Salina ran to him, throwing her arms around his neck.

"Oh Goddess, I thought…" The rest drowned out by her sobs.

"Its okay, Salina. It's okay. He's going to be all right. Logan's too tough to die." Nairn held her tight against him as he leaned against the stone railing. By the Goddess he'd missed the feel of her.

"You big idiot!" Salina eased back from him a little. "I know he'll be okay. I was worried about you!"

"Me?" That confused him. After their last meeting, she literally kicked him out the door, buck-naked. She tossed his clothes out the window minutes later, yelling some colorful phrases about his anatomy and questioning his parentage. He couldn't for the life of him, remember what began the fight.

"Yes, you." She stepped away from him arms crossed over her stomach. "You come in here all smoky, dirty, and bloody. Pale as a ghost. Why didn't you come back?"

"Excuse me?" Nairn shook his head trying to keep up with her.

"Why didn't you come back to the townhouse?"

"I thought you didn't want me around." He remembered the night. Two hours after their fight, he'd seen her through the window in the arms of Logan, accepting his comfort. Nairn had slunk off. By the next morning, Nairn had worked up a good lather and stormed over to Logan's place. Only to find his best friend gone. Nairn then stormed over to find movers at Salina's townhouse, but no Salina. When he checked with her staff, they informed him Ms. Dubois had gone to America with Mr. Kincaid. Adding insult to injury, her new address was the same as Logan's American estate.

"It isn't the point," she said as he watched a leaf

waft down from a tree falling across Salina's face. She flicked it aside with a sassy jerk of her hand. Logan's majordomo opened the terrace door that moment, clearing his throat.

"Excuse me, sir. Mr. St. Clair, there are a Janissary and feeders which need to speak with you."

Naira and Salina eyed each other and Nairn gestured for her to go first through the door.

Chapter Twenty-six

LOGAN AWOKE TO a mouth, fever warm, trailing kiss after kiss along his collarbone. He lay on his back and enjoyed the sensations in a drowsy half-sleep state. A wicked little tongue darted out to skip along his jaw and down his neck. He felt a lithe body slide over him straddling his hips and deftly slide him into a tight, moist, hot, sheath. Logan clenched his teeth and gave a half smile to the pleasure washing over him as womanly hips rocked against his. Eyes still closed a small gasp escaped his lips when nails raked teasingly over his bare chest to nick his nipples in a wondrous torment. He felt long silken tresses brush his rib cage when she bent her head to run the tip of her tongue across his mouth. She stopped to nibble on his lower lip pulling it slightly into her mouth and then he felt them.

Feeding teeth.

His eyes snapped open in surprise.

She clutched his shoulders and tried to pull herself down to his neck. Her strength surprised him but he held her fast. Logan looked up into his lover's eyes—dark blue, smoky with passion, and the hunger all Tarczals were born with.

He'd grabbed the hair at the base of her skull. Allyson opened her mouth and softly cried out as he applied more pressure to stop her actions. He ran the thumb of his free hand across her lower lip to feel it quiver under his touch and her mouth opened wider. He stared in amazement. He'd not thought them to form this fast. There, just behind her front teeth, a hundred times harder than normal bone, were two slender completely retractable and razor sharp feeding teeth. Allyson moaned and squirmed on him, he grinned at her impatience.

"Is my lovely lady hungry?" He ran his free hand over one breast to cup it, to knead it, and then slid his hand down to rest lightly on her buttocks. She squirmed more and tried to nod her head. He pulled her closer to his face; they stared eye to eye. Hers were fever bright as the change, cell deep, burned out the damaged and unneeded in her body, to replenish, nourish what was to be the new.

"The first lesson you must learn, my love, is never, never to take without permission. You must always ask. Do you understand me, Allyson?"

Her eyes pleaded with him as her hunger built, twisted, gnawed, and clawed throughout her gut to make it known. Forever now a constant company to her new life. He tightened his grip and she gasped. He pressed the issue. "Do you understand, Allyson?" He expected an answer in some form of recognition in her eyes or at best, a moan.

"Yeeesss." She licked her lips and in a hoarse whisper answered.

He was surprised and pleased she could speak this early in the change, especially with all the damage done to her in the crash.

"Good." He gently released his hold on her and meant to sit up until Allyson pressed her hands to his chest.

"It will be easier if I score the skin for you the first time." He reached for the small dagger on the nightstand. She placed her hand out to stop him, leaned into nuzzle him along his neck, tentatively grazing her new teeth against his skin.

"So you want to try it on your own the first time?" he chuckled.

She nuzzled his neck more, hesitated and waited.

"Yes, you may." He leaned up and all but purred the words into her ear then opened his mouth in a silent oh as she punctured his skin expertly and rode him to a glorious climax.

Afterward, Logan sat against the headboard watching Allyson soundly sleep, tucked in the covers beside him. She'd awakened twice to feed since the first time and mounted him each time to bring him and herself to several extraordinary orgasms. He was smug with self satisfaction on how quickly she had learned to feed. He shook his head though, in silent amazement over her choice of how to procure nourishment. He'd fed from her during lovemaking; it was natural for her to do the same. He shrugged his shoulders in a happy sigh. *I must be more careful when I allow her to feed from me and check the amount she takes or else I just might die a happy man.*

Nairn knocked softly then half stepped from behind the bedroom door, moving to the bedside when Logan motioned him closer.

"How's the lady doing?" Nairn nodded toward the sleeping Allyson.

Logan tucked the covers around her. "She's acquired her teeth already."

"I'll be damned. That's quick." Nairn rubbed the back of his neck. "I'd ask if it were normal but we're kind of in uncharted territory, aren't we?"

Logan blew out a pent up breath. "Franchot was the last change we know of and already half Tarczal. Allyson…" Nairn placed a hand on his shoulder and squeezed. Logan nodded. "I have to be positive right? If she's of Alaza's line then this will work."

"Hate to admit it but dad's usually right about this stuff." Nairn chuckled.

"Let's hope Lucien is right this time." Logan hugged Allyson close to him. "Any chance there's a feeder or two downstairs?"

"Feeders, buddy you've got them lined up around the block. Yours, mine, the houses, the clubs, and even a few of the old townies are waiting downstairs." Nairn positively beamed.

Logan sat there stunned.

"Thought it might surprise you. I've every last one of my Janissary and their feeders signed up to pitch in and do what's necessary."

Logan sputtered. "All of them?"

"Down to the newbies."

"Damn. Why? I only know a handful of them personally. Why would they risk all? The Alliance will be livid when they find out what I've done."

"As I said, they're loyal." Nairn shrugged his shoulders then gave a devious grin. "Oh, I don't believe you'll have to worry about reprisals."

"Why not?" Logan's eyes narrowed. "What have you done?"

Nairn chuckled, "Me? Nothing, well hardly at all. I passed on the broadcast from the mic Thomas wore during the altercation in the plant."

Catching Logan's attention. "Thomas was wearing a wire?"

"Yep, not sure why, guess he figured the odds of him coming out of this alive and telling the tale weren't good. What he captured has been recorded, played and the transcripts will be in the Alliance's hot little hands by morning." Nairn's shoulders slumped. "I'm sorry about your parents and Thomas's part in their death."

Logan forced down the lump in his throat. "Me, too. It's hard to think of Thomas as anything other than a friend."

Nairn nodded. "Good news is, the mic also picked

up Franchot's confession he acted alone when he murdered Michael. I made sure the local guys are receiving right about now."

Logan gave a chuckle. "Thanks. I guess I'll be saying it quite a bit in the next few days." He shook his head in disbelief. "Janissary, feeders, everyone else, this is going to cost me a bundle in thank-yous." Logan ran a hand through his hair, a silly grin of relief on his face.

Nairn chuckled softly. "I've instructed all feeders downstairs to the protocol when they enter your room. I seriously doubt we'll have any trouble with Sleeping Beauty there. This lady is peaceful as a lamb." Nairn straightened and shifted his gaze to Logan. "You my friend, must be hungry, want me to send the first one up?"

"Yes." Logan sighed and Nairn slipped out into the hallway.

It was quiet Paige, much to Logan's surprise, Nairn let into the room. He observed she paused to allow her eyes to adjust to the dim light in the room. She tiptoed over to him, no doubt remembering Nairn's words not to make any unnecessary sounds or movements. He eased off the bed not disturbing the sleeping woman beside him. Nairn warned the feeders concerning Allyson's heighten sensitivity to the world around her and her lack of control quenching her newfound thirst. They all were in uncharted territory.

Logan had slipped on a pair of jeans before Paige

entered the room. He pulled a sweater over his head as she approached. Taking her hand, he guided her to a comfortable high-backed chair on the other side of the room. She gave him a quick peck on the cheek before she sat.

He was nearly finished when a low, ominous growl came from directly in front of them. Paige stiffened in his arms.

"Don't move and don't make a sound." Logan softly whispered against her neck. "Try not to let her know you're scared, fear will only feed her anger more." He could feel the young woman's heart slamming against her ribs.

Logan eased his head up to look directly into the snarling face of his lover. Sitting a little straighter in the chair, his hands shifted Paige's body slightly more into his and away from danger. Allyson's eyes tracked the movement.

Soft and low Logan murmured to the girl. "I won't let her hurt you, Paige."

"Allyson, go back to the bed." He issued the command to her in a steady and calm voice. Funny, because he didn't feel either.

"Miiinnee!" Allyson hissed in a deadly whisper, her hands clenched and unclenched at her sides.

"Yes, I am yours, but I need to feed, too. Would you deny me nourishment?"

"Feeeed from meeee." The whimpered plea came.

Logan's heart squeezed when he noticed the desire

and pain etched on Allyson's face as she stared at him. She stepped forward a half step, her hands still flexed.

Damn it. Logan gave a quick glance at the bedroom door. Where was Nairn? He or one of the Janissaries was supposed to be standing guard on the other side of the door. Couldn't he hear what was going on in here?

"I can't sweetheart, at least not yet. Go back to the bed and wait for me." Slowly, painfully, Allyson backed up. Just as slowly, Logan stood and placed his body between the two women. He reached out to stroke Allyson's cheek and she leaned into him, nuzzling against his hand, eyes closed.

"Stay behind me at all times." Logan turned his head slightly to speak to the feeder. He felt if not saw her nod of agreement. She put her hand on his waist to steady herself. They began inching toward the door. With the first shift of their weight, Allyson's eyes snapped open.

"MIIINE!" She snarled and lunged only to rake the air as Logan caught her by the wrist.

"NO!" He roared. He shook her hard once then let go of her so quickly she stumbled back onto the floor. Allyson gazed up at him from a half crouch, grief etching her face.

"Enough, Allyson!" His voice cracked like a whip. "Go back to the bed and wait, for me."

"Feeeed frooom meeee." She trembled, yet rose to stand defiantly before him.

"No." He commanded and pointed towards the bed. Allyson turned as though to do as he bid and they moved slowly for the door again. Later, Logan would thank his superior night vision for catching Allyson's lightening quick dive. He whirled catching her around the waist in mid air as she made yet another lunge for Paige.

Allyson howled in rage when stopped, then in surprise as Logan calmly sat down on the chair, threw her over his knee and soundly spanked her. In one fluid motion, he stood and placed her on her feet. Allyson scurried over to the bed, paused to rub her backside and then slipped into the bed's center. She snatched a pillow up to hug it tightly to her chest, eyes narrowed as she glared at Paige.

"You can leave now, Paige. Allyson will behave."

✧　✧　✧

PLACING FIRST ONE foot in front of the other, Paige carefully made her way to the door. Her hand fell on the doorknob; Logan's voice caused her to turn.

"Thanks, for your help, Paige. I hope you understand." He frowned slightly and sighed. She nodded with an understanding smile before slipping gratefully out the door.

✧　✧　✧

THE SNICK OF the door latch barely evaporated when

Nairn, charged down the hallway, nearly bowling her over.

"Are you all right?" He grabbed her and yanked her away from the door. "I stepped away, for just a moment, I am sorry." Nairn eyes raked over her body checking for injuries. "What the hell happened in there?"

"Simple." Paige took a breath, shuddered, and sat heavily into the chair Nairn had occupied earlier. "The boss's lady has a jealous streak longer than the Nile."

LOGAN OBSERVED THE length of her nails making a mental note to trim them soon. He walked over to the edge of the bed and sat down. Allyson scooted towards the headboard still hugging the pillow to her, keeping her face turned from him. He reached out to capture her chin between his thumb and forefinger, turning her to face him. Tears glittered in her eyes before spilling down her cheeks and a shudder racked her body.

He leaned to her, brushing his lips across hers. She opened her mouth in an urgent need to taste more of him. He eased closer and she pressed into his arms. All he wanted at the moment was to lose himself in her, but he knew her lessons were just beginning. He tilted her head back to gain her full attention sliding on his sternest face.

"You will not attack my feeders ever again."

She frowned and opened her mouth to protest.

"No." He silenced her. "Now listen to me. You must do as I say or a Janissary will be brought in here to restrain you while I feed." She blanched. *Good,* he thought, *I have her attention now.* "I can't feed from you; you need to keep all you have. I need to feed, so you may feed." He watched as she pondered his words and then snuggled against him like a kitten. He schooled his grin. He wasn't about to be fooled by her coquettish attempts again. He wrapped her hair around his hand close to her nape and snapped her head back, a gesture which surprised her. Eyes wide she stared at him. "You will leave my feeders alone. Say it, Allyson."

"Yeeesss. I leeave feeeders aaalone."

She spoke almost entire sentences, amazing him. According to what information recorded on changes, most in this infantile state were like newborn kittens, blind with the need to feed, oblivious to all else. He searched her face to see if she might try to deceive him. Satisfied she'd comply, he brought his mouth down on hers in a hot hungry kiss.

"You will be good." Logan tucked the covers around her and lingered over her. A knock at the door drew him away. Nairn waited anxiously.

"Think you can get another feeder to volunteer?" Logan asked his friend.

"Possible, you want me to come inside?" He studied Logan's face.

"No." Logan replied then lowered his voice. "But don't go too far. My once sweet kitten has developed the attitude, claws, and teeth of an angry she-tiger."

Nairn raised an eyebrow and mouthed a silent 'O' He thought of mentioning to Logan about switching to a male feeder then quickly dismissed the idea. Watching Logan watch Allyson, Nairn smirked. Allyson wasn't the only one, he mused, who could have a jealous streak.

"I'll see if anyone is brave enough to enter the lair." He didn't even try to hide a grin.

Marcy cautiously entered the room, shoulders straight, chin up. Logan walked to her, raised her hand to his mouth, placing a quick kiss on the back it. They both heard Allyson draw a breath between clenched teeth. Marcy froze, but Logan placed an arm around Marcy's shoulders leading her to the chair.

"You don't have to worry about Allyson. She will behave herself, because she knows I only plan to feed." He said it loud enough for Allyson to hear then settled Marcy on his lap, bent his head close to her neck, only to bite his lip in an attempt not to laugh aloud.

As Marcy whispered, "Wait 'til you get our bill for hazardous duty pay, Mr. K."

❖　❖　❖

THREE DAYS WENT by without any more incidents.

Allyson healed at a remarkable velocity, she fed as though she'd been born with the ability, and her night vision developed at an unprecedented rate. However, the only light she could tolerate was still candle. Each hour, each day, Allyson became more alert and while this delighted Logan, it caused him a trepidation which nagged at him; their telepathic connection seemed to have been severed. Logan wondered if all was going a little too well.

Logan woke to find himself alone in the bed and nearly panicked. He found her in the bathroom. Allyson locked in, the faint sour sweet smell of vomit wafted from beneath the door.

"Sweetheart," he knocked gently. "Let me in please. I need to know you're alright."

The door lock clicked. Opening it, he found her seated before the toilet, shoulders hunched, naked, shivering and crying. Logan stepped back into the bedroom, snatching his sweater from the chair. Entering the room, he slipped it over her head then handed her a glass of water, telling her to rinse her mouth. He knelt beside her, holding her as she cried.

Her tears slowed and she sniffled. "Am I going to die? I feel like I am." The last eked into a whimper.

"Baby," he tried to keep the concern out of his voice. "I need to know what you've brought up."

"I can't remember what day this is." Allyson held on to him as she shivered "Yesterday's lunch and breakfast I think."

"Any blood?" Logan attempted to sound calm, matter of fact.

"Nooo," she held her breath until he spoke.

"Good. Then your body is just discarding what it doesn't need right now as it changes the food but it's accepted the blood which it needs. This is good, real good and baby?"

"Yes, Logan."

"You won't die." And she began to cry and vomit again. When she'd exhausted herself, he carried her back to the bed and cradled her in his arms. Logan insisted she feed from him and later when she fell asleep in his arms, he still held her.

The soft, golden pink rays of the morning sun peeked under the drapes. Logan felt the side of the bed dip slightly. His voice lightly teased, "Where are you off to?"

"I just wanted to see." She turned to him; with one hand, she reached to touch her cheek. He slid across the bed sitting up, pulling her between his legs, wrapping his arms around her waist to rest his cheek against her stomach. "Come back to bed." He looked up into her face. "It's still too soon; give yourself another day or two."

"It was…was it awful?" She shuddered and he hugged her tight to him.

"Yes." He drew her into the bed beside him and arranged the covers over them. "You've healed quickly already, better than expected, just give your body a little more time before you see yourself."

"Am I…I never thought I was vain." She pressed her face to the crook of his shoulder.

"You're still gorgeous," he whispered against the softness of her hair. "More so with each day." Her tears of relief wet his skin.

Chapter Twenty-seven

NAIRN UNDERSTOOD HE was all wrong for Salina with his job's demanding and dangerous venues. He'd never have enough time for her and worry someone would hurt her because of him. Logan and Allyson's near disaster was warning enough. No, a relationship wasn't a good idea.

The night before on the terrace, her body drew his gaze. She wore yet another one of *those* dresses, too tight, too short, and it showed off her compact angular little body to perfection. Nairn knew that body as well as his own. Every curve, hollow, and swell. He acknowledged what she wanted and recognized he couldn't give her what she craved. Home. Family. Security. His career wasn't one that a man could expect a woman to understand, to put up with. Gone at a moment's notice, sometimes for days or weeks, or possibly not coming back at all. He hated contacting families when that happened. Unable to confide in any others than those who shared the same responsibilities, hell, he couldn't even share a third of his work with anyone. *That's what you get for being the boss.* Yes, not giving in to her was the right thing to do, his head told him. His heart squeezed, painfully telling him how wrong he was.

✧   ✧   ✧

SALINA TOOK HER time heading to the stairs for the umpteenth time that morning. She chided herself on her behavior of the previous night. They'd been so freaking civilized to each other. She expected, hoped after him nearly losing his own life and his best friend's, Nairn would've come to his senses and appreciate how precious life should be with the person you loved. No, instead of sweeping her off her feet and proclaiming his undying love, he'd gone off to lecture the Janissary and feeders. If she'd…if he'd…oh, bother, when was she going to admit the fact that he… She turned the corner and stopped abruptly as Nairn walked out of his room into the hallway.

"Hello, Nairn," dumb struck, that was all she could utter.

"Salina." Nairn thanked his lucky stars he didn't betray his thoughts by whipping his head around like some lovesick adolescent at the sound of her voice.

"You…" They both had spoken at the same time and each gave a nervous laugh.

"You go ahead."

"No, I insist you go ahead, ladies first." *If all else fails, remember your manners, they won't let you down*, he told himself.

"I was just going to say you look nice in that shirt."

Salina rocked on her high heels.

Nairn grinned. "Thank you." *Manners, oh thank you, Mom.* "You look great in that dress, but then you always look great." *Shut-up – Nairn! How could anyone have such exquisitely long legs?* He groaned inwardly at the sweet memory of those legs wrapped around his waist. Another time. Another place.

"Flatterer," Salina blushed.

"Aaa, Salina…" *Watch it Nairn. You're headed for dangerous ground here.*

"Yes, Nairn?" She took a step forward staring at his mouth.

Nairn's stare settled on hers and he swallowed hard. That sultry little mouth of hers set in that pixie face. Those hazel eyes that turned up at the corners, cat like and exotic. Did she have any idea what she did to him? He clenched his jaw, grinding his teeth, or worse, did she know and use it to torment him? If she licked her lower lip one more time.

Nairn's father, Lucien, words echoed in his head. *A man likes his liquor hard and his women soft…and don't ever confuse soft with stupid. Some of the sharpest women come in the supplest of packages.* Nairn regained the power of speech. "Guess we should go downstairs. I've got a million things waiting for me on my desk." By the gods he should be drawn and quartered for his stupidity and never have lain in her bed in the first place. Too late again his father's words came back to haunt him. *The only way to get a woman*

out of your system is to bed her, but in doing so you run
the risk of losing your heart and soul to her.

Nairn had lost both to her decades ago.

"Yes. *We* should go down." Salina strode by him giving him an ample view of her backside as she worked her legs and high heels to their best advantage.

✧   ✧   ✧

NAIRN WORKED THE morning away in his office but he couldn't focus on the spreadsheet on the computer screen. He picked up a CD and slid it into his stereo. The hard driving beat flowed out and Nairn smiled and breathed out a, *yeah*, then reached over and cranked up the volume. A couple of pencils found their way into his hands and he dived into his own drum accompaniment to the song blasting out.

✧   ✧   ✧

OUTSIDE THE DOOR to Nairn's office, Salina stood with her hand on the doorknob and smiled listening to the music blaring. She was getting to him. Well, she intended to burrow a little more under his skin. Yeah, and maybe cause a nasty rash while she was at it.

The door to his office opened and Salina stood at the threshold. Nairn stopped mid drum beat, seeing tears glistening in her eyes. He grunted and reached back to turn the music down then thought better and turned it completely off. Salina shut the door behind her, hesitating. Nairn rounded his desk. He pulled out a chair for her and handed her his handkerchief.

"What's wrong?" Nairn's clenched jaw twitched.

Inwardly Salina smiled, not often did she pull out the tears but she had to make this bluff believable, his clenched jaw meant she'd struck a nerve.

"I spoke with my mother."

"Awh, crap, how is Clarice holding up?"

"She isn't." Actually, her mother was thrilled with all the attention from the fallout of Franchot's reign of terror.

"I'm sorry, is there anything I can do to help?"

Damn his civility. "I'm going home."

"I'm moving back, permanently," Salina held her breath.

She noticed the telltale tick at the corner of his left eye and let the breath out slowly.

"That may be for the best."

Damn him! Damn him, he was calling her bluff. He wasn't going to win this time.

"Yes, mother needs me, and when she doesn't, well, I've always enjoyed the European countries more that the states." She stood, flashed him a quick smile before turning for the door. That's when she noticed it missing.

"It's gone." She gazed at the bare space on her wrist.

Nairn, stood when she did, now he came around his desk. "What is?"

"My bracelet." She examined the floor. "The one

Logan gave me for my birthday."

Nairn searched the floor not finding it. "Hey, don't worry." He placed a finger under her chin lifting her face. "I'll find it. I know how much it means to you. I'll make sure you get it back."

"I'm leaving in the morning," Salina stammered.

"Not a problem, I'll have it hand couriered to you. I'll find it, don't worry, ok?" The pad of his thumb stroked her lower lip.

"Yes, sure, ok." She turned to leave.

"Salina?"

"Yes?" This was it, what she'd hoped for.

"Have a safe trip."

"Thank you, I will." Carefully she closed the door behind her, smiling pleasantly when staff personnel went past bidding her a nice day. Salina walked at a normal pace to her rooms. Inside she fumed; well if he wanted her to leave she'd do just that. By the gods, *she wanted to kill something, and that something was Nairn St. Clair.* Well if he wanted her gone so be it, she will leave him alone. She smiled; it would only be a matter of time before he'd beg her to come back to him. And she'd make him do all the crawling.

✧   ✧   ✧

NAIRN RESTED HIS forehead against the closed door. He ached to grab her, crush her to him. Letting her walk out the door was the hardest thing he'd ever done.

Chapter Twenty-eight

LOGAN SAT IN a darken corner of the study, the hour was long after midnight. At this time of night the room was usually deserted, they way he liked it. A log in the fireplace shifted, sending a shower of sparks up the chimney. He'd stoked the fire earlier and realized he still held the poker in his hand. Leaning forward, he place it in the holder then took a drink. The whiskey scalded its way to his gut. Unfortunately, taste was all Tarczals got out of alcohol. They couldn't get drunk; an oddity of being different than the rest of mankind.

Life finally had taken a turn for the better, in some ways.

Allyson's body healed at an impressive rate. She handled feeding like a pro, wasn't squeamish about consuming blood, could probably see better at night than he could, and her strength was impressive. A smile tugged the corners of his mouth as he remembered walking into his-their bedroom to find she'd decided to rearrange the furniture all by herself. Some of the suit pieces, like the matching armoires, weighed a considerable amount.

She'd taken the news of sterility calmly, claiming it didn't matter since she'd received the same diagnoses before the metamorphosis. She handled each change with grace and dignity.

But, was she happy? Did she accept all this because the only alternative held death?

An oddity is what he'd turned her into, his Allyson, his T'yhiél. Logan savored the gift. A wife, mate, beloved, whatever the title a one in a lifetime love, one in a trillion, Dr. Legrou informed him were the chances of a Tarczal finding a T'yhiél Tarczal mate. Finding someone such as Allyson, a person who held the genes of Alaza before her change by Kharzarin, the odds were incomprehensible.

Logan regretted he'd changed her without a thought to her wishes.

He would man up to whatever decision she chose on their fate. With or without her, he'd accept her choice.

He sat staring into space and then as if on cue from a play, Allyson stepped into the doorway, hesitating like a young deer testing the scent of its surroundings. She wore a peignoir the color of the palest pink, a virginal blush. The silk clung to her and shimmered with every rise and fall of her breath. Her hair, with its many shades of blonde, hung like a silver waterfall in the moonlight down her back. Unconsciously, he rubbed the tips of his thumb and forefinger together remembering the silky texture of her hair in his hand. Her skin fairly glowed with health. No one would guess several weeks past, her supple body nearly died from horrible injuries inside and out. She stood exquisitely beautiful in the faint glow of the room.

"Logan, there you are." She glided over to where he sat. "I woke up and you were gone."

"I couldn't sleep and came down for a night cap."

"Hmmm, I haven't tried alcohol yet, I wonder how it will affect me." She reached for his glass.

He shifted it away from her. "You should ask Dr. Legrou first. It probably wasn't a good idea for me to consume any yet, since I'm your sole source of sustenance. I'm sorry, I wasn't thinking."

Hands on her hips, she confronted him. "Logan, what's wrong? Except for when I take nourishment, you've been evading me when you possibly can." Avoiding his eyes, she picked a piece of non-existent lint from her gown. "Are you sorry you changed me?"

He was stunned.

"How do you feel about this? The life I've condemned you to?" There he'd said it; he steeled himself for her answer.

Her head shot up. "Condemned? You haven't condemned me. You've given me a whole new world to explore. You gave a second chance at life, at love." Her eyes softened. "Is this because of Flora?"

"I offered this to her and she…"

"Rejected you because she didn't know the real you; she didn't love who you are." Allyson sat down on his lap, taking his face in her hands. "Logan, I'm not Flora but I understand her and why you thought her innocent in spite of her indiscretion with you. While she wasn't a virgin in the true sense of the word, she was completely innocent to the rest of the world around her and especially to her own emotions." Allyson withdrew her hand from his face to place it over his heart. "Flora was never going to grow up, no matter her age. Sadly for her, she was a product of her time. She couldn't accept anything outside the safety of her world and Franchot shattered her world. Face it, she chose death instead of the reality of you and the life you two could have had together. She was a small town girl with impossible ideas of what the world held. Even without the gift you offered, if the two of you had run off, it would only been a matter of time before she'd have rejected you. Flora couldn't accept a Tarczal world or a Tarczal man. It wasn't in her realm of reality to do so."

"I didn't ask your permission to change you."

She kissed the tip of his nose. "Thank goodness you didn't wait around for me to give it. I'd be dead right now. Ever think about that?" Allyson jabbed him in the chest with one finger.

"Yes, and because of me, you were put in harm's way."

"No, Franchot put us in harm's way. Can we talk about something else? I don't want to remember Franchot or what he put us through for one night."

"You're tied to me," Logan sighed. "You're my

T'yhiél. You can't feed from anyone but me."

"Yes, it's going to make a few things a little tricky," she agreed.

Logan took a deep breath. "It makes divorce impossible."

"Divorce?" Allyson bolted up. "We aren't even married yet, and you have us divorced? I thought Tarczal's mated for life."

"Yes. Do you mind being tied to me?" Logan's voice held hope and fear.

"Tied? Yes. Married, no." She titled her head giving him a coy glance. "If you ever get around to asking me."

He kissed her long and slow, sighing against her neck. "You allow me to forget who I am, what I am. You make it possible for me to be just a man, nothing more. A man in love with the most beautiful woman I know. And I thank the gods for her existence and I love you more every day."

"I love you, too," she whispered back to him.

He trailed kisses along her jaw and down her throat. "Ah, music to my heart."

Allyson pulled back to gaze in his face, an impish smile danced on her lips. "Well?"

Logan's eyes held worry and wistfulness. "Allyson, will you do me the honor of becoming my wife?"

"YES!" she shouted and covered his mouth with hers in a long, slow, wet, kiss.

Chapter Twenty-nine

ANDRÉ DELACROIX AND Lucien St. Clair sat across the table from Logan. They'd flown in two days before to help Logan and Nairn clean up the mess left behind by the Alliance member's quick departure. They sat quietly as Logan shook his head at Nairn.

"Giving me a report is worthless, don't you think?" Logan rested his chin in his hand and doodled on a scrap of paper.

Nairn shrugged. "Habit I guess, I might as well tell someone with authority."

"Authority? I believe it flew out the window when the members disbanded." Logan snorted.

Nairn grumbled. "Do you want to hear what I've got or not?"

"Don't get pissy. Go ahead." Logan lay his pen down, focusing his attention on Nairn.

"I found her."

"Who? Daisy?" Logan straightened. "Is she all right?"

Nairn leaned back, hands behind his head, grinning like a Cheshire cat. "Happy as a proverbial clam."

Logan leaned back in his chair; eyes closed in relief, and sighed. "How is she? What does she need?

How can I help?"

"I slipped the home's administrator some money and sent a few Janissaries over to help out with repairs."

"Repairs?"

"She's in a county home for retired farmer's wives. You'll like this, the house is a little over a hundred years old and still in pretty good condition. It's much like the old Rainey farm."

"Good. Daisy's found a home at last."

"She's happy and she said she was sorry for all the trouble she caused you."

"Did you tell her…?" Logan started then stopped when Nairn waved him off.

"I told her it was all okay and you'd be contacting her. She said she'd appreciate it if you would."

"Thanks, and I will." Logan made a note to himself to set up a fund for her and her new family. "I'll make sure they have whatever they need."

"Kinda thought you would, I told them you'd be contacting them about finances. The home raises smaller animals like chickens for the pot, and eggs, some rabbits, and they have a nice size vegetable garden."

"Do they have flowers?" Logan asked anxiously, his eyes turned to a memory. "Flora always loved flowers. I'll see they receive some seeds and plantings."

"Thought I should mention, there's a small cemetery on the property, too. I made sure George has a nice headstone. There's no body in a grave but I thought he should have one, anyway."

"Which reminds me, I never asked about the old warehouse. What happened to it?"

"George was good at his work. He set enough explosives so nothing but rubble remains. My crew went in as Hazmat and EPA to clean the rest up. There weren't much of the bodies left to bury or identify who was who."

"Thank you, for doing it for him. Does Daisy know about the stone?"

"She visits him twice a day."

"I owe you."

"Speaking of." Nairn placed a few receipts in front of Logan. "You can write me a check for these."

Logan glanced down and laughed at his friend's audacity.

André cleared his throat. "We should discuss why we've come together. I have a petition signed by over a thousand of our people. You're the perfect choice." André insisted, nodding to his nephew.

Logan shook his head. "Considering how I handled things, I don't think so."

"Your uncle is correct," Lucien interjected. "Who better to form a new panel for the Alliance?"

Logan scoffed. "I'd think people would want me to resign."

Nairn slap his palms down on the table. "The Alliance needs punished for what they did to you and your parents."

Lucien placed a hand on his son's arm. "They've all resigned in disgrace. André and I agree with Logan. It won't do anyone any good to tell the populace what those men did to Salina's father or Logan's parents."

"Letting them off with acquiescence, what does it say about our society?" Nairn said with a snarl.

Resignation lined André's face as he reasoned with Nairn. "We are willing to accept our mistakes and turn a heinous wrong into something worth rebuilding. Our hope is this will make our people realize we have a strong leader at our helm. A leader with a clearcut vision for their future, who's willing to admit he doesn't have all the answers, but is willing to listen, adapt, in his governing of them."

"Quite a bit to live up to." Logan blew out a pent up breath. "You really think I can do this?"

"Yes," answered André and Lucien in unison.

Logan picked up the petition, briefly glancing over some of the names on it and impressed with some of the family names. "I have their vote." He lifted the papers. "I have you three, Jovy, and her Rroma gypsy's of Machavaya in my corner. Maybe I can pull this off."

"It's still hard to believe she and Allyson are related." Nairn ran a hand threw his hair.

"Tell me about it." Logan shook his head, still not able to wrap his own mind around the revelation. "The arrogance of the woman. She insisted I ask her for Allyson's hand in marriage."

André lifted an eyebrow. "Nephew, did you?"

"Allyson thought it was funny and insisted I did." Logan grinned. "I got Allyson back; I suggested Jovy have free rein making the wedding dress."

The four men laughed until tears ran down their cheeks. A release they all needed.

André slapped Logan on the back. "Don't forget your connection to the legend."

Logan groaned, "The damn legend. Who'd have guessed Allyson and I are to help breed the next generation in Tarczal evolution?"

Nairn snickered. "What, not up for the job?"

"You're so not funny." Logan threw his pen at him. He turned to his uncle.

"Does the legend mention any way to circumvent Allyson being sterile after the metamorphosis? If we pull off such a miracle, I'll start believing." Logan sobered, listening to the men adding their two cents on the subject of procreation. Children, the one thing he'd never be able to give his gorgeous wife.

"Maybe Jovy and her crew have a potion for it, too." Lucien joked but the look in his eyes told Logan he believed all things possible.

Logan looked at the men around him and thought of the men and women who were pledging their assistance and faith in him. Maybe it was time for a new beginning, for him and the Tarczal race.

Chapter Thirty

JOVY, LOGAN'S AUNT Maryse who decided that her nephew's wedding was worth leaving her home this once, Logan and Allyson were seated at The House's long dining room table.

Sketches, fabric samples, glossy magazine pictures, and dusty ancient Tarczal books littered the table's surface.

As the Delacroix matriarch, Maryse had elected herself in charge of Allyson's education into Tarczal wedding customs and traditions. She was detailing the actual wedding ceremony when Logan quietly excused himself and left the room. Allyson tilted her head to Jovy and then placed a hand on Maryse's, "Excuse me a moment, please. I believe someone…" nodding towards the door Logan had just exited through "needs a hug."

Maryse patted her hand and chuckled, "Go see if or what we old women have done to upset him. We three, I believe, are the only ones he shows just how sensitive he is in the matters of the heart."

Allyson found Logan in the study staring at a small painted miniature of his parents. She stepped between him and the picture, forcing his gaze to her.

Coyly she batted her lashes, "Do you have a minute for me in your thoughts, Sir?"

Logan placed a hand on either side of her face. He bent to kiss her delicately on the lips. She swallowed a tiny sigh, his kiss made her feel as though she were made of a fine crystal that would shatter under pressure save that, that he'd just applied. He withdrew so slowly, it was a moment before she opened her eyes and realized he was smiling at her from his full height. He gathered her to him, her arms wrapped around his waist. They stood for a moment, her head resting on his chest, an ear pressed closely listening to the sound of his heart rhythmically beating. He held her with one arm as he stroked her hair with the other. She felt him take a small breath before he began to speak.

"How is it, my little cat, that you always seem to know just when to jump into my lap and demand attention. Making it quite impossible for me to concentrate on what troubles me, and forcing me to share it with you?"

"If I do it so well," tilting her head back to look at him, "it's because you taught me well with the many times you jumped into my lap." He gathered her even closer to him. She pressed, "Tell me about your mother and father's wedding." Logan kissed the top of her head, an indication to her, she had guessed correctly at his thoughts.

"Theirs, even in their time, was a wedding of very old tradition and customs. I remember my mother telling me how beautiful, romantic and solemn it was. I can still see my father standing nearby smiling proudly as she told me. I remember how as she spoke of their vows to each other, she and father would pass a secret look, eyes sparkling. Though I was too young to fully understand that look, I remember clearly thinking *this must be what it is like to truly be in love.* Mother's description of their wedding…well it sounded so perfect. I guess I always wanted my wedding to be like theirs. A silly thought for a man is it not?"

Allyson stood on tiptoes to kiss his mouth lightly, "No it isn't silly. It's completely romantic. Let's make ours a remembrance of theirs."

✧   ✧   ✧

IT WAS THE wedding of the century, thanks to Aunt Maryse and Jovy's planning and Logan's money.

Allyson's off the shoulder gown, designed by and a gift from Jovy, made Logan's part in the ceremony easily obtained. His wedding finery left her unconsciously chewing her lower lip. He wore an attractive antique white cravat at his throat, the tails of which lay three inches down his shirt, a shirt with many tiny buttons.

On occasions, if the bride and groom were of equal height, the ceremonial feeding from each other was accomplished with the two standing. Logan could easily rest his chin on the top of her head so he'd have to be seated with her on his lap for Allyson to perform her part of the ritual. First, she must prepare him for her part and to help her do so, one of the new Alliance, members placed a chair behind Logan. He removed his waistcoat, handing it to the waiting Alliance magistrate. Carefully pulling her on to his lap, Logan gallantly spread her silks out to form a fan.

Allyson took a deep breath, she unwound the cravat, removing it from his neck and not looking to see who took it, she placed it in an out stretched palm. Her fingers fumbled, trembled as she undid the first button of many on his shirt. Glancing up into Logan's eyes, he momentarily caught and held her there. His eyes and smile told her of his love and pride for her, reassuring her she could complete her task. With new confidence, she undid the shirt from neck to just below his sternum. Placing her hands under the material at the small hollow of his neck, she pushed back the starchy whiteness to expose his muscular tan neck and shoulder.

✧   ✧   ✧

LOGAN MOVED A silken, honey-blonde lock to expose her shoulder and neck. An Alliance magistrate stepped forward to swab a small spot on her neck and shoulder and then Logan's. The swab held a bitter, pungent smelling liquid, meant to prevent the marks left by each from healing cleanly, ensuing tiny scares would be left.

Logan and Allyson would be in effect, marking each other for life, making it clear to all their claims on one another. Earlier, Logan had instructed Allyson to puncture deeply. He warned her to expect the taste left by the swab to be bitter.

✧   ✧   ✧

AS ANOTHER ALLIANCE magistrate came to place a hand on each of their heads, Allyson was struck by how quiet the room, save for the beating of her heart, had become. Which she was sure the entire room could hear.

The man smiled down at them, "Please repeat after me." And so they began their vows.

"I, Logan, take you, Allyson, as my mate and willingly share my life's blood with you now and forever. May it nourish your body in times of feast and famine, so you may know the depth of my love and devotion to you." A moment later, Allyson declared the same vows to him. He squeezed her waist reassuringly as she paused, overwhelmed by the love she felt for him.

Then André begged a moment of everyone's time as he approached Logan and Allyson.

"These were your parents'. They wanted you to have them." André presented Logan with his parents wedding rings dug from the ashes of where they died locked in each other's embrace and

Logan nearly lost all his composure.

"Thank you Uncle." Logan said and kissed his uncle's hand. Allyson wiped Logan's tears from his cheeks with her thumbs as André slipped back into the crowd.

When they finished their vows, the Alliance magistrate nodded to them and they simultaneously punctured each other. The Alliance magistrate finished with "Let all those who witness these marks, heed your claim to each other."

Even with Logan's warning, the bitterness from the herb swab nearly made her gag. She felt Logan's hand on her waist flex. He, too, was unprepared for the taste. They had agreed to count silently to three, then swallow, then release their hold as this was only to be a taste not a true feeding.

Custom dictated an Alliance member to step forward at this time and inform the groom he may kiss the bride. Long before the gentleman could move, Logan pulled her closer. She wrapped her arms around his neck. Their mouths met, tongues darting inward to duel an ancient duel. She tasted her life's liquid on him and thrilled in knowing he tasted his on her.

In the distance, a man cleared his throat and from the twittering from those around them, Allyson and Logan realized it wasn't the first time he may have done so. Bowing her head to stare at Logan's bare chest, she felt the heat rising quickly to her cheeks.

Glancing up, she could see a smug male grin on Logan's face. The Alliance member chuckling softly addressed Logan, "You may now kiss the bride again." Beaming, Logan whispered a quick *I love you* to her, before placing a brief chaste kiss on her upturned mouth. They stood and well-wishers crowded in, showering them with flower petals as the customs of old.

✧　✧　✧

SHE LED HIM out onto the dance floor. Pausing when they reached dead center, Allyson, much to Logan's amusement, placed his arms around her waist. She slid her hands up the front of his shirt and whispered to him, "It's already been too long since I felt your arms around me." She pressed back the still open shirtfront to place a kiss on his bare skin.

They'd stopped dancing. His mouth covered hers in a possessive, yet controlled kiss. He bent his head more allowing her to place her arms around his neck and as she did, he bent farther, placing an arm behind her knees scooping her up. He cradled her protectively to him, never once breaking the kiss. Allyson nestled against his broad shoulder as he scanned the crowd daring anyone to protest or try to stop what he was about to do.

In ancient times, if a challenge were made for the bride, this was the occasion. When the groom prepared to leave with his bride and make his final claim on the woman he'd chosen.

Several of the older men smiled knowingly, some of the older matrons' faces reflected memories of their wedding dance. Younger women, some unattached, some not, wore blatant envy written on their faces. A small hand full of young men felt the flare of challenge rise in them as their ancestors might. Wisely, they thought better of it, either civilization reared its head or they headed the message of Logan's determined forceful stance. Logan strode forward and the well-wishers courteously stepped back leaving a wide path.

Tarczal men possessed the strength of twenty or more normal humans. Realizing this and knowing Logan also worked out every day, he still awed Allyson by carrying her up the three flights of stairs to his, now their room.

Reaching the door, he proceeded to pop it open with a kick. Logan crossed the threshold, and walked over to the bedside, gently placing her on her feet. Returning to the door, he softly shut it, throwing the lock latch in place. He stood there, back leaning against the wood, silently appraising her. Allyson made a half turn exposing her back to him. She reached with one hand to pull her long hair to one side, letting it fall down across one collarbone and breast.

She nearly jumped when he placed his hands on her shoulders. She hadn't heard him approach. Kissing the one bare shoulder briefly, Logan went about the task of unbuttoning her gown. As he undid the last button, the heavy silks rustled to the floor. Allyson stepped out of the dress, now clad only in a bustier, panties, stockings and shoes. Her back still turned to him, she heard him remove her gown from the floor. Skilled fingers deftly unfastened the hooks of the bustier, sliding it from her. She turned to face him, it was her turn now.

Shyly, she undid the waistband of his trousers, tugging the half-unbuttoned shirt from their depths. He placed an upturned palm out taking the freshly wrestled cufflinks from her, dropping them into a trouser pocket. Freeing him from his shirt, she slipped it from him. Logan caught it at one wrist, tossing it aside. Immediately, she stepped back, unsure what to do next. In doing so, the backs of her knees collided with the bed, seating her; her gaze averted from his face. When she looked again into his face, a small gasp sprang from her.

Logan and she had made love numerous times before and she hadn't been some unenlightened virgin when first they met. This time, this place was new, and to be different from any time before or after. She stared into his face, his eyes gleamed with a feral light and his face filled with primitive possessiveness of a man about to take the woman he claimed as his.

Reaching for his trouser zipper, he lowered it more provocatively than a stripper. He removed his shoes; hooking his thumbs in his briefs and trousers, he removed both in one fluid motion.

Allyson had seen Logan aroused before, but at this moment he appeared fuller, longer, it standing stiff and high from him. His mouth twitched at the corners; with a knowing smile, he placed one knee than the other on the bed. He grasped each ankle pulling her legs down, out and spread wide on either side of his as he knelt there. Placing the palm of one hand on her stomach, he slowly, deliberately moved his hand from side to side. She found herself shivering and whispering, "Please." Why, or what she was pleading for, she didn't know.

Logan still moved his hand gently on her, watching her. The hand on her stomach snaked out, snatching her panties from her before she realized what he'd done. The hand, along with its mate, caressed her hips; he cooed soft ancient Tarczal words.

He bent forward, kissing the area between her springy hair and navel, working his way up. Balancing his weight on one arm, still kneeling, he reached to stroke and knead one breast; his tongued laved and suckled the other. His gaze never left her face, he still murmured more words when she shifted or arched to his touch.

Logan stopped, resting his weight on his hands as he stretched his length out over her. Allyson's breath was in short shallow gasps. He lowered himself more, she found herself placing her palms against his chest to stall his descent. Her legs jerked up bent at the knees. He kissed her panting mouth, her chin and nose. His tongue and lips trailing a path down her jaw and back up to nuzzle a pink shell of an ear. Still he whispered words that had no meaning to her, yet reassured and comforted her at the same time. His weight now flattened her breasts. She felt her nipples hardened as the dark silken hair decorating his chest caressed them, his arousal pressed against her slippery folds.

Logan's mouth covered hers. He entered at an agonizingly slow pace. Hands that once vainly tried pushing him away immediately tried to pull him closer. Just as he was about to be encased totally, he withdrew causing her to wrap arms and legs about him as she sobbed, "Please Logan, Please!" Placing his hands under her buttocks for deeper penetration, he squeezed the mounds roughly, before plunging his need deep into her depths.

Again and again he plunged, stoking the fire burning deep within her. The control Logan held so carefully on his own emotions and desires earlier, he vainly fought to hold. Nipping, kissing, licking, caressing, pinching, fondling he worked his way back up her body. Tangling his hands in her hair, he forced her head back roughly, and growled, "Now, and forever you are mine! Say it, Allyson!"

She ran her hands up his body, raking him from buttocks to nape, drawing blood. "Yes! Now and forever I am yours." Her hands tangled in his hair jerking his head back as he bent to kiss her. She finished, "And you are mine, Logan!"

He stared into her eyes, dark with the need of him, "Yes, I am yours, now and forever!"

Chapter Thirty-one

Seventy-five years later

WHEN THEIR TIME came to move, since staying in one place and not aging as those around you could lead to problems, Logan and Allyson relocated to the quiet and serene French county side of Logan's birth. André retired from the wine-making business, turning it over to Logan. Maryse said it was about time she finally had her husband all to herself. Allyson blossomed, roaming the countryside, painting to her heart's content. Life was wonderful.

✧　✧　✧

ALLYSON NOTED IT started slowly at first, a morning here or there. She'd bring up a breakfast or an occasional lunch or dinner. Residual effects from the metamorphosis the local doctor assured her, nothing of concern. She attempted to hide the problem from Logan but it became impossible when her blood intake increased by double, then triple. Logan contacted his trusted friend Dr. Dennis Legrou, bringing him to the Delacroix estate in France.

Dennis came back into his office on the estate, a

huge smile on his face. Logan jumped to his feet still holding Allyson's hand. "Sit back down, Logan, and ease up on the poor woman's hand." Dennis nodded to Allyson's attempt at removing her hand from her husband's death grip. "I believe we've discovered what's causing your increased appetite, the lethargy, and the nausea."

Logan kissed his wife's hand before releasing it. "Is it serious? Can it be cured?"

"Serious and cured, mmmm, yes and no. But it's certainly monumental."

"Well?" Logan pressed him.

"You're pregnant."

"We can't be," sputtered Allyson.

"Then you two haven't ever…."

"Okay, we could be, but how, oh, I know how, I just mean." She threw up her hands. "Everyone before, before I became Tarczal, told me I was sterile and afterwards this isn't supposed to happen."

Dennis chuckled. "No it isn't, and I don't' know the hows or whys, but you definitely are. I personally ran the test three times myself."

Logan kissed her full on the mouth. "Gucss we've done it again sweetheart. Tell us doctor. How far along is she?"

"Three months give or take."

"You're sure?" they said in unison.

"Yes, I'm, quite sure."

Epilogue

Six months later

ANOTHER CONTRACTION RIPPED through her and Allyson hissed out a breath between clenched teeth. The doctor slid up to the bed and pulled off the sheet covering her raised legs.

"Well, well, it looks like we're going to have a baby soon." He came up smiling after checking her. Allyson shot an arm out to grab the doctor by the knot of his necktie and pulled him down so they were face to face.

"Do something," she snarled at him. "I've been in labor for sixteen hours and you keep telling me, soon!"

Logan helped the doctor pry Allyson's fingers from his tie.

Between clenched teeth, Allyson growled, "Stop saying we, there's no we in this. You're not having it damn it; I'm the one in labor!" She hissed a breath when another contraction rolled over her.

"Can you do anything to help her?" Logan asked taking the doctor aside and safely out of his wife's reach.

"She's doing fine. Just keep her breathing the way I showed you. It won't be long now," Doc said as he stepped into the hallway.

Logan went back to his wife's side, placing one arm behind her, the other arm she clasped to her.

"Breathe, sweetheart, breathe, remember, he, he, he."

"Breathe yourself, damn it!" she snapped then completely changed emotional gears pleading with him. "Logan, please make it stop, please?"

"I see a head!" the nurse who had come in to check on the progress of the birth said, hurrying out to find the doctor.

"Logan? Something doesn't feel right." Allyson sat up quickly bearing down hard.

Logan saw the baby's head, she pushed again, he could see the baby's entire face.

"Where's the damn doctor?" Logan muttered under his breath.

"LOGAN!" screamed Allyson and pushed one last time as the child slipped from her into her husband's arms. And she slipped into oblivion.

✧   ✧   ✧

WHO WRAPPED HER *head in a cotton ball?* Allyson blinked against the light.

"Hi, welcome back." Logan dabbed her forehead and cheek with a cool washcloth.

Allyson licked her lips. Inside and out, she felt so dry. "Hi." Her face rapidly contorted in fear, she tried to sit up. "The baby, where's the baby?"

"Shush now, lay back." He signaled to the nurse standing there and she hurried out of the room.

"Logan?"

"Everything is fine, sweetheart."

The nurse cheerfully stepped in the room. "Here they are."

Allyson stared as two nurses came in, each carrying an infant. One blue blanket and one pink swaddled the babies.

"Two?"

"Yes, look what we did," Logan said proudly.

"Two," she repeated in awe.

"You only get out what you put into something," he said with a straight face.

Allyson just rolled her eyes; butter would melt in his mouth at the moment, she thought. Logan wore a self-satisfying typical smug smile at the all male comment.

✧   ✧   ✧

THEY NAMED THE fraternal twins in honor of Logan's parents, Jean-Pierre and Genevieve Vashti Kincaid.

Logan kissed the top of his wife's head. "You scared us after you delivered him and then passed out." He would tell her later how she'd gone limp after birthing their son and how blood had poured from her. How the doctor in his attempt to staunch the bleeding discovered the second baby's head and pulled the infant, screaming her tiny lungs out, from Allyson's womb with his bare hands.

For now, he would let her regain her strength and rejoice in the birth of their children before he'd tell her how she'd scared the hell out of him.

The nurse placed the blue-blanketed child in her arms.

Logan scooted in bed with her. "Look at this little one." Holding the baby, he offered her a glimpse of their daughter.

She stared at the babies, their tiny mouths drawn up in a pucker, their eyes an indigo blue. For now, at least, their son had his father's coloring while their daughter had hers.

"Let me hold her, too."

Logan went to place their daughter in her arms but the baby began to cry and fuss. Logan held her and cooed to her, immediately she stopped fussing.

"I guess we know who's a daddy's girl!" Allyson laughed.

"She's comfortable and didn't like being disturbed." Logan smiled down at the pink, squirming bundle and the little girl smiled back at him. "Look at her, she smiled!" Much to Allyson's amazement, he made silly baby talk to the infant. Oh, if the rest of the Alliance could see their new leader who spoke so elegantly reduced to incoherent baby-babble.

Their son began nuzzling her breast through the

material of her gown.

Holding his daughter, watching his wife and son, Logan felt whole and content for the second time in his life. The first time being when he met Allyson. He marveled at his daughter's tiny, rosebud mouth, button nose, and big blue eyes. The baby chose this moment to grab his finger tightly in her tiny hands. He glanced at Allyson contentedly feeding their son. "I wonder what mischief you and your brother have in store for us little one," he whispered to their daughter, whose answer to him was a Mona Lisa smile before drifting off to sleep.